—

OLD

—

GREEN

—

WORLD

—

JASON DEWEY CRAFT

———

OLD

———

GREEN

———

WORLD

———

A NOVEL

CRAFT FICTION
Old Green World
Jason Dewey Craft

ISBN: 978-0-9961538-2-9 (ebook)
ISBN: 978-0-9961538-3-6 (paperback)

Editor: Sandra Spicher
Cover and Interior Design: Derek George

http://www.craftfiction.com

1

Albert was responsible for the garden. He inherited it at the age of eight and never gave it up. Every year or two, he would bring a younger student under his wing, but the apprentices lost interest once they realized Albert would happily do all the work himself. Sister Alice, the old teacher, never pushed the issue, and Sister Clare, the new teacher, never had the time to care.

The garden and Albert got along well, like old friends. He knew how to tend to it, when to leave it alone, how to harvest it, and how to take it back down to the ground when the season was done.

He poked radish seeds into the cool dirt of early spring with his thumb and then covered them. He used to be able to do this with an effortless precision, with perfect spacing of the seeds and rows, but it was a challenge now. His movements hadn't adjusted to the size of his hands. He had grown three feet this year, and was taller and wider now than anyone he knew. He was still cowed by them, the hands he owned, a strange man's hands.

He scratched at his beard, which was just beginning to

grow in red patches. The itch got on his nerves. He looked over at Thomas, surrounded with sheets of parchment covered with calligraphy and sketches and weighed down with small stones. Thomas was trying to read one of the sheets and fought it a little as it curled in the wind. Albert watched his lips move as he focused on the page. Thomas always did that. Then Thomas scratched at his own beard and Albert smiled.

Albert looked at the seeds he had planted and pictured the radish plants they would become. He pictured the smaller boy he had been a year ago. Time passing. Sister Alice had taught them that time was an illusion. "Every moment: this moment," she had said to them in class. "That's it."

"Not the apocalypse, though?" he had asked. "That was a different moment, wasn't it?" He had felt so clever. The apocalypse had happened four thousand years ago. They talked about it at school all the time.

"Every moment is the apocalypse, Albert," Sister Alice had answered.

Albert finished the row and looked to Thomas again. "I'm hungry," he said.

"It's lunch," Thomas said. He pointed toward the pine bell tower, which jutted into the sky, ragged and sturdy, four times the height of any other structure in the square. Albert followed Thomas's gaze and saw one of the caretakers ascending. The tower was now five years old, three of those years in the building. The bell tower rang once an hour, at the hand of one of ten volunteers who kept watch on the water clock housed in the bank next door. The Adepts had initiated the tower project to teach the people of the town the importance of precise time.

"Why do we have to pay attention to time, if it's an illusion?" Albert had asked Sister Alice in class.

"Everything is an illusion," she had said, "and that's precisely why we have to pay attention."

A child burst from the schoolhouse, a tiny version of the boys, wearing the same clothes and the same close-cropped hair. He ran toward them, a little ball in loose blue wool knickers and tunic. "Albert!" he screamed.

Albert dropped to a nimble crouch and then leapt toward the child. "Don't run into the garden!" he said, grabbing the child with a gentle tackle. The child shrieked giddily and Albert laughed.

"I escaped," the child said.

"You're not supposed to escape," Albert said. "You're causing trouble for Sister Clare."

"Hannah," the child said, "Hannah made a mess, and Sister Clare was talking to Hannah, and I ran out the door." The child pointed back to the door.

Sister Clare burst from it. She wore the same blue wool, but hers was draped as robes, with simple, sharp embroidery. Her head was covered. She looked wildly in all directions. She was five years older than Albert, at most.

"Here, Sister Clare," Albert called. He tucked the child under his arm and carried the kicking bundle toward her.

She exhaled, closed her eyes, and reopened them with slightly more calm. "Harald," she said to the child. She held her fingers in front of the child's face and gave a weary, flabby snap. "Presence."

The child began crying.

A wetness crept into the wool of Albert's sleeve, at the point where he cradled the child with his arm. He scrunched his nose. He handed the child back to Clare and smiled at her. "It's going to be all right," he said.

Sister Clare pursed her lips. "How is the garden?"

"It's fine. I'm almost finished."

"Wonderful, so this afternoon you'll read your . . ." She trailed off, a blank look on her face.

Albert waited a moment, then said, "Military history. I'll read military history and strategy this afternoon."

"Wonderful," Sister Clare said. She looked at Thomas for a moment, as if she had something more to say, then reconsidered. "Thomas is fine, isn't he?"

"Yes. He's reading physics," Albert said. "No one's watching the children, Sister Clare."

Sister Clare closed her eyes and furrowed her brow, as if she were trying to read something from behind her eyelids. After a moment she said, "It's all right." Then, a moment later, she said, "Wait, no. No, it's not."

Her eyes snapped open. She hastened toward the schoolhouse, the child in her arms. He looked back to Albert and waved good-bye.

"We're going to lunch now," Albert called after her.

"Wonderful," Sister Clare called back.

Thomas stood, gathered his sheets of manuscript, collected them in a satchel. They began walking across the square. They passed the tower and approached a cluster of buildings just beyond: the town's hall of government was there, and Thomas's house sat just beside it.

The breeze stirred the patchy grasses. Three stray cats walked in the square: one cringed against the breeze; one ignored it, staring intently at something unknown; one put its face right toward the breeze and seemed to enjoy it.

"It's cold," Albert said. He huddled close to Thomas. "Do you think Mister Ewan has made soup today?"

"Maybe. You're right, it is cold, come in closer," Thomas said, shouldering in as they crossed the square.

"How's the physics?" Albert asked.

"It's difficult. But it's interesting, so that helps. It's called causal relations."

"What does that mean?"

"I'd explain it to you, but I don't understand it yet."

"I don't even understand why you have to learn physics."

Thomas shrugged.

The Adepts taught what they taught, Albert knew. Most of the time it made sense, but not always.

"I'm glad I don't have to do any more math or physics," Albert said. "I like koan study better. Just ask me a question, and I'll say 'Shut up! Ha-ha!' and then you'll smack me. And then we'll both become enlightened."

"You know it's not as simple as that. That's one of the subjects you're best at. You know koans are work."

"Or are they? Shut up! Ha-ha!"

Thomas smiled, then kneeled down to scratch a cat behind its ears.

Albert kneeled next to Thomas, leaned close into his ear, and whispered, "You're supposed to smack me now." Thomas pretended to ignore him, then stood and walked ahead. Albert shrugged. "Missed opportunity," he said.

They walked around the side of Thomas's house to a back door, smooth and elm, with a bronze knocker. The door opened as they approached, and an older man in a smock greeted them. Mister Ewan led them into the kitchen. "Stay in here for a while," he said. He stretched his arm up to ruffle Albert's hair and pointed out some cheese and biscuits for him to eat.

"Mother's busy?" asked Thomas.

"Sister Alice is here," Mister Ewan said. "She arrived early this morning, and they have been meeting ever since. I'm not sure, but I think it's the Baixans."

"Baixans, I can't wait to fight some Baixans," Albert said, smiling through a mouth full of crumbs and cheese.

"I'm sure it's serious if they've been talking all morning."

Thomas looked at the door a few times and picked at some food absently. "I hope they aren't moving inland."

Albert chewed through the rest of his biscuits. A bell rang, and Mister Ewan went to answer after handing Albert a sandwich he'd hastily prepared. Albert swallowed when he noticed Thomas staring at him. "Are you all right? What's wrong?" Albert asked. "It's just a sandwich. I'll still have room for lunch."

"I'm fine. Please don't joke about the Baixans, Albert."

Albert stood still. He didn't know where to look, so he looked at his sandwich. "I didn't mean to make you upset."

Mister Ewan returned behind Thomas's mother. Lady Newton was chewing on the stylus that she always chewed. She wore smooth, flowing gray wool, much finer than the schoolteacher robes and embroidered in red thread. She smiled at Albert. "Dear. I trust you and Thomas had a productive morning?"

Albert, smiling in return: "Well, we did some exercises, and then I turned and planted the school garden while Thomas studied physics. And I invited Thomas to become enlightened with me, but he declined. So that's on him."

Lady Newton laughed, her arm drawing Albert close. "We'll have to work on Thomas. Sister Alice is here, dear, so you'll eat in the kitchen with Mister Ewan."

"May I eat in the kitchen, too?" Thomas asked.

Lady Newton frowned at him. "Of course not. Don't be ridiculous. Go to the table."

Thomas glared at his mother. He took two chicken eggs from the clay bowl on the rough-hewn sideboard and threw them onto the tiles on the floor.

"Would you care to explain that? The process that brought you to this moment?" Lady Newton said. "Mister Ewan's going to have to clean that up. Is that what you hoped to accomplish?"

"What makes Sister Alice so special that Albert has to miss his lunch?" Thomas pointed at the hallway like he was criticizing it.

"Miss his lunch?" Lady Newton replied. "It's lovely here in this kitchen. I wish I could eat in the kitchen. And this isn't about Albert, it's about you and your selfish—"

"Because you're ashamed, you put on an act for Sister Alice, you can't do what is right—"

"—your behavior, every act you take brings us closer to either civilization or chaos, do you appreciate that? Does it even enter into your mind that your tantrums, your irresponsibility, could eventually ruin and destroy everyone in Eden-town?"

Thomas slammed his hand on the sideboard and stormed out.

Everyone was quiet for a moment. Lady Newton put her arm back around Albert and gave him a squeeze. "Enjoy your lunch, dear. We'll all eat together tomorrow, all right?"

"Have a good lunch," Albert said as she walked out. The Newtons had a hallway. The Newtons had more rooms than anyone in Eden-town: rooms just to cook, rooms just to eat, rooms just to stand between other rooms.

Mister Ewan reached toward a stack of cloths on the sideboard. The cloths were clean-edged, precisely cut from old clothes. He soaked a cloth in a basin, kneeled to the floor, and began cleaning up the eggs with the wet cloth. "It's just you and me again," he said from the floor.

"I'll do that," Albert said. "You go ahead and finish getting ready for them." Mister Ewan filled three bowls, put them on a flat wooden board, and walked out into the hall. Albert rinsed the towel in a basin. The basin was bigger than the egg bowl, but it was similar workmanship. Geoffrey Pauli made all the pots in town and always stamped a "G" into the bottom.

Albert sat down at the kitchen table. Mister Ewan came back in and filled two more bowls. It was barley porridge. Mister Ewan made it at least once a week, but Albert never got tired of it. It was always full and savory, with greens from the forest and a runny egg on top.

"I miss sitting with you for lunch," Albert said. "We haven't eaten together since . . ." He trailed off. He had almost said *since Mayor Newton died* but it felt wrong to say that.

"Lady Newton is soft-hearted," Mister Ewan said. "It would be easier if you and I just ate in the kitchen every day. There's a table for the people who run things, and a table for everyone else. The old days are over.

"We used to all sit together, even the Adepts, did you know that? We used to live in longhouses and eat at the long tables together. That was how it was when I was a little boy. Then they decided we would have towns, and that there would be mayors, and separate houses, and people serving people. My father refused. He just ran off into the woods. So it was just my mother and me, and Lady Newton and her parents. Even then, we used to eat together, all of us. Then the Adepts decided there needed to be a house with a room just for eating, and just for them. Now we act like that's how it's always been. There's no going back."

Albert stared at his bowl and kept eating. "Maybe it just takes time. Maybe we'll all eat together again once we're finished building civilization."

"When's that going to happen? When will it be finished?" Mister Ewan said. Albert didn't say anything. They ate quietly for a while before Mister Ewan said, "It's all right, though. It's good for you to eat with them. You're good for Thomas."

Albert and Thomas were quiet when they walked back to school, until Thomas began bumping into Albert on purpose and stepping on his feet. Albert bumped him back. Thomas dropped his satchel, grabbed Albert around his shoulders, and started wrestling him.

"You're going to lose. You know you're going to lose," Albert said.

"I'm going to win this time," Thomas said. He tried to mimic a wolf call.

Albert wrestled him down into the grass, sat on him, held Thomas's arms down with his hands. "I give up, I give up," Thomas laughed. Albert let his arms go but stayed straddled on him. Thomas kept his eyes locked with Albert's and very gradually put his hands onto Albert's thighs, as if his hands were operating secretly as he held Albert's attention. They were still for a while, catching their breath.

"Mother and Sister Alice are worried about the Baixans. They talked about it all morning. They wouldn't tell me much, though."

"We'll fight them eventually, right?" Albert said. "It's what I've trained for."

Thomas turned his head to the side, looked away from Albert, toward his house. "I'm getting married to Cynthia," Thomas said. "We talked about it at lunch."

"I know," Albert said. Thomas was engaged to Cynthia Kelvin, whose father was the mayor of Over-town. They had been engaged since they were babies. When they married, they would unify the north. It was for civilization.

"I mean soon, though," Thomas said. "Before the year is over. We're going to Over-town in a few weeks to meet them."

"Oh."

"I have to do it. I don't have a choice."

"I know."

+   +   +

After school each day, Albert practiced fighting. He shot things with arrows and struck them with swords. Four days a week he practiced with the militia, a group of older boys and men who knew less about fighting than Albert did. The other days, Albert practiced archery at home with Mama Mura. They practiced the bow in a space they had set aside for it. It was a mulched row with a hay target, near where the forest bounded their farmland.

The east side of the farm approached the village. Between them sat the Plancks' farm and some low trees and clearings. The west side of the farm touched the old forest. It took a full day of travel through ancient trees to reach Overtown. To the north of them was the channel, and to the south it was trees for leagues and leagues, all the way to the Old City of the Island.

Albert drew, fired, and struck the bull's-eye slightly to the left. "Good," Mura said.

Albert winced. "I'm pulling to the left." He stared at his right hand. *My hands*, he thought. *Me*. He then fired two more in close succession, each of which struck closer to the center. He looked back at Mura and smiled. "I think I got it," he said, and approached the target to free his arrows.

"Good," Mura said. The setting sun cast itself right across her face, and Albert could see the variegation in her color that only came out in full light. There were small flecks of gold in her dark brown eyes. Her hair was cut close to the scalp, but he could still see the reds that mottled the dark brown. "Are you all right?" she asked.

"I'm fine. I'm just thinking, I guess." He ran a hand across his own short red hair. Sweat showered from it, a mist. "I won't be shooting targets for much longer. I'll be a soldier, like you were."

Mura shrugged. "I guess you could call it 'soldier'? We didn't have a word like that. It's different from what we have here. We were just a group of people with weapons and a goal."

"You met Mama and Papa then," Albert said. He plucked at the bowstring absently, firing nothing into the ground.

"We fought near the village where Mama and Papa grew up," Mura said. "There were raiders there, making chaos, and we were trying to stop them. But we failed. Some of us escaped, but the village was razed. I think you already know about that. It was tough. A lot of people were killed."

"So you saved Mama and Papa when you all escaped," Albert said.

Mura smiled. "It's probably truer to say we saved each other. But yes, we escaped. There were others as well. We all got away together."

"What happened to the rest of the people?"

"The trip was difficult. Some people didn't make it. Most of us did, though. We found a village in Baixa, and most of the group settled there. You know the rest. Mama and Papa and I kept going. We wanted to get far away. We wanted to make sure we were somewhere peaceful. So we crossed the sea and found this place and made a life, and we had you."

Albert drew and fired several bull's-eyes silently before speaking again. "So you and Papa and Mama are married, right? Thomas has to get married to that girl in Over-town. It's the same thing, right? Just that Administrators have rules and ceremonies for it?"

"I don't know, really. I don't understand what their ritual is all about. It has more to do with land than anything else, I think. Papa and Mama are village kin, and Mama and I love each other. We all raise you together. Maybe Thomas can tell you what that would mean for them." Mura studied Albert for a moment. "Why is this so interesting to you all of a sudden? Is Thomas putting something into your head?"

"No, of course not. It's not Thomas at all. He doesn't want

any of it," Albert said. "Maybe he'll say no. I don't think he should do it."

"I see." Mura sighed. "Of course."

He said nothing. He was scared of what would come out if he spoke. He did as he first learned from Sister Alice when he was very small: he stood very still, turned to the sound and feeling of his breath, and let the things he held in just wash over him.

Mura stared at Albert for a long time, then gave him a kiss on the cheek. She crossed her arms, hugged herself, turned, and walked toward the house.

Albert took some time to collect himself. He shot a few more arrows: all true. He could shoot an arrow, no matter how he felt. When he felt calm enough, he headed toward the house.

Mura tended to the fire. Mama Lini and Papa Arto were making supper. Lini was the tall, stout epicenter: her red hair cascaded from her head in all directions, and the energy of the room danced around her. Piles of chopped soup vegetables sat before her in a frozen orbit. Arto was a compact block of a man, short and sturdy, with a thick black beard the only hair left on his head. He held down the floor with his gravity. He was dropping biscuits for cooking.

The Todorovs spoke a casserole of dialects. The languages of the White Island and Viru made the meat of it, but it was seasoned by everything in between. Arto said to his son, "I need you to help pack the cart before we go to market tomorrow morning, all right? It shouldn't take too long. But you should sleep early for it." Albert gave a faraway nod.

Lini paused her chopping. She went to Albert and cradled his head in her hands. She felt his forehead. "You look sad. Are you sick?"

"I'm fine, Mama," Albert said. "I was just practicing a little extra."

"He does us all proud. He's ready for whatever Baixans they throw at him," Mura said. She put new wood on the fire and poked at it.

Lini winced. "You know I don't want to talk about the Baixans. The Newtons are well? You behaved yourself today?" Albert nodded and worked his way toward Mura and the fire. He stared quietly at the pot. "Really, what's wrong?" Lini said. "Did you eat enough for lunch?"

"Leave him be," Mura said, looking intently at Lini. "He's fine."

"Oh! *Oh*." Lini's eyes snapped wide.

"What? What's going on?" Arto asked.

"Shush, it's fine." Then, in a comical stage whisper: "A crush." She then turned to Mura to confirm. "A crush?"

"I don't want to talk about this," Albert said. "Please stop."

"Is it a nice girl at school?" Lini asked. "Not the horse-keeper's daughter, she's hideous. Is it your teacher? What is the new Adept's name? Julia?"

"Clare," Mura said. "She's been his teacher for a year and you never remember. It's Clare."

"Right, Clare. So it's her?"

"Please, please stop," Albert said. He had already turned to face the wall.

"He's right," Mura said. "Let it rest."

Arto said to Lini: "There's no girl at school. You never pay attention." And then, to Albert: "Thomas is a good boy. You'll make a good home together." And then, to Mura: "The family is ruling class, though, is that going to be a problem?"

"Everyone should stop talking," Mura said with considerably more intensity. Albert was already out the door.

He looked out across the field toward the forest. It was still twilight. The glow of dusk illumined everything and made the familiar seem unfamiliar. He could see details at the point where the woods met their farmland: leaves, needles, and underbrush, and the spaces in between. Vague layers of forest lay beyond that, dark branches that webbed across all his field of vision. Then the greenish black shadow of the forest dissolved into the enormity of itself, on and on and on forever.

He spent some time staring at it, listening to his own breath and listening to the wind caress the trees, feeling it cool his ears. At one point, when everything was still, he thought he saw something, or a shadow of something, several layers in: an indistinct figure moving in the depth of the forest.

He stood and focused on the woods. He felt the wind grow colder as the sun set, a chill on his neck and in his bones. He had lost the shadow, though, and couldn't get it back.

There were things out in the forest. Maybe it was Mister Ewan's father, or the ghost of Mayor Newton, or the Baixans. Maybe it was a crowd of spirits, all those millions of people who died when the world ended, all of them piling on one another in layers and layers. Maybe when he died, he would go and live there, too. He would become just one of those things.

After some time, he turned toward the house and went in to supper.

+   +   +

He dreamed he was in the forest, the deepest of all, with every tree spidering out of the ground and into the other trees. He could see the pattern of every tree inside the leaves, and he knew that the pattern of the forest was the same as the pattern of the tree.

He didn't know the edges of the forest, or how to get out. He was inside a thicket, and it felt like shelter. The shadow came over him. He couldn't see the shadow, but he could feel that the shadow was warm, and wanted Albert, and Albert wanted him back. And when he buried his face into the shadow, feeling its pulse and skin and warmth, he was the shadow, too, and they were the forest, too. When his father woke him, he had a moment of not knowing where he was.

Arto put out some of last night's biscuits with a strong cheese and some radishes from the garden. He made some eggs and barley tea while Albert loaded up the cart.

They ate in quiet until Arto said: "You haven't talked since last night. We didn't mean to embarrass you."

"I know."

"And we won't speak of it. Mama Mura told us that it's difficult."

"There's no *it*. There's nothing to talk about. Everyone's made up a story about nothing. I'm fine. I love food and fighting and shooting arrows. That's all."

Arto smiled and patted his hand. "Probably it will die down at the market around lunch, and you can go out and hunt a bit." He took a sip of his tea. "I want you to get some things to read from Harriet today. You haven't been bringing books home. You didn't think I would notice, did you? I told Harriet I would trade some vegetables and beer. Get whatever you want."

"No, don't do that," Albert said. "It's not worth the cost. I'm almost out of school, and I won't need to read after that."

"You need to read for the rest of your life, all right? You don't know how good it is, that you and all the children in Eden-town get to spend years in school. In the rest of the world, you don't have the Adepts healing everyone and teaching them how to live. When you get away from the Islands, you're lucky to eat, much less go to school. You aren't going to waste that."

"Do they read in wars?" Albert said. "You've been in one, and I haven't, so I don't know. I didn't get the impression that there was a lot of reading, though."

Arto looked away from Albert. He gave more attention to his bite of biscuit and cheese than it needed. "You're smart, aren't you? Smarter than your father."

The Adepts had taught them in school how to identify emotional states in their bodies: they taught it when the children were very little, using games and play. Albert remembered the lesson about shame, about the tightness of breath in the top of his stomach, just beside the ribs. That was where his shame lived, and it sang to him now. "I'm sorry, Papa. I don't govern myself."

"Yes," Arto said. "You are going to war. And I don't sleep anymore because I know this. But what happens when you get back? This is what I try to think about. I try to think about when you come home. Maybe someday I will think about it enough to sleep.

"And, when I finally sleep, I'll dream that you come home with honor, and that you move into a nice house. Maybe a farm, or maybe you will live with Thomas . . . or, no, because you don't love Thomas, do you? But you'll be home. On the Island, in civilization. You taught me that word. Do you remember that? I don't need much from civilization. It's not really my world. Civilization means we have this farm, and no one is trying to kill us. That's all I need. But you, civilization is your world. You learned everything from the Adepts, and you learned it better than anyone, better even than Thomas, although only his mother is brave enough to say that out loud.

"So I'll dream of you coming home a gentleman, with strength and honor and the power of your mind. All the riches you will have!" Arto said, with a burst of enthusiasm that took him halfway out of his seat. "I can barely imagine. I told you how it was in Viru, it wasn't like that at all. Everyone was poor always. Hell, one winter it was so bad somebody tried to eat *me*."

"That's right, the one time, and the man was crazy and you had to run away." Albert had heard the story many times and very much wanted to preempt hearing it again.

"You'll never understand until you see it," Arto said. "All these things that have been part of your life since you were a baby. 'Book.' When I was a boy, I didn't know 'book.' There was no such thing. What is 'book'? What is 'read'? I never read anything, and I never will. Your mother, sewing with needles now? There was no 'needle' in Viru. There was no 'market,' no 'farm.' When we got here, Mal Planck and the Adepts taught us what farming was, and why we should care. Before then, all our lives, it was nothing but hunt and fight and eat and die. You couldn't even understand." He trailed off. There was a long silence.

"So," Arto then said, picking up and biting a radish, "you are going to keep reading. No more protest. Once you have a book, then you can read it and then trade it for more books. That's what Harriet said. And then, when you become a gentleman, and you live in your big house, probably without Thomas, but maybe with Thomas—when you live there, you can remember that we bought you a book, and you can invite us to live with you in your big house."

Albert put his hand on Arto's. "I don't know if it will work out like that. But thank you, Papa."

"We should head into town," Arto said.

They started down the road from their farm to the market square. The road was smooth enough, marked mostly with their wagon wheels. They shared the road with the Plancks, who had the farm just one over. Arto always sang a song while they rode: once, when he was little, Albert had asked Arto about it. "It's a folk song from Viru, wishing good travel. It's lucky," Arto said. "It doesn't sound lucky. It sounds scary," Albert said, and Arto laughed.

Now Albert sang along, although he barely understood the song. All the words were familiar, common words they used in the house, but together they became gibberish, or a code. He sang along all the louder for that, full of hope that someday the veil would drop, that he would be granted a sudden understanding of something real and deep about his father.

There were thick woods for a while between their farms and the town, but when they came out from the woods the town and the Castle stretched before them like another world. The breeze kept Albert alert but not too cold.

When they approached the market, just at the foot of the Castle, it started to get crowded with throngs of people and carts. "If you please," Arto smiled to another farmer as he pulled ahead of him into their spot. The Todorovs had a good spot, near the front of the market.

There were carts with piles of kale greens, beetroot, and mushrooms, carts with big sea fish ready to be split open, fileted, and salted. One cart only sold cut firewood. It did quite well. There were distractions and luxuries: books, spices, wool scarves, and iron jewelry, hot barley and pine teas and boar meat pies. It smelled of food and butchery and harvest. The market was loud with greetings and with the hashing out of bargains and with gossip. Arto and Albert put out their flag.

Mister Ewan was their first customer, as usual. "What do you have today?" Mister Ewan asked. Arto said, "I brought the salted fish you asked for, and the cheese. I have apples and beetroot and greens, lots of greens. And I have your beer. And I have these morels, these mushrooms, take a look at these mushrooms, tell me that you don't want those, Lady Newton could eat like the noble she is just on these mushrooms. And this, you should try it." He handed Mister Ewan a small earthen crock. "This is good, it's salt and peppercorns and bits of the pig's head."

"Do you have stockings? Both the Lady and Thomas have holes in their stockings."

"I do. New ones! Lini just finished these." He pulled them out. They were a vivid red. Mister Ewan laughed and said, "Yes. These are lovely."

"Thank you, Mister Ewan," Arto said as he took some coin from him. The Adepts had recently introduced money to the White Island. "Do you know why we immigrant Todorovs do well at market?" Arto said. "We do well because you always come to us first and trade with us. You trade for the Newtons. And you always have, since the very beginning."

"It's selfish. You have the best cart," Mister Ewan said. He looked at Albert. "I remember when you were a baby. Your father had just started to bring the cart. You would roam around all day talking to everyone. Charming everyone."

"He loved the butcher," Arto said. "One time he disappeared for hours, have I told you this story? I was terrified. His mothers would kill me if I lost him. And so I run around the market in a panic, and turn over every rug and every cart, and then when I get back to ours he is just sitting there, covered in blood and offal, and smiling and saying, 'I was helping the butcher.'"

Mary Hawking drifted over to them from her cart. She sold spices. Arto was talking, but she interrupted him. "The Baixans are sneaking in, did you know that? On their boats. All quiet-like. If they knew what was good for them, they'd turn around and jump back into the sea." She punched Albert's arm. "Before we send you at them."

Samuel Bohm had joined in by now. He built furniture. "I heard they're down south, somewhere with nothing but rocks and beasts. I heard they're going to settle in and make a town. Then, when they have a town, they'll attack us and say the Island is theirs."

Geoffrey Pauli sat in the cart next to Arto's, selling his pottery. His son Harald sat next to him and ate a small rhubarb cake that Albert had given him. Geoffrey wiped some cake off of Harald and then made a face at Samuel. "How do you know all this about the Baixans, if there's nothing where they are?"

"Mal Planck heard it from one of the Adepts," Samuel said.

"So the Adepts know this. The *Adepts*," Geoffrey said. "And, knowing this, they are just letting the Baixans do it."

"I don't know, maybe the Adepts have something up their sleeve. Maybe they're just waiting for Albert to finish school in a few weeks, so he can send them all crashing back into the sea." Samuel gave Albert a gentle punch on the arm as well. Albert had gotten a lot of gentle punches recently.

"I'll believe it when I see a Baixan," Geoffrey said. Samuel started to say something, but Geoffrey was already walking to the other side of the cart.

They sold out of most of their supply in a blur of a morning. By lunch, everyone had gotten their shopping and their gossip out of the way. They sat quietly while Arto counted the money. Most of the White Islanders still found money bizarre and frightening, but Arto had taken to it. "It stands in for things you trade. We had something like this in Viru. I understand some things," he had said to Albert.

Albert went to get pies for his father and himself from a cart down the way. On the way there, he went to the book cart. Harriet sat in the middle of the books, her back to him, her hair long down the back of her head in brown and gray lines. She was trying to lure a cat over with some crumbs of food. The volumes around her were large, sewn with hide on the front. When she realized he was there, he had already started to leaf through one of the books. "The sisters put the words on them at school," he said to Harriet.

"We just have ones with words on them already. Because I'm not an Adept." Harriet smiled. "I have plenty of books, though, and I know them all. So you can come and talk to me. And I can talk to Sister Clare if you want something I don't have."

"Do you have any physics?" Albert asked.

Harriet picked up a volume, a thinner one. "This is called the Feynman Lectures. I tried to read it once. It's difficult. I didn't understand it!" She laughed. "Do you study physics at school?"

"Thomas does. Physics is mostly for Administrators, I guess." Albert said. "Do you have any sutras?" She had a book with sutras and stories of bodhisattvas. He paged through it. It had pictures: images of the Buddha and mandalas.

The traffic at the cart picked up a bit right after lunch, but then dropped off again. Arto was relieved; he was running low in stock and hated to turn people away. They sat in the cart, and Albert told Arto about the books: which ones he wanted to read first, what a sutra was, and what little he knew from school about the people who wrote sutras, people who were ancient at the time of the ancients. After that, they just sat and watched people go by. The afternoon sun settled into the horizon.

Thomas stopped by the cart. He had his bow. "Hello, Farmer Arto! How was business?"

"Good, better than we deserve, Master Thomas. Thank you. You look very official," Arto said. When they were in school, both the boys wore uniforms, but when they weren't Thomas wore Administration clothes: the fine gray wool, the red embroidery. He looked like an adult to Albert. He looked like someone to be proud of.

Thomas and Arto made small talk. When it started to taper off, Thomas stood around and picked at loose splinters at the edge of the cart.

"It's a nice day still," he said to Albert. "I thought I might go out and hunt."

"What a lovely idea you've had, Master Thomas," Arto said. "Albert, we're closing up. You should go with Thomas. Master Thomas, I've been putting money into your bank!" He showed Thomas the money.

"Yes, Albert said! Thank you. More people are starting to do it. Sister Alice is very excited. She says the bank is very important for civilization."

"Sure, I suppose that makes sense," Arto said.

"Does it?" Thomas asked. "I'm glad. I wish someone would explain it to me." He smiled.

"We'll head up to the north forest, Papa," Albert said. "We'll be careful."

Arto kissed his son on both cheeks. "Have fun," he said. He began tying down cargo and packing up as Albert and Thomas started walking north.

They approached the edge of the forest, where the atmosphere started to change. The murmuring of town activity fell away. The woods swallowed the sounds of the world. Albert closed his eyes for a moment to take the silence in, but then Thomas broke it, saying, "I don't want to go to Over-town. I don't want to get married."

"We'll figure it out," Albert said. "Let's talk about it later if we're going to hunt. You'll scare everything away."

Thomas hit a tree with his bow. "I only said that for your father. I don't want to hunt. I wanted to talk to you, damn it."

Albert usually let the tantrums pass, but he didn't today. "Stop it. Someone worked hard for a long time to make that bow. Stop disrespecting it."

"Stop talking like my mother."

"Your mother's usually right. Stop acting like a baby."

He thought Thomas would either tackle him or run away. Thomas didn't do either, though. "Fine," he said. Then they walked some more.

"I have to do things, too," Albert said. "I have to go fight the Baixans."

"We don't know for sure that we'll fight the Baixans," Thomas said.

"Seems like we're going to fight eventually."

"That's different, though. You like fighting."

"I like practicing. It feels different now that it's really going to happen."

"But you get to go fight, and then you'll come home . . ."

"If I live."

"Well, I'm assuming you'll live. Then, when you get home, you won't have to fight any more, and you won't be married either. You'll be free to choose." Thomas was still hitting things, but he had grabbed a loose limb to replace the bow. "I guess I thought I could just be an Administrator by myself, and not get married."

"I kind of always thought we would get married," Albert said.

Thomas got very quiet at that. Albert was terrified. He had been sure that Thomas felt the same way, but the feeling changed when it became words. It turned into something clear and real and dangerous. He couldn't undo it. He wanted to say that he had just been joking, but he hadn't been. So he let the terrifying moment be. They walked a little farther.

"Do you want to stop here for a bit?" Thomas said. "It's a good clearing." They were near a glade where deer would bed. At the edge of the clearing they found a fallen trunk to sit on. Albert picked up comforting smells of moss and rotting leaves. Some low trees framed the clearing, and it was dim and still with the shade and the aging afternoon sun. Albert would have picked somewhere with clearer lines of sight. He still was thinking of hunting, a little.

They sat for a while in silence, with just the rustle of wind in leaves and the calls of faraway birds echoing across the canopy of trees. Thomas, in small increments, crept across the tree trunk, closer and closer to Albert. Soon, their knees touched, and Thomas began to barely brush the back of his hand against Albert's leg, in a way that at first could be passed off as distracted movement, but became more deliberate and intense when Albert avoided protesting.

Touching each other wasn't new to them; they had played and hugged and grabbed at each other constantly for years. This was different, though. It wasn't affection in and of itself, but something with a goal. It came upon Albert like a swell, a thunderhead: the unspoken thing between them. He looked at Thomas and said, "I—," but Thomas interrupted the thought by clamping his mouth over Albert's.

They crashed against each other, feverish, sweaty, and swept out of reason. Thomas tore the collar of Albert's shirt, then pulled his own shirt off. They pawed off one another's remaining clothes, sprawled on the forest floor, and wallowed in a shared, wild, virginal amazement: that they could actually be naked together like this, that they could put their hands and mouths all over each other, that this was possible outside their minds and in reality. The overwhelming truth of that alone drove them like a wave through their first and second times; by the third, they finally began to come back to themselves, to be intimate with it, to talk through it and tickle each other and laugh and finally rest in each other's arms.

Albert nodded off for a short time against Thomas's

chest, but heard a *psst, psst* and came to. He rose up and followed Thomas's eyes across the glade. A large stag stood within range.

"What do we do?" Thomas whispered.

"Shh," Albert cautioned. His bow was near, and he grabbed it and an arrow silently. Standing was a different matter, and he had to spend a few seconds planning it out. He thought about pulling on his pants, but after consideration just stood naked with his bow.

He looked down at Thomas and whispered, "I have forest all over my ass," and it was Thomas's turn to caution. "Shh."

It didn't feel awkward at all: indeed, he'd never felt so right in his life. He drew and struck the stag in the heart, a perfect shot.

+   +   +

They gutted the stag and dragged it together out of the forest. It was the size of three men. They found a spot near the edge of the forest, covered the stag's body with leaves and branches, and went to town to find a wheelbarrow.

They headed toward the outer edge of the town. The sun was setting, and they walked quietly, side by side. Just before the walls, Thomas grabbed Albert and gave him a sloppy kiss. "I wanted to do that one more time, before we have to be proper again," he said.

They saw something ahead of them on the road, a pile. They thought it was spilled cargo from a cart. As they got closer to it, though, they realized it was two bodies, one lying on top of the other. Albert turned over the body on top.

"That's Seamus. I train with him," Albert said.

The other body wore old, rusted chain armor, with new and clean regalia draped over the breast: black cloth, with an orange serpent. Both the boys had learned this symbol in a lesson Sister Clare taught just a few weeks ago. She told them it was the new insignia of the Baixan army.

They looked at each other in a silence that Albert finally broke. "You take Seamus's sword and shield. I'll take the Baixan's. We need to be armed."

They crossed through the gates. It was too quiet for an early market evening. Shutters were closed and bolted, and no one was out on the street. *Everyone knows,* Albert thought. *The word has gotten out.*

They stuck close to the outer walls of the houses and crept along slowly and quietly as possible. With the sunset, the temperature began to drop again. Albert felt a gentle but cold wind through the thatched houses, and he listened to it, tried to pick up anything that interrupted it. About six houses in, he saw a group walking toward them, too far away at first to be distinct. He put his right arm across Thomas, pressing him against the nearest wall. They waited until they saw the black and orange on their chests.

There were three of them. The orange of their nation hung on them limply. They stumbled into each other with a manic lack of focus. When they were about twenty feet away, Albert stepped toward them. He had already nocked an arrow. "Stop. You're . . . under arrest," he said.

The soldier in front and center, the largest one, looked directly at him. He looked bedraggled and wild. Albert noticed his eyes, a weird luminescent green, greener than the distance between them, brighter than the twilight around them. The center soldier started taking awkward, interrupted steps toward him, his drawn sword hanging limply against his leg, bouncing against it.

Albert paused. He had expected a fierce charge. It always happened that way in militia training. He didn't know how to time himself. He felt an awkward tremble, somewhere just below his belly. He pushed it down, drew his bow, and fired directly toward the soldier. The Baixans wore helmets, but their faces were exposed. He aimed there and hit there.

As the big one fell, the other two let out a shrill shout and fell toward them. Their fear and hostility comforted Albert. *Obviously looking for trouble.* He dropped his bow and drew his sword. "Now, Thomas," he said. Thomas hesitated, but then drew his sword and ran to join him.

One soldier held an axe: Albert went to him, leaving Thomas to work with the second, a smaller soldier with a short sword. *That's safer,* he thought.

The soldier with the axe made clumsy swings, opening himself up each time. Albert dodged the first couple easily, with surprise. *These are the Baixans?* At the third swing, he struck at the exposed weapon arm, a downward chop at the bicep. The soldier screamed wildly, tried to pull back, and lunged at the sword with his shield edge. Albert pulled his sword free and took a second swing at the neck. Baixan armor left much of the neck exposed. He hit flesh and the soldier fell.

Albert could hear Thomas making practice sounds as he fought. "One, two, parry, up, down, block," he murmured. Nervous, defensive whispers.

Albert dropped his sword, took his own opponent's axe, and brought it down on the final Baixan's shoulder and neck from the side. The Baixan collapsed, moaning.

"Put the blade through his neck, Thomas," he said, a gentle command. Thomas hesitated, then did it, with a little battle cry performance.

It was over. They caught their breath.

"You used the Baixan's axe," Thomas said.

"I wanted to keep the sword sharp for a little while."

"You were so fast. I'm not as good a soldier as you."

"Don't say that. You did well. You just need to be ready to kill them. Remember that they want to kill you first. Mostly, though, stop worrying about it. Otherwise, you'll freeze up. You'll be fine with a little more practice."

"You sound like our fighting classes."

Albert smiled. "I'm just saying what the teacher says."

Albert heard a cold ringing in his ears. He had practiced fighting daily since he was a child, but he had never killed another person before. How well he did it frightened him. He felt smaller and nervous. He wanted to say, *Be careful. I love you*, to Thomas, but this wasn't the forest. They had to be different. They started toward the Castle.

Their footsteps felt loud against the dirt as they walked. The twilight deepened into darkness, and it was empty and quiet all the way to the square like any cool spring night. The buildings opened up to the square on the far side, opposite the school and Thomas's house. They walked across the old rocks and grass in the stillness, trying to stay in the shelter of the buildings.

As they crossed the square, they saw a figure with a pale glow, equidistant from the school and house. They got closer and realized it was Sister Alice. She seemed calm, if focused, and she gazed far up in the air. She held a small box in her upturned hands, the source of her glow. As they got closer, they saw the detail and shape of the shining, humming box.

"It's a magic box," Thomas whispered to Albert. Suddenly, Albert realized they were sneaking up on their old teacher. He felt like a schoolboy doing something he wasn't supposed to. He called out, tentatively, as gentle as a yell could be. "Sister Alice, it's Thomas and Albert, can we help?"

"I'm fine, boys, just a moment, please," she said. Polite as always, and only a bit more curt than usual. They moved more closely toward her. Albert didn't understand why she stood in place, or why she gazed into the sky so intently. He tried to get closer, to see what she was seeing.

He looked up toward the sky. In the fading twilight, he could see a dark, squirming mass, far, far up in the air, hundreds of feet. It shook, and little wiggling appendages extended from it. He couldn't make sense of it, until he saw that it was growing. Slowly, almost lazily, figures floated up from various points in town to the mass, into the sky, each of them flailing, each of them unable to control what was happening to them.

Thomas crept up next to him. "What is it?"

"It's a bunch of men. She's floating up Baixans and binding them in the sky."

The last figure floated up into the mass. The group of them writhed, a beast of many arms and legs. Albert guessed at least twenty Baixans were up there, defying gravity against their will.

"Please stand over here by me, boys," Sister Alice asked, and they did. Once they were standing next to her, Albert heard her exhale, and saw the glowing box fade to dark. Then he saw the mass fall from the sky. The men landed on the opposite side of the square with a sick, wrong sound, at once both wet and metallic.

Sister Alice sighed and turned to them. "My apologies, boys, that was vulgar. There were too many of them to do anything more precise. I wish you hadn't had to see that." And then, after an uncomfortable silence, she said, patiently, "Are you boys all right? We're under attack, now, so we need to be sharp."

"Yes, ma'am, it's . . . all right, ma'am," Thomas said.

Albert waited a moment, not sure how to deal with what he had seen. He pretended she was still his schoolteacher. "Sister Alice, we came here from the north forest," he said. "What are they trying to do?"

"There aren't many of them," Sister Alice said. "It seems that they wanted to sneak in and cause trouble."

"We . . . we killed some of them," Albert said. "Do all Baixans have those green eyes, like monsters? They don't seem real."

"Where did this happen? Please visualize it for me, Albert."

Albert had done this dozens of times in school; the process was natural at this point. He set an intention for the memory, relaxed his mind, and let the memory arise in flashes and chunks. It never made sense that the randomness of his mind could tell a story, but the less he tried to understand it, the better he seemed to do in school. So he calmed himself now and let it happen.

Sister Alice closed her eyes, put her hand on Albert's shoulder, and focused. ". . . There. This is a very rich visualization, Albert, very good." She was quiet again, looking as if she were trying to access something in her mind. "Thank you, Albert."

"Was that all right? Could you see it?"

"Yes. The green eyes are unusual, Albert. I hadn't seen it in the others. This is a good discovery."

"What does it mean?" Thomas asked.

Sister Alice paused. "It's . . . nothing. A forest sickness." She gestured to the coast. "Many of the militia have gone down coast to where the Baixans landed, and they have that under control. I think we have most of the troops that got into the city now, but only most. Please keep patrolling. Help the militia with any stragglers."

"Yes, Sister Alice," Thomas said, standing a little taller and speaking with a voice that sounded especially adult.

"Head toward the coast south of town, but be sure to cover all the side ways and corners. I'll stay here and protect the main square. You can send people to me if anyone's worried or confused."

"Thank you, ma'am," Albert said. They headed out of the

square and down the Castle, walking diagonally through the town and toward the coast. It was dark, and the moon had risen. Out in the distance, they could hear the faintest clamor from the coast, which they figured must be the militia. This part of town, though, like the north gates, was eerily quiet.

Albert saw a cat walk lazily along the street, not trying to conceal itself. It came up to them, and Albert scratched it behind the ears. It nuzzled his leg. The town had lots of cats, and because they were everywhere, people tended to ignore them, or even killed them like pests, which Albert couldn't abide. He liked cats. They were good hunters.

"Stop playing," Thomas hissed at him. "We need to be on patrol."

"There doesn't seem to be much to patrol," Albert said. "I think Sister Alice dropped most of them." He trailed off when he saw some movement ahead. It was a man, who promptly dropped the sword and somewhat rickety looking shield he was carrying. The man walked toward them with hands raised.

The man spoke to them in a Baixan dialect. Albert understood some phrases from it. Terra Baixa had a hundred dialects, but Albert's parents had spent a long time crossing it, and they had taught the words and phrases they learned to him.

"Be careful," Thomas said, "I bet it's a trick."

"Maybe," Albert said, "but maybe not. He probably saw all his friends drop out of the sky, after all." He approached the Baixan and tried to use the dialect that he heard. He managed to say, "Hello, please stay, we are not going to kill you."

The Baixan fell to his knees and shook. He looked incapable of harming anything. He looked up at Albert. His eyes were normal to Albert: brown, with a bloodshot red tinge, pink at the edges. Albert drew closer to him and put together the sentences: "Please get up now. You will go with us to the beach."

The Baixan's response was rapid and desperate, and it took a few seconds before Albert could understand. ". . . You take us and you lock us up, you (*something*) us, I am so hungry, and then (*something something*) us, here, and now we are here and you fight us? Just to go to (*something*) again? I don't understand. But it's fine, it's all right, all right? Just please don't kill me, please don't kill me."

"What is he saying?" Thomas asked.

"I don't . . . it doesn't make sense. I don't understand what he's saying. He says he's hungry, and please don't kill him."

"All right, that's fair," Thomas said, and then to the Baixan, slowly and loudly, in the White Island language, "*We are not going to kill you.*"

Albert sighed. "Let's just take him with us to the coast."

They put the Baixan in front of them, at swordpoint. Albert let Thomas handle the prisoner management. It seemed to give Thomas a sense of pride, and it allowed Albert to talk more with the prisoner.

"Please say more things to me about your past," Albert said. "I don't understand the words you are saying. Please say it to me in the most simple way."

The Baixan sighed, exasperated. "You! White Island! Hurt us! And put us here! And then my friends fly in the sky! And then . . . (*crashing noise*) . . . Incredible! Why? Why do you do?"

Albert had no idea what to say. "I don't understand."

They walked farther southeast from town. The landscape changed as they drew toward the coast. They came across a cluster of smoldering houses, with broken-in doors and windows, trampled gardens, and toppled cisterns. The occupants of the houses stood outside, brooding over three dead Baixans.

"They lit the roofs and then broke in and attacked us. My brother has a terrible wound in his stomach, the bastards. But we took care of them. If the idiots had waited an hour, we would have all been in bed. How about you, you bastard?" the homeowner said, pointing to Thomas and Albert's prisoner. "Let us kill him."

"He surrendered," Albert said. He stood as tall as he could in the face of a mob of his elders. "I'm taking him to the Adept."

"He'll get White Island justice," Thomas said. Albert recognized the voice Thomas always took on when talking to townspeople: clear as a bell, emphatic without being overbearing. "That's how we show them that we are better than they are." The crowd accepted Thomas's statement with a clear lack of enthusiasm. Albert and Thomas walked on with their prisoner.

They reached the spot where the Baixans had landed. Albert recognized several militia members. Ten enemy soldiers lay face-first on the shore, their hands bound behind their backs. Samuel Bohm, furniture builder and senior member of the militia, watched over the proceedings, giving a few orders. The whole business seemed to be winding down. The militia were practicing military formality but were visibly excited that they had come out victorious. Albert wasn't sure whether they should approach Samuel directly, but Thomas clearly had no qualms. He strode up to him, and Albert prodded the prisoner so that they could follow.

"I told you," Samuel said to Albert.

Albert shrugged. "Yes, sir, you did."

Samuel gestured to a spot on the shore where the other Baixans were tied, and Albert took the prisoner there. His friend Aengus was watching the prisoners. Aengus had been a few years ahead of Albert in school, but hadn't challenged Albert all the time like the other older students had. He would sit next to Albert in class sometimes and tell older-boy stories, raucous stories, his arm around Albert's. Albert had always worried that Aengus would get him in trouble. "Hallo, Aengus, here's a prisoner."

"All right, Al? Aye, we can put him here. I have some rope."

"Can they breathe all right? They're stuck in the sand."

"They can turn their heads back and forth. I don't think we need to coddle them. They did try to invade us, after all."

"Yeah, I guess so," Albert said. "This one seems pretty confused."

"Of course he does, he's a Baixan," Aengus said. "They don't have Adepts or towns or civilization or anything. They're practically animals." Aengus paused for a second, then said, "No offense intended, Albert."

"What?" Albert said. "Oh. No offense taken."

Albert and Thomas took their leave of the militia members. Albert noticed that Thomas bowed to Samuel, as if this were a ceremony.

As they meandered back toward the Castle, Thomas leaned against Albert from time to time. When they got to the square, there was no sign of Sister Alice, nor of the Baixans she had dropped. "What do you think she did with the bodies?" Albert asked.

"I really don't want to know," Thomas replied.

"You should go check in on your mother. She's probably worried."

Thomas paused for a minute. "Will you come in?"

"My parents will be worried, too. I don't know if they know about the attack, and I'm out so late."

"I wanted to stay over with you tonight."

Albert smiled. "I wanted that, too. Come over tomorrow, and we can spend some time on the farm."

Thomas went inside, and Albert walked on. The full moon shone on the town now, lighting his path. Albert strolled toward the farm with his dreams as company. After the war, he would be a hero, worthy of living with Thomas. Cynthia would surely understand. They could all live together. Thomas would rule Eden-town, and Albert would keep him safe. Thomas and Cynthia would have children, and he would teach them how to shoot a bow and ride a horse. They'd all sit at the table where he'd had lunch for years, happy and fed and content. Every night, Thomas would come into their room in his nightshirt, climb into their bed, and put out the candle as they held each other. It would be perfect.

The west side of town had some candles and fires lit, some rustling and murmuring. A woman called out for her husband from a window, "You have to eat."

"I have to finish," the husband called back from the garden. "I'm late because of the Baixans."

"We never even saw a Baixan," she said, backing away from the window.

The darkness grew thicker and cooler as he walked outside the town walls. Two militia members stood at the gate now. Instead of their usual wave, they gave Albert a formal salute.

The little light that remained at the gates disappeared when he was beyond them. The breeze was cool, and he walked briskly to stay warm. He looked into the trees that surrounded him on the path. He thought about going back to get the stag but decided it would take too long. He regretted killing it. It would be a waste.

Ahead of him on the path, about halfway to the farm, he saw a shape just at the edge of the trees. It moved enough that he knew it was alive, but it was calm and still. As he drew closer, he realized it was a lynx. A good-sized lynx: it stood about five feet tall, eight feet long. Albert should have been on his guard, should have drawn his bow, but he didn't. He just walked toward it, listening to his breath, and to the breath of the lynx.

The lynx stretched as Albert approached, extending its front arms and pulling its haunches back and into the air. It yawned. It still had a full winter coat, gray with black patches at his throat and ears and back, the gray shining in the moonlight. As he drew closer, Albert could see the imperfections in the coat, the scars. The right eye might have been blinded.

Albert reached out to touch the lynx, not knowing why. Naturally, it slashed at Albert's hand, cutting into it deeply. Albert reared back at the hot stinging.

"I'm not your pet," the lynx said.

Albert looked down to his hand in the moonlight, expecting the bath of blood that was to come. He didn't see anything, though. When he gingerly touched the back of his hand, it was whole and dry. The lynx wasn't there.

He emerged from the woods into the farmland. The Plancks' farm was still and asleep as he passed it.

As he approached his home, he noticed a lack of firelight from the house. Everything was as dark and quiet as the surrounding night. That was wrong; they wouldn't have just gone to bed. He started running to the gate at the entrance to the farm.

It sat open, with two bodies at the threshold. They were dead Baixans, each with several arrows in them. Another body lay halfway between them and the house. Albert walked to it, hurried but absent, as if he weren't directing himself.

The body was Mura. She still had her bow in her hand.

She had taken a blow vicious enough to go through most of the neck.

Albert couldn't move. He stood there and stared. *Still and the sound of breath*, part of him inside said, and another part howled, howled and tore at his head and face from the inside. He was like that for moments, hours, trying to feel his lungs beneath the screaming, to hear his breath, to center on the world around him. He finally realized he had to find Mama Lini and Papa Arto.

Albert walked through the front door, which stood open. There had been a fight just inside the house; the furniture was turned over and thrown. The fire had burned down to just embers. Lini lay beside it, absolutely still. A large pool of blood spread beneath her. Arto lay just beyond. Splayed beside him was a final Baixan, with an arrow in his side.

Albert checked them for breath. Lini had none. Arto breathed, shallowly. His head was wet. Albert made sure that the Baixan was dead. He thought he saw marks around the Baixan's neck, though it was hard to tell in the dark. "You killed him, didn't you, Papa?" Albert said to no one. "You tried to keep everyone safe."

He lit a candle. With the light, he could see blood coming from his father's ears. He found cloth for bandages, and cleaned and bound the wounds on Arto's body. He didn't know what to do about the ears, so he gingerly put some cloth around Arto's head.

He cradled his father's head and took him to his room. He dragged the Baixan out of their house, and threw him on top of the other ones. Then he brought Mura in to the house, and put her in her bed, and then took Lini, and put her beside Mura. Then he straightened the furniture.

He went back to his father and sat beside him. He sat there for a long time, staring at the changes the candle made against the wall as it flickered. He didn't know what to do. He realized at some point that he was just saying, "Papa, wake up, Papa, I can't hear you anymore," over and over. That prompted him to get up.

He walked to the Plancks'. He saw the faint glow of a fire and smoke from their chimney. *No Baixans bothered to attack them*, Albert thought. He went to the door and knocked, still disconnected from what he was doing, still alien to everything around him. He knocked gently, knowing he would be waking them up. And then he was telling a sleepy Mal Planck that he needed help and that his mothers were dead.

+ + +

By sunrise, one of the Planck boys had gotten to the Castle and back, bringing along a cart with the Newtons and Sister Alice. They hurried out and found Albert in Arto's room, holding his hand. "He doesn't move or make sounds or anything," Albert said.

Lady Newton took Albert and gently led him from the bedside. "We're here to help. Sister Alice is going to examine your father. Is it all right if we have a few minutes alone with him?" She handed him off to Thomas, who took him back to the main room. Sister Alice closed the bedroom door behind them.

Thomas took Albert in his arms. "I should have been here."

"It was all over when I got here. They were lying here, right there." Albert pointed across the room, and his face contorted with the enormity of it.

They sat on a bench by the fire. Albert buried his head in Thomas's shoulders. He felt the warmth and darkness there, and he wanted that to be everything. He wanted to escape there and stay there. Thomas kissed the top of his head and murmured, *Shh, shh.*

They settled like that for a while. Albert started to feel closer to himself again. The ringing and cold started to fade from his nerves. Then Lady Newton and Sister Alice came from his father's room. Lady Newton said, "What are you boys playing at here?"

Albert sat up and Thomas stood. "I was comforting him, Mother. For mercy's sake," he said.

"We're all here to offer comfort, and we can do it without indignity," Sister Alice said. "It doesn't help Albert or anyone else to cow over him like that."

Sister Alice looked at Lady Newton and said, "Marie," as if it ended a conversation, and then went back into the room.

Lady Newton took a minute to collect herself. She bit at her stylus absently, then worried it with her hands. Then, she put it on the supper table and turned to Albert again, as if she'd just noticed he was here. "Albert, may I speak alone with you for a moment? Thomas." She pointed Thomas to the door with her eyes.

Thomas stormed out of the room, and Lady Newton pretended not to notice. "Let's sit down for a second," she said. Albert thought to himself, *Just tell me, I don't need to sit down*, but in the end he realized he did.

Lady Newton sat more tightly and narrowly than she usually did. "Sister Alice has looked into your father's mind. His mind is gone, Albert. The best thing we can do is put his body to rest as well. Sister Alice is doing this now."

"But . . . no, I mean, he's breathing, we just need to give him a little time." Albert stood up abruptly and began to walk toward his father's room. "We just need to give him a little time!"

Lady Newton stood up after him, grabbing his shoulder. "Albert! Stop. I know it's confusing, but I need you to accept it. The mind makes a life. It would be cruel to let your father die without some kindness and guidance. That's all Sister Alice is doing."

Albert stared at her, wanting desperately to be angry, but realized the truth of it. He deflated.

"You have to accept this, Albert." She looked toward his father's room. And . . . and you have to be strong about this yourself." She stopped there: awkward, unfinished thoughts hanging over the room.

Then, Lady Newton put her head in her hands. The movement was typically controlled and elegant, but also unlike anything Albert could imagine. In this position, she exhaled several times. When she brought her face back from her hands, it was sad and gray.

"Thomas was ten years old when he first told me that he loved you. I should have stopped it then. I should have sent you home and asked you not to visit us anymore. But I couldn't. I couldn't bear the thought of the house without you. By then I loved you, too.

"All this has happened to me: my mother, my father, my husband," she said. She pulled at her fingers, as if she were keeping count. "I wish it weren't happening to you. You're going to want to be gone, too, like your parents are now. You're going to want to walk into the woods so far that you lose yourself, and then just sit and let everything stop. You can't do that, do you understand? You have to keep going."

She paused. She glanced at the stylus on the table. "You and Thomas, whatever's happened already between you has to stop. If Thomas and I were the Plancks, and we lived next door, nothing would make me happier than to have you two together for the rest of your lives.

"But we're not. Our family is a part of the Administration, and we have a responsibility. We are responsible to the White Island and to the re-creation of human civilization. We have to build. Thomas and Cynthia will unite the north of the White Island by their marriage. This is the next step in the path. It will help all of us live in peace. I am willing to sacrifice so much for that. Do you understand?"

Albert stood and stared down at her, speechless.

Lady Newton met his gaze and spoke. "If you . . . if you need to hate me for this, it's all right. Do you understand me? It's all right, if that's what it takes to keep you going."

She stood. She reached up and took his face in her hands. "Just don't stop. I'm begging you. You have to promise."

He felt very far away: between him and the world were layers and layers of shadow and helplessness. From his far-away place, he could hear himself promising Lady Newton, promising her he would keep going.

Sister Alice came from his father's room. She gently closed the door behind her. "Marie," she said in a whisper.

"A moment please, Sister Alice," Lady Newton said. Even in that moment, Albert could hear her coming back, could hear the unbearable sadness and tumult begin to recover itself in rationality and propriety, could hear her returning the world to its order and its common sense. She stood taller, and put herself back in order with some sort of magic gesture. She put her arm around him in a way that made him think, for the barest of a second, that things were going to be all right.

"You should say good-bye to your father. And to your mothers, too, if you haven't yet." She picked up her stylus from the table and placed it in a pocket. "We will all wait outside while you do that. Take as long as you need."

+ + +

Albert walked outside. The sun felt too bright, and he squinted against it. They were all gathered in a circle: the Newtons, Sister Alice, some friends from the militia. Lady

Newton put her hand on his shoulder. She was herself again, kind and orderly. He could see it now: the cordial steel layer between what she felt and what she showed.

"This is a tragedy," Lady Newton said. "We will miss your family terribly." Albert stared as everyone bowed their heads. Lady Newton started to hum something. Albert had heard strains of it before: it was one of the old songs of the White Island, from before civilization. Before he could make out the melody, though, he saw Sister Alice raise an eyebrow. Lady Newton abruptly stopped humming.

Everyone came up after that, each offering their own condolences. Thomas hugged him, but stiffly. All of his comrades hugged him warmly and whispered kindnesses in his ear. *They really mean it, too,* he thought.

Lady Newton started heading back for the cart. She signaled for Thomas to join her.

"I'll stay for a while and help," Thomas said. "I'll walk back later."

Sister Alice looked at him directly in the eye and said, "You're going with your mother. Now."

Thomas silently nodded. He waved to Albert and headed behind his mother.

Sister Alice turned to Albert. "Mila and Will and Aengus will stay with you tonight. They can help you start getting things back in order. You can put your family to rest. We would like to come back soon and pay our respects."

Albert nodded. "Thank you." And then, as soon as the thought came to his mind: "We'll go to war soon, won't we? For this."

"Yes, of course," Alice said. "Your family will be avenged. And we'll bring the boon of civilization to Baixa, so that this won't happen again."

Albert looked out across the field. "What will happen to the farm?"

"We'll station people to watch the forest from here, to watch for Baixans. I expect the Plancks will tend to the farm for a while."

Albert didn't say anything; he just listened to his breath. It sat there steadily, beneath all the things falling apart.

"Albert, look at me," Sister Alice said. "This is a moment to be aware. Your parents came from the wilderness and became a part of us. They were citizens, real citizens. They always had my respect because of that. If you live as a citizen, then civilization will provide for you. I know you know this. Correct?"

Albert knew the drill. "Yes, Sister Alice. I know."

"It's going to be all right, Albert. You have my respect, as well." It was the nicest thing Sister Alice had ever said to him. She climbed into the cart with the Newtons and they drove away.

Albert sat on the stoop in front of the house. Aengus came up, sat beside him, and put his arm around Albert's shoulder. They sat like that silently for a long while. It didn't feel strange to Albert at all. He wanted someone there and didn't care if it felt proper.

When Aengus spoke, he spoke gently and slowly. "You haven't slept for a while, have you? I think it would be a good idea for you to rest. How about we get you cleaned up and in bed?" Albert looked down and realized he still had blood all over himself. He nodded.

Aengus took him by the hand, and led him to the side of the house, where the rain cistern was. Albert absently took off his clothes, leaving them in a pile, grabbed a bucket, and poured a bucketful over his head. He then grabbed lye soap from the stoop—soap his mother had made—and started scrubbing himself with it.

Before long, Aengus came back. "I found a towel," he said, and wrapped it around Albert, who was limp and shivering at this point. When Aengus faced Albert, Albert buried his head in his shoulder. He didn't know what else to do. He couldn't move.

Aengus stepped back and looked him in the face. "I'd carry you if I could," he said. He led Albert into the house and into his room. He wrapped Albert in extra blankets and drew a shade over the window. For a while after, he sat and watched over Albert, but Albert had fallen fast asleep.

+ + +

He dreamed of two men in the forest, a smart man and a strong man. The strong man had taken ill, and the smart man tended to him. He brought clean water, and food, and cool cloths to soothe the strong man's hot brow.

"I should be well, I should be well," the strong man groaned.

"Just rest. I'll take care of you," the smart man said.

The smart man did everything he knew to do. He made poultices and potions; he made the strong man's bed cool and warm; he fed him broth and water and porridge with herbs. None of it worked, and the strong man grew weaker and weaker.

At the end, the strong man leaned his head against the smart man's chest. "Thank you. I'm dying, but these last days have been my happiest. Thank you for taking care of me. I love you."

The smart man wailed, "I love you, I can't lose you. Why is this happening?"

The strong man kissed the smart man's cheek. "This is the forest still. This is what happens."

The strong man slipped away. Albert could feel him die, could feel his breath leave him. Albert watched the smart man bury him, in a clearing surrounded by trees. The smart man sat by the strong man's grave, for years, forever. And Albert could hear him repeating, over and over, a chant, an oath to destroy the forest.

When he woke, light was still peeking through the shade at his window, and Aengus was at the door.

Albert looked to the window and said, "I guess I didn't sleep for very long."

"You slept for an entire day," Aengus said. "Take your time getting up. There's food."

Albert joined him out in the main room. Aengus had fried some lentils and greens. Albert ate three bowls with a bigger hunger than he could remember. Afterward, he and Aengus sat out on the porch.

Aengus let the silence rest for a while and then said, with almost painful gentleness, "So, we want to find a nice place here to rest your parents. We thought this spot over here"— he pointed over their shoulders and behind them, to a point behind the house—"where it looks very pretty and quiet, but isn't too far away. But we can pick wherever you think is best. You let me know, and we will do the digging. I don't want you to have to worry about that right now."

Albert said, "I . . . that would be a good place, sure. Thank you, Aengus."

"I'll tell the others," Aengus said. He headed off.

Albert looked out the front porch. He could see the bodies of the Baixans piled on top of each other, to the side of the footpath. When Aengus came back, he found Albert standing beside the bodies.

"Al? Al, are you all right?"

"For a second, I thought I might cut off their heads and put them on stakes. And put the stakes at the front gate, so the Baixans would know what we would do to them. But that's too terrible."

"Let's tend to your family," Aengus said, taking his hand.

"That's the important thing right now. When that's done, we'll build a fire and burn them."

Albert turned to Aengus with a dark, sad smile. "I don't know if we keep extra stakes around, anyway."

Will and Aengus dug the graves, while Mila helped Albert get the bodies of his parents ready. They cleaned them all, dressed them, and wrapped them in some fabric Lini had woven. When the graves were ready, they lowered them down with rope.

"Do you want to say anything?" Aengus said to Albert.

"I don't want them to be dead. I want to say that." All he could think to himself was, *I used to be able to hear them, I could hear them all the time. And I can't hear them anymore.* He couldn't look at them in the graves like this. His stomach started to lurch under him. "I need to walk away for a minute. Is that all right?"

"Of course, Al. Go take a little time."

"Don't . . . don't cover them yet, all right?"

Albert walked into the forest, far enough that the house and farm were just out of sight. He found a small clearing and lay face-up in it, staring into the canopy. He thought to himself, *It's all right to let them go. I'll still love them.* He started to calm down, but he still didn't want to go back. He lay there and listened to the leaves.

Eventually, he could hear the crunching of footsteps approaching him. Aengus had found him. "Are you all right?"

"I just needed a little time away. I feel better now."

Aengus kneeled beside Albert and, with a little hesitation, ran a hand through Albert's hair. "I understand. This is a lot."

"It's fine to finish. I'm sorry to hold everyone up."

"There's nothing to apologize for. We have plenty else to keep busy. Will is cleaning up the house now. Do you want to stay here? I could bring you a mug of ale, and you could relax," Aengus said.

"No, I'll join you. I should help. I want to."

They finished burying Albert's parents and cremating the Baixans. They cleaned the house. They took care of the livestock, harvested some greens and beets, and killed and cleaned a chicken for supper. Albert cleaned out his room and Arto's, so that the others could sleep there, and moved himself into his mothers' room. He realized there were moments he could create by focusing on the quotidian, moments where he could forget.

As the afternoon went on, they started to slow down. Albert and Aengus tapped a cask of ale to drink. Will and Mila insisted on letting them drink and rest while they made chicken stew with the vegetables from the garden for supper. After drinking ale on the porch with Aengus, Albert insisted on coming in and showing Mila his father's way of making biscuits.

They sat down to supper in warmer spirits. Everyone told stories of good memories they had of Lini and Mura and Arto. They each claimed to have a very favorite sweater, or pair of stockings, or pillowcase that Lini had made. Albert didn't know whether to believe it, but he chose to.

This was a different kind of meal, he thought. It was different from the table of the Newtons, which was laden with manners, and expectations, and unspoken problems, and goals that might never be achieved. It wasn't the table he had shared with his parents his entire life, either. He had fed here since he was a baby. This had been a table so natural to him that he couldn't imagine it having contours; he couldn't perceive its peculiarities or boundaries. Now, he sat in the same place but in a different world. He noticed things here that he had never noticed in this place before:

the light, the acoustics of the room, the interplay of the people and food.

After a while and enough ale, Will suddenly brought up the Baixans. "So we're going to war with them in a week because of why? Because they made a piss-poor attack on our shore? They're primitives. What's the point?"

"For fuck's sake, shut up, Will," Aengus said. "Have some decency."

Will froze and stammered, "I . . . Al, I didn't mean it like . . ."

Albert tried to give a reassuring glance back. "No, don't worry, Will, it's fine. We should talk about this. It's . . . um. Natural."

Aengus put his hand on Albert's. "I'd kill a thousand Baixans for what they did here."

"This isn't about revenge," Mila said, glaring at Aengus. "This is about civilization. The Baixans don't have the world we have here. They resent it. They want to wipe it out."

"But they're crap at it," Will retorted. "If the wolf wants to eat my baby, I don't go to war with it. I just put the baby in the house."

"You're drunk, and whatever point you just tried to make was nonsense," Mila said.

Will shrugged and took a healthy swig of ale.

"No, no, Mila has a good point, listen," Aengus said. "Al, you were there during the attack. The Baixans don't have what we have, and it makes them desperate and vicious. I feel bad for them, I do. But until they learn about civilization and become a part of it, then there's nothing to stop them from doing terrible things, awful things, like what happened to you. I don't want what happened here to happen ever again. Aye, I'll go to war for it." Aengus sounded a little choked up. He was in his cups as well.

Everyone was quiet.

"I want to go, too," Albert said, "but not because I think it will fix anything, or because I think the Baixans will wipe us out, or because we have some civilization they don't. I don't know. I don't know anything. Nothing makes sense. I want to go there and see Terra Baixa, and see whether they really are a nation of terrible killers, or if they are savages needing us to take them over, or . . . or if this is just some shit game. If I go to Terra Baixa, at least I can find out for sure.

"I think I've had too much to drink," Albert said to the silence that welcomed the end of his speech. "I'm going to go to bed now. Thank you all so much for supper and for everything today."

He stood up and went to bed. Will had meticulously cleaned his mothers' bed and put new bedclothes on it. He put on a warm nightshirt that Lini had made, and he climbed in.

He heard somber murmuring outside the room, and then the sound of supper being cleaned up. After a while, Aengus came in, stumbling a little. In a loud whisper, he said, "Will and Mila are gonna stay in the other rooms. Is it all right if I share with you?"

"Sure, of course."

"Thank you, Albert. You're such a good man." Aengus stripped down to his underclothes and just kept on going, tripping over his underpants and ending up naked. Albert peeked at him in the moonlight streaming through the shutters. Aengus had always been an expressive boy, big and vital and aware of his own body. Albert remembered staring at him across the room when they were in school. Aengus's chest and arms were as big as they'd always been, maybe a little bigger with the fat of age. He was getting a belly.

He climbed in behind Albert and, without any pretext or

ceremony, spooned him and pulled him close. "We upset you, I'm so sorry. Will should've just kept quiet."

"It's all right, Aengus," Albert said, and couldn't help stroking Aengus's forearm in reassurance. His forearm was broad and covered in blond hair. "Thank you. I couldn't have made it through today without you."

"You don't deserve this, love, you don't deserve any of this," Aengus whispered against his ear. "You're a good boy. I'm so sorry." With each word, Aengus's affectionate speech became less speech and more breath against the back of Albert's neck. Around the point of "I'm so sorry" it had become mostly just rough lips on his skin.

Albert lay there silently for a minute, not sure what to do. He thought about Thomas. Thomas's love was his childhood table, so natural that he had never noticed its contours, its peculiarities, its boundaries. Now, he was amazed that he had never seen the chasms around it or beneath it. He was in the same place, a familiar place, but in another world.

He flipped over and kissed Aengus. Aengus's face was soft and stubbly. It felt nice. After that, he just let everything happen.

2

The solid gray sky spat rain as they landed. The wind froze them and tossed the boats as they crossed the channel, and, when they landed, it kicked up muddy sand and blew it on their faces.

Albert looked back from where they had come. They'd spent far less time on the water than he'd expected. He had never been away from the White Island, and, in his mind, Terra Baixa was the other side of the world. Really, though, it was nothing between them; he could look across the water and still see the cliffs of the land they had left.

As they brought the boats ashore, he found himself staring across the water, until the commander shouted, "Make a perimeter!" and slapped him on the back. He gave himself a little grief for not being alert.

They had marched for six weeks, starting in Edentown and heading down the White Island coast. They had walked through the midlands, and through the North Umbrian lands, where the oldest and biggest trees in all of the White Island stood. They had gone past one of the hot places, where the people before the end had kept infernal machines, where the machines had collapsed and their fires had tainted the very ground. Over time, the hot places had lost their fundamental sickness, but they were still strange, treeless places. The one they visited in North Umbria had been peaceful and uninhabited. They crossed it on a sunny day; the sun shone down on the grasses and heathery crags, and they could see butterflies and bees as they walked.

The forest kept them company through the whole march. It sat always to their right, its trunks and canopy and animals and eternity hiding beyond the tree line. "I wonder if the forest changes as you go south, like the coast does," Aengus had asked Albert, as they stared into the green.

"Sure it does. I don't know exactly how, but it has to, like anything else." Albert said. "I guess that's what makes Eden-town and Over-town special. That's the best road from east to west on the White Island, isn't it? It's the only place where we can imagine just going right west. Otherwise, it's all like here. Stuck between the woods and the water."

Aengus smiled then, and looked a little less weary. When they had started the march, Aengus was full of jokes and vigor, but then he began to complain about the walking, the orders, the monotony, and the blisters on his feet. His complaints had gotten gradually louder and more frequent, until the commander yelled at him to shut up.

He and Albert shared a tent, but the romps of the first few nights had turned into long, worried heart-to-heart talks, and then the quiet, worn nights of the final weeks.

"I'm so tired, but I can't sleep," Aengus would say to Albert, who had been trying. Albert turned over and watched Aengus staring up at the roof of the tent. "This is the right thing, we're doing the right thing," Aengus reassured himself. "But I'm so tired. Are we even going to be able to fight like this?"

"Let's try to sleep," Albert said. Albert looked at Aengus and tried to picture the boy at the farm who drank ale on the porch and acted confident and cantankerous to make Albert feel better. Aengus was so much better at comfort than he was, Albert thought. They didn't need to trade.

They found some respite in village stops along the way—King's-town, and North-town, and Inland-town. They were all like Eden-town: kindly, hardworking people, small, cozy squares, and happy, safe children. Everyone was excited about the effort. Militia from each town joined them as they went, until Albert lost count of the troops. Kids would follow them out of town and cheer. In King's-town, a little girl gave him a drop biscuit, like his father used to make. It was wrapped in a little cloth napkin, with butter and honey. He squinted through his wet eyes and thanked her.

The terrain turned to marshes. They came to the estuary of the Dark River, where it met the sea. A boat full of Adepts waited there for them. The Adepts had sailed from their home, the White Island's Old City. The boat was taller than a house, and its wood glowed a burnished deep gold in the setting sun. It stood between Albert and the sun as he and Aengus took their small pinewood dinghy across the river to the south shore. It would follow them the rest of the march.

Finally, they made it to the launch site at the Headland. They could not have set out farther north, as the land rose into the cliffs and no one disembarked from the Abyss. It was very bad luck.

The Abyss was a decaying stone wall, not far upcoast from the Headland and built before the apocalypse. Someone or something had carved great round openings into the wall that led straight to hell. The Adepts disputed the existence of hell, of course, and claimed that you could travel through the caves to Terra Baixa. Albert had heard that the

Old People had powers to travel through magic doors, and he wondered if the Adepts were trying to sell a similar idea. But he knew, regardless, that it was madness. Nothing that went into those holes came out, and to even be there was to tempt demons. Everyone knew that.

The militia stopped at the Abyss on the way. Albert wasn't sure why. He thought it might be some sort of ritual. Maybe they had to face the horror of the Abyss to gain courage, so that they would stay strong in Terra Baixa. Or maybe, he thought, they needed to connect to what they were before the Old People arrived, before there were Adepts and farms and houses. Maybe they needed to remember when they were savages, like the Baixans, not so long ago.

They all stood in front of the holes, in front of the wall and the doors to hell. Then the commander, the hard-ass who had shouted them all the way down the coast—the hard-ass who was taking away Aengus's soul, bit by bit—the commander screamed at the Abyss, just screamed at it. The troops gradually joined in, until hundreds of them were yelling at the wall, at the wounds in the world that shouldn't exist.

The Abyss took all the wrath of five hundred young soldiers taken from quiet lives and brought to an effort that barely made sense. In the middle of the screaming, Albert turned to look at Aengus and mouthed, silently, *This is crazy*, and Aengus, with a look of overwhelming relief, mouthed back, *I know!* Albert realized he had pulled Aengus back from a lost place just then. He'd done something worthwhile that day.

After the yelling died down, a cadre of officials—Adepts, Administrators, and a little man, one of the Old People— appeared on horseback at the top of the Abyss hill, facing the soldiers. Albert thought, *That one looks like Thomas*, and then realized that it was.

Thomas and his mother had left for Over-town the same time he and Aengus had started marching. The last time he saw Thomas was the morning he went to do business with Lady Newton.

"What is this about?" Aengus asked as Albert left the farm.

"There are things to do with the bank after your parents die. I think she's going to give me the money my father gave to the bank."

"Do you need a bag to carry it?"

"I don't know. I'll borrow one if I do."

When he approached the house, he had seen Thomas staring at him from the upstairs window, but it wasn't Thomas at the door. Mister Ewan showed him to Lady Newton's office. Lady Newton didn't mention Thomas but was very friendly. Mister Ewan brought them tea. It turned out the money was his now, and he could just leave it in the bank.

As they finished their business, they heard a sudden crash and a call from Mister Ewan. "Oh, no! Oh, milady, come quickly, the supper for tonight, I think it's ruined."

Lady Newton pursed her lips, tapping them with the stylus. "Albert, just a moment, please. I should attend to whatever he's on about." She left him in her office. He drummed his fingers, then looked at the paper she had asked him to write on for the bank. The writing didn't make much sense. Then, Thomas came in.

"Thomas? What's going on?"

"She wouldn't let me come down to see you. I asked Mister Ewan to create a distraction."

"You're a grown man," Albert said.

"Could you shame me later? We have two minutes at most, and I'm leaving for Over-town at the end of the week." He took Albert's hand. "I'm sorry I haven't visited. I miss you."

"I miss you, too," Albert said. Then he felt something hot

rise inside him, and he let it say: "But what does that matter? With marriage and war going on. Are you not going to get married because you miss me? Does missing me turn me into someone you can marry?"

Thomas just stared at him.

Then the voice coming from Albert said: "Maybe we could just leave. Maybe we could walk away and go live in the woods. That's what we'd have to do, isn't it? Are you ready to leave it all? I'll try if you want to."

Thomas looked away. He was supposed to say, "Yes, of course, Albert, yes," but he didn't.

Albert crossed his arms and said, "Exactly. So let's stop acting like children and try to act like citizens."

Lady Newton burst back in and said, "Thomas," much more loudly than anything Albert had ever heard her say before.

"What did you say to him?" Thomas shouted at her. "I hate you."

Albert turned to Thomas. "I'll write you. We'll figure something out." He then turned to Lady Newton and said, "Please don't take this out on Mister Ewan. He was only trying to help." Then he showed himself the door.

He told Aengus all about it that evening on the porch. "They were the closest thing to family I had left," he said. "Now it's all ruined."

"They're still your family," Aengus said. "You're just upset. You're going to miss them. You should have said a more proper good-bye."

"There's no point in it. Everything's different now."

"You can't just leave what you two have. You're kidding yourself."

Albert looked at him. "What do you mean, 'what we have'?"

"We were all in school for years, Al. Everyone knows. It's

best to be honest about it. It's fine, I don't mind." Aengus looked away from Albert.

And then, there at the Abyss, Thomas stood before them, surrounded by importance. His bearing had changed: he wore the armor of the White Island and held a confident, grave expression over the troops. Albert tried to catch Thomas's eye, but there were too many people, was too much noise, too much hell, between them.

During the crossing to Baixa, as he bilged the dinghy that Aengus tried desperately to steer, Albert stared across the channel, at the boat that held the Adepts and Old People and Administrators. He wondered if Thomas was on it. Even in the wet grayness he could admire the boat's size, the quality of its polished wooden hull. A carved horse's head graced the bow. When the militia landed, the big horse boat sat at the center of everything, soldiers milling around it.

"Half of us help them out, while the rest of us fend for ourselves," Albert said.

Aengus shrugged, then moved to help another soldier who was fighting his boat out of the waves. Suddenly, the commander jumped onto Aengus, pushing him away from the boat and screaming.

"No! No! You *make a perimeter*! That's not your boat. What the hell are you *doing*? You . . . make . . . a *perimeter*!" Aengus, flustered, tripped over his own feet and fell over. The commander, continuing to scream, kicked him.

That was enough.

Albert came up behind the commander and swept his leg. The commander fell to the ground while Albert drew his sword.

The commander rolled away from Albert and hopped back up to a crouch. He snarled and drew a knife. The commander was older than Albert, maybe as old as Lady Newton or Albert's parents. Albert realized that the commander had probably been born in the forest. He might have even grown up in the forest. When he went to battle, he didn't even think of the sword: he'd rather wrestle and stab with knives. Albert laughed. This would be easy.

The commander lunged forward with his knife, but Albert was already out of the way. He kicked the commander in the back, putting him face-first into the sand. The commander rolled over onto his back, but now Albert's sword was at his throat.

"You try anything stupid right now, and it's over. Stay down."

"I'll kill you," the commander said.

"I doubt it. If you tried, I would kill you first," Albert said. "You might as well just drop that idea.

"All of your . . . behavior is going to stop. Stop harassing us, and start acting like a leader. If you say no, I'll run you through."

The commander glared at him.

Albert said, "Take your time if you aren't sure which way to go. I'm not in any hurry."

"Traitor!" the commander said. "Brat. Fucking Baixan. You're going to be strung up for this."

"That isn't helpful," Albert said. He pressed the blade into his neck a bit, making a little dent.

The commander's eyes welled. He howled at Albert in rage, a mad look in his eyes. Albert moved the sword to the right of his Adam's apple, just afield of the jugular, and pressed in, just until the skin was broken. The mad eyes widened and glazed over in helplessness.

They were surrounded by soldiers. All of them murmured to one another, but no one did anything. Then a little man emerged from the crowd, one of the Old People. Albert had always known about the Old People, from school and from stories, but he'd never seen one until the Abyss. He thought this might be the same one. The Old Person looked frail and small, only six feet tall.

"What's going on?" the Old Person asked. He asked it gently, like they were greeting each other on a walk.

"Stop him, Brother Richard," the commander said. "Make him stop. Please."

Albert took a dry swallow and then spoke. He projected for the crowd. "Hello, hail, Brother Richard. Sir. Sir, our leader fails to understand the distinction between discipline and abuse. It's hurting our morale. I've asked him to correct his course. He had a particularly poor moment." For a second, then, he became aware of himself. His words felt like Adept words, from the military training and the schooling that Sister Alice had passed to him. He felt strong and clever.

"He's lying, Brother Richard," the commander pleaded. "He's a traitor."

Richard looked at each of them for a moment. Then, he said, "Albert, Nikola. May I take a moment to observe your memories?"

"Yes, sir," Albert said. "Thank you for asking." The commander whimpered an assent, the sword still at his neck.

Richard closed his eyes, held still for a couple of moments, then opened them with an exhalation. "Albert, you're obviously being insubordinate. You're also right.

"Nikola, dear. This isn't working out. We talked about this, yes? About this need to dominate others to feel secure. We agreed it wouldn't become a problem, didn't we? But now, here we are, and you are contributing negatively to the effort."

Nikola started crying. His last bits of dignity flooded out of him. Richard kneeled beside Nikola and almost invisibly moved Albert's sword away as he did so. He touched Nikola on the forehead.

"There, there. Don't blame yourself. I made an error in judgment. This is a new world, and it can be difficult."

Nikola curled his big head into Richard's tiny shoulder and wailed.

"We'll send you back with some supplies. You'll meet Brother Calvin at the outskirts of the Old City encampment. We will help you work through this."

Richard then looked at Albert. "So. You are the commander now."

"What?" Albert said. "I mean, excuse me, sir?"

"You've just undermined this one's authority and made a successful argument against his ability to do the job. What would you suggest I do?"

"I don't know. Shouldn't you punish me, send me back or lock me up or something?" *Float me up a mile in the sky with a magic box and then drop me?*

Richard smiled. "I'm trying an experiment. Let's hope I don't regret this decision, dear. Please allow Nikola to stand."

Richard walked Nikola away. Everyone turned to Albert and stared.

Albert turned to Aengus. "The boat's all right?"

Aengus and the soldier next to him nodded dumbly in unison.

"Right," Albert said. "So, I guess we need to make a perimeter."

+   +   +

The next morning, he received a note from Brother Richard, calling him into the Adepts' camp for a first briefing. The Adepts camped several hundred yards away from the troops, on clearer and more even ground. The tents gleamed in Albert's view as he approached. They were a clean white, formed of the same oiled canvas used for sails, sturdy and waterproof. They were laid out at right angles, with good spacing in between. Albert and Aengus slept in a tent made of animal skins and shellacked wool, with plenty of leaks, and they had one of the best in the militia.

Albert approached the center tent. Richard emerged just as he came to the entry. Albert reared back and yelped.

"Nothing to fear here, Albert," Richard said.

"Thank you. I'm still not used to, um." Albert stopped himself.

Richard gave back a smile, wry but open. "It's fine. Please come in."

Sunlight cast a warm beige glow through the canvas. Beds and animal skins covered the ground, and a long but very low wooden table sat in the far corner. The table held a desperately organized set of books and papers: military history, maps with arrows, but also some diagrams that Albert recognized from Thomas's physics. One map was marked up extensively with pins and with lines and dots in many colors of ink.

"I'll make some tea, Albert," Richard said.

"Thank you, please, or, that is, you don't have to, I can make tea . . ."

"That's kind of you to offer, dear. I'm fine. Please sit."

He did. The stool was like a baby's stool, but he managed to squat on it. He looked over the papers on the table. He tried to scoot closer to the table but banged his knees on the edge of it. "These are the plans for the incursion?"

Richard nodded. "This is Terra Baixa. You know from your lessons at school, yes? This," he pointed, "is us. This, here, is our destination. The march will take a few weeks. First, we will wait here for all our troops to assemble, and then we will take the front to the Baixans."

"Will we have surprise on our side?"

"I doubt it. We're very visible, even now. We have a significant advantage in numbers, though. Were I a Baixan, I would feel a sense of inevitability about it."

"Won't they send some Administrators to negotiate with us or something, then?"

Richard smiled and patted his hand. "They don't have Administrators, Albert." He looked directly at Albert in that Adept way, eye contact that didn't break, no matter how uncomfortable it got.

"They aren't organized in the sense that we are. That's much of the point. We assume many things about how people work, how groups work: those things are not true here. There is no central Administration to negotiate with. There's only us, against the chaos that is Terra Baixa."

"But they attacked us and want to invade us. Right? How can they do that if they don't have an Administration?"

"*Invade* is a strong word." Richard paused. "There's no doubt that they are aggressive. They were lashing out at us, and we had to respond."

He took a longer pause, lost in thought. "I could hear some skepticism in your voice just then, yes? Please trust that we are doing the right thing here. We will tame the chaos here and bring our civilization to Terra Baixa. I know you can see the benefit in that. Your parents made their way across this land. They told you stories about this place, didn't they?"

Albert nodded.

"When we finish, Terra Baixa will be a happier place, like the White Island. That alone will make this all worth it."

Albert shrugged.

"How are your troops?" Richard asked.

"I think they're glad to have someone human in charge. They talk to me a lot."

Richard smoothed out his robe. "That's to be expected. And how are you? Are you well?"

Albert said the first thing that came to his mind, surprising himself. "I saw Thomas—Thomas Newton—at the Abyss. Where is he now?"

Richard smiled, squeezed Albert's hand, and looked him in the eye. Even though Richard was standing, their eyes were almost level. "Of course. Thomas trains right now at our support camp in the Old City. In London." Albert blinked and gasped when Richard used the sacred name for the Old City. "He's part of a program we've undertaken. We are teaching the next generation of Administrators about war and how it should be waged. This is the first war we'll fight, but it won't be the last, unfortunately. War is an engine of civilization."

Richard poured a tiny draw of the steeping tea into his cup, checked it, then put the pot and cup back down.

"The future lies in the growth of Thomas and other Administrators, Albert. We and the Adepts can only begin civilization. For it to last, you must learn to civilize yourselves.

"You miss Thomas, don't you? It's fine to miss him. You two were very close."

Albert wanted to speak but kept silent.

"Full disclosure, Albert: primogeniture is part of the experiment. Do you know what that is?"

"I don't." Albert paused for a moment. A guess popped into his mind. "Something to do with Administrators and marriage?"

"You're right, Albert! Such a quick mind. Primogeniture existed before the apocalypse, for hundreds and hundreds of years. In these early stages, we need to manage the economy of Administration, to ensure a continuity of property and rule. Primogeniture helps us do that. It keeps things stable. It had faded away from our world before apocalypse, but when we first began rebuilding, we thought it might have some value as a model."

"I don't see the point. Why this one man and one woman rule for Administrators? It makes things less resilient. Less adaptable."

Richard smiled, took the lid from the teapot, looked inside, then put it back. "Good. It's a valid question. I would argue that it's more about the children than the marriage, and that, at this early stage, stability supersedes resilience and adaptability. But I'm certainly open to a healthy discussion." He tented his fingers before his face, tapped them against each other.

"More disclosure, Albert, to reward your thinking. We first introduced primogeniture with a range of experiments: a range of genders, numbers. We were wary of bringing an antiquated model back to the world. The Administrator class took strongly to marriage as we have it now, though. They liked the strictness of it.

"These aren't hard rules. We're trying things, and we may change. Frankly, it's trivial that you and Thomas are both male. If your union would move progress forward, we'd find other individuals to help you all produce children. It's not difficult." Richard then paused, smoothed out his robe again, and returned to the tea. Albert felt something on the edges of him. *He got excited. He said more than he planned to,* Albert thought.

"Our union wouldn't do that, though." Albert said. He felt cold. "Because I'm not an Administrator. The problem isn't that we're both boys. The problem is that I'm common."

Richard gave a furtive stare at him, said, "No, of course not, dear. You . . ." then stopped himself, locked his gaze to the teapot, and said: "Yes. Perhaps that will change some-day. But, yes."

Richard poured into tiny cups. He placed one before Albert with his small, delicate hands. He closed Albert's right hand around the teacup and gently touched a spot on it, the tender point where thumb and forefinger meet.

Then he spoke. "There are the systems that organize us, and then there are our lives themselves. We have to respect the systems. Without them, there is no meaning. In my enthusiasm, though, I sometimes forget when God is in the details."

Albert, confused, looked at him helplessly.

"I could say I've had to deal with far worse in my life. And I have: far, far worse. But that's not the point. I'm sorry, Albert. Drink your tea, child."

Albert drank. It was perfect: full and the perfect temperature. It smelled like flowers. Albert had never tasted anything like it. "Thank you, sir."

Richard looked at him a moment and then put a hand to Albert's face. It felt like a child's hand. "Of course, son. This new world, with its big, sad boys."

+   +   +

They built a beachhead. They found a decent source of water, and set up routines for fishing and hunting, and scheduled patrols and defenses. Albert had to think differently: organizations and dependencies, individuals working in concert, the orchestration of work and people. It was complex. He'd helped his parents with the farm for years, though, and knew complexity.

The beachhead grew over the weeks, with troops arriving from the west of the White Island and from the Green Island, which lay beyond. The rocky cliffs in the north of the Green Island held immense power. Every Adept trained in the shadow of those cliffs. Every Adept was created there.

Albert and Aengus went to the shore to greet the Green Island's boats when they first arrived. The troops from the Green Island wore breastplates and gorgets made of beautiful black iron, the handiwork superior to anything the White Island could yet produce. They saw the tallest and meanest-looking of them and assumed he was Peter, the commander from the Green Island. Aengus gave the salute they had been taught in training. Peter started laughing, then kissed Aengus full on the mouth, then punched him in the shoulder, hard. "They taught the babies well," he said. He looked at Albert. "What are you supposed to be?" he asked.

"I command the White Island's troops," Albert said.

"Do you, now?" Peter leaned in toward Albert. "They're playing army games with you now? I guess I shouldn't be surprised." He sniffed at Albert, then cleared his throat and spat at his feet.

Albert stood taller and put his hand on the hilt of his sword. Before he could do anything more, Peter shoved him hard, sending him back several feet.

"Don't do something that will get you killed," Peter said. "Stay out of our fucking way. That goes for both you and your troops." He walked away without another word.

The camp and the exposed beach were a mere lip on the edge of the vast hills and forests of Baixa. They watched the woods intently, but nothing emerged from the Baixan forest onto the beach. Albert would sit with the camp guards sometimes. He talked most often with Henry, who was from the Western coast of the White Island, a place called the Horn. Henry had sailed to the Green Island before.

"We went a few times. You lived by the water, too, didn't you? You never got on a boat?"

"I've been on a boat, sure. My father and I would sail up and down the channel," Albert said. "We just never sailed that far. My parents had traveled for years. They didn't want to go anywhere."

"We went a few times to pick up Adepts. That's where they come from," Henry said. "They don't have to use a boat. They can open doors and go anywhere, is what my mother said. I don't know why they took a boat. Maybe they wanted to be more like us."

"What was the Green Island like?" Albert asked.

"It's like magic, like you're dreaming when you're there," Henry said. "The Green Island is madness. All you folk from the east, I don't think you'd be able to handle it."

"We can barely handle being here," Albert said.

One day, Albert found Aengus comforting a soldier in their tent. He stepped back out to give them some privacy.

"I want to go home," he could hear the soldier sniffling from within the tent. "I just want to go home."

"I know, I know. We all do," Aengus said. "It's going to be all right. We're doing a good thing. We'll tell our children about these days. They'll be proud of us."

They talked for a while and grew more quiet. Finally, the two of them emerged from the tent. The soldier looked at Albert sheepishly. Albert tried to smile at her. His smile didn't feel comforting.

"They're all homesick," Aengus said later. "It's not just me."

"Of course not," Albert replied. "It's all right to be home-sick. We've all been taken away from our homes, after all."

"I feel better not to be alone. Is it bad that I feel that?"

Albert smiled. "No, not at all."

"Maybe I'll talk to more people. We could use some cheer around this place. It's Midsummer's Night tonight—did you even know?"

Albert let out a short laugh. "I hadn't realized, but it is, isn't it?"

"No one realized! I guess it's my job to tell everyone," Aengus said. He stood, stretched out, scratched at his chest, smiled. He started to head out of the tent, but then stopped and looked at Albert. "Is that all right? Did you need me to do anything?"

Albert wanted him to stay. He could see a glimmer of the old Aengus, and he wanted that all for himself. But now he was the problem. Most of the soldiers on the beach arrived after Albert took command. They didn't know that he had been just another soldier. They treated him with deference and distance. He was a commander now. He could feel himself drifting away. He wanted Aengus back, but he couldn't be Albert for him anymore.

"Go meet people. Help them out. I'm glad you're feeling better."

+ + +

Albert spent his evenings checking on the patrols and guards, making sure everything was in order. The camp was beginning to run smoothly and needed less and less. He found himself chatting idly with guards sometimes, then stopping himself, realizing that he was doing something for which he reprimanded others.

He tried to find things he could do alone. He pored over maps of Baixa and of the Old City they approached, all of them vague with large swaths of undocumented country. He read a physics book Richard had made him. Richard had chosen a book for people who weren't very smart at physics, though he had put it much more politely. Albert was glad it was a simple book, though. It told a story of the smallest parts of the universe and how they work. The story said that the smallest things, seen up close, were completely unpredictable and chaotic. Somehow, though, all that chaos resolved by the time everything got bigger, so that our world could be predictable, with things like gravity and velocity and physical matter. It made little sense to Albert, even said simply. He decided to just take it at face value.

He wrote Thomas letters, as well. Richard promised to see them delivered.

"I don't want to ruin his wedding or anything," he said to Richard.

"I know you don't, dear. It's good for you both to stay in touch."

"You keep saying that, and Lady Newton said it, too. We can't be together, but we should stay in touch, and we'll always be 'great friends.' As if that means something."

"This war won't last forever," Richard said. "It may not last more than a few months. You'll go back to the Islands and tend to your farm. It's natural that you and Thomas will see each other. As long as it's a private affair, and doesn't interfere with his marriage, it seems like that's in everyone's best interest.

"Civilization isn't just about laws, Albert. It's about the mutual happiness of the civilized. You and Thomas will do what you need to feel happy, and that's fine."

Albert had come to believe that Richard never intended to make him feel common or unworthy. That made these moments worse.

+   +   +

Dear Thomas,

Everything is fine here, and we are safe right now. We are still on the beach of Terra Baixa. I saw you at the Abyss before we left. You looked like you were already mayor. I was proud of you. Did you meet Richard, the Old Person? He and I are friends. He has given me a physics book, and I am learning about quantum physics.

I am tired of this already, and I want to be a good citizen and farmer when I get home. I hope we come home soon. I miss you.
Albert

He went to bed early. Aengus came in several hours later, unsteady on his feet. He stripped down, spooned Albert, and began to nuzzle against him. Albert pretended to sleep.

+ + +

Albert met Richard for another briefing the next morning. They were now talking daily, planning the impending march and the fortifications between the coast and the forest. They would soon go inland and battle the Baixans.

"We'll march south," Richard said. "We may hit some enemies on the way, but the worst will happen when we get to the stronghold here," he tapped the map, "in the ruins of one of the largest Old Cities."

"That's where they keep the bulk of their troops?"

"I believe so, yes." Richard smoothed out his robe again. Albert could tell he was holding back, but he let it go.

"So, we fight them there. I guess we will beat them. After that, we occupy their city, and Terra Baixa, and make it civilized," Albert said.

"Have we ever had a conversation about occupation?" Richard said. Albert couldn't tell if he was being skeptical or forgetful.

"You teach us history in your schools, and you say a lot of things in these meetings about civilization," Albert said. "It's not hard to piece it together."

Richard smiled. "Yes, the Old City will be the seat of a civilized Baixan nation. From there, we will bring civilization across Baixa, and to Viru. Eventually we will cover the world. This will be a good start."

"When do we begin the march?"

"The day after tomorrow."

Aengus shook when Albert told him they were heading out. "I knew we would head out soon. It's just sooner than I thought. We just got settled." Aengus scratched where his neck met his shoulder. He stared at the spot where the canvas of the tent met the scaffolding, where some light came through. Albert knew by now that this was his comfort spot.

"Don't worry. We'll be marching for months. It'll be well into summer before we get to their Old City. All these troops will take a while to get through the forest." Albert held him, with one hand at Aengus's neck and one in the small of his back. That was what settled Aengus best. "We're here to do this. You'll feel better when you're moving around, when we're all on the march," Albert said, with as much enthusiasm as he could.

"I'm trying to just look at what I feel, like Sister Alice would always tell us," Aengus said. "But when I do, it's shaking all through me, and bells ringing, and burning all over. It's too big for me. I'm too scared, Al."

Albert held him a little tighter. "I got some ale, and some bacon that we can cook tonight. It can just be you and me." They stood there together quietly for a second. "Don't be scared. I'll do my best, all right?"

+ + +

The mass of troops and Adepts and equipment of warfare marched into Terra Baixa slowly, slowly. Someone, something had once dug rough trails through the forest, but nothing dependable. An advance group inched its way into the forest with saws, machetes, torches, and an Adept carrying a box to handle the thick stuff.

On a good day, the Adept would push herself and get four or five miles in. Most days were not good, though. Most days saw as little as a mile or two of progress, and a lot of sitting and waiting. Most days they stirred up something big, some inhabitant of the forest.

The second day from the beach, they kicked up a giant bear-dog, eighteen feet long and easily a ton in weight. It dove on one of the soldiers helping to clear the way and took his whole head in one bite. It mauled a second as the crew fled.

Albert got to the scene before anyone else from camp. He saw the bodies splayed before him, and the bear-dog slowly stalking the Adept, who had stayed behind. He recognized his teacher, Sister Clare. He knew Clare had joined them, but he had only seen her from a distance. She looked so young to him now. It had just begun to rain, a sudden downpour.

"Can you cast it away, ma'am? Can you throw it into the trees?"

"That's more energy than I have right now, unfortunately. I'm trying to calm it," she said. She said it evenly, with composure; she said it like they were at school. "It's challenging."

"At the count of three, can you give it your best shot? Put all the sleep into him that you can."

"Yes. I can do that."

Albert counted to three, and Clare focused and allowed her eyes to close. The bear-dog's breathing slowed, and its eyelids fluttered. Albert jumped at it and put his sword between its ribs. He had seen some bear-dogs before, but not many, and never one this big. He gave his best guess as to where the heart was.

He got it right. When the bear-dog died, it was quieter and easier than he had expected. Sister Clare had done a good job with the sedation. It fell away from Albert in a large but muffled *thump*.

They took some time to catch their breath in the moment afterward. They looked at one another. Albert looked up to the rain and let it wash his face off. He felt that moment of comfort he often felt with Adepts. He knew his thoughts were open to them, and that made things simpler. Sometimes he felt that he knew theirs.

Clare spoke for the both of them. "This is its home, and we're tearing into it. It was scared and angry. There's some shame in what we do here."

They buried the lost crew. They also dragged the bear-dog into the woods and rested it in a quiet spot.

Albert usually patrolled with the forest watch, since the alternative was boredom. The Adept did most of the work and was rotated regularly. Often, at first to Albert's surprise, it was Richard. The other troops were as unfamiliar with Old People as Albert and followed him closely, attentively, like parents with a child, until he earned some distance by throwing a wild boar across the forest with his mind.

After they had walked for a while, Albert found it easier to talk to Richard. One day, they took a break together after working through the morning. Richard shared some wheat cakes and a bottle of tea.

"Where do you come from?" Albert asked. "Where do the Old People live?"

"Our home is across the sea, on the Green Island. I spend most of my time in the Old City, though. London." Albert had learned that Richard used the sacred name pretty liberally.

"You were born on the Green Island?"

"Sort of. Not really," Richard said, then noticed Albert's

confusion. "I apologize, that was glib. I was born in London. A London."

Albert paused for a minute. He could feel something on the edges of Richard. "You were there, weren't you? You, the Old People . . . you were at the apocalypse."

Richard showed some surprise. He was quiet for a long time. "Yes."

"And you escaped and you came here. How did you do it?"

"It's a bit complex. There's physics to it."

"You can try me," Albert said. "I know a little physics now, from the book you lent me."

Richard didn't speak.

Albert pushed a little. "Say it simply. It was thousands of years ago, right? How can you still be here and alive? How did you escape?"

"There are ways to step out of time and space as you know it. We did that. I don't know if I would call it escape."

A question came to Albert. He wasn't sure whether to ask, but Richard was quiet, and his mouth and shoulders seemed to say that he wanted to be asked. "Did you cause it? The apocalypse?"

Richard sighed. "I don't know. We may have. I don't know." He paused. "Does that make you hate me? To hear that?"

Albert shrugged. "The apocalypse is a story. It never did anything to me. If I had to swear whether it happened or not, I couldn't. I'm just here, where people point at things and call them *apocalypse*."

Richard smiled thinly and wiped a tear from his face. "It felt good to tell someone that. Albert . . . we don't tell people that part. Will you keep it secret for me?"

"Sure, no problem." Albert thought for a minute. "You said *a* London." It felt dangerous and exciting to him just to say *London*. "Just because it was older? Isn't it *the* London?"

"Do you know when you are in the forest, deeply in? It's

all trees, and you know all the trees, because you've seen these trees before. But when you're lost, are you sure they are the same trees? They're familiar, but you don't know if they are right or not. That's part of what it means to be lost, isn't it?"

"So you know London, but you don't know if it's the right London?"

"Right," Richard said.

Albert smiled. "You might not even know if it was the right apocalypse."

Richard looked at him. "You never cease to amaze me."

Albert then said, half seriously: "Did you make the Abyss, the holes to hell? Is that what made the apocalypse?"

Richard laughed. "Don't be silly, boy. It's a tunnel. It's a road."

"It goes into a rock in front of the sea. Where the hell is the road supposed to go?"

"Enough!" Richard said, laughing freely and still crying as well. "I can't explain modern engineering to a ten-foot-tall giant-boy. Just trust me on this."

"*Giant-boy?* I'm normal-sized. It's you that's wee. And I don't think you know what 'modern' means."

Richard wiped the tears from his face. He rested his head on Albert's arm for a moment. "I like you, Albert Todorov. Thank you."

Albert smiled. "We should get back to patrol."

"Yes," Richard said, and walked into where the forest encroached again. He walked ahead, until he was several yards away from Albert. He then stopped, turned left, and approached the edge of what had been cleared. He froze suddenly and looked back. "Albert. I never heard them. Run!"

Before Albert had time to think, a mass of bodies rushed from the forest and slammed into Richard. The mass covered him in a violent blur, and when it uncovered him again, he was torn apart. After they finished with Richard, they stopped and scanned about. They looked at Albert.

They looked like animals. They didn't wear Baixan regalia; they wore rags. They shared the eyes Albert had seen in the very first Baixan, a weird glowing green. He squinted, and it seemed like the green glow was an aura around them, strongest at the eyes.

Albert had his bow and he drew it. Somewhere in the back of his head, he realized that he was done for if they went for him as a group. He kept that idea in its place.

Three arrows shot from his bow as they were regrouping. Three wild Baixans fell. Another second passed, as the rest processed what was happening. He was sure it was his imagination, but he thought he saw their green glows fade for a moment.

"TROOPS!" Albert yelled at the top of his lungs.

Then they came after him. He stood his ground. They were far enough away that he managed to take out two more as they rushed him. That still left three.

They ran at him with amazing speed and strength, given how hungry they looked. They were on him even as he drew his sword. Then he fell on his back, their blows and their smell on him. One grabbed his arm with a yank that he thought would take it out. The other bit at his shoulder, and he felt it through the armor. The mouth reared back, bloodied, its teeth damaged. Albert kicked and managed to hit one and rammed his head into the chest of another. He knew this was all just struggling and delays. There were too many of them, and they attacked with no sense of self-preservation. They started to pull at him. The biting mouth kept coming in at his face. He held his sword in front of him, but the mouth, the face—the face was slicing itself against the blade just to get at Albert.

Suddenly, the mouth fell back. Albert felt some of the weight of the others go away. The other troops had arrived. Aengus had skewered the biter. He finished the biter off and then ran to Albert, leaving his sword in the biter's chest.

"Are you all right, Al?" Aengus shouted.

"Aengus, your sword. Get your sword. I'm fine," Albert said to him. He tried hard not to show impatience.

Aengus went back to get it. "I was upset," he said to Albert when he returned to him. His voice was quavering.

"Worse things are going to happen to us. We have to keep our heads, all right?"

They looked around. The patrol had killed most of the savages. They held one survivor down. "This one is wild. Do we keep him alive for questioning?"

"We can't let him escape. Let's hold him down as long as we can. Pile on. Aengus, we need some rope, and we need to get word to the Adepts. The rest of you, get on patrol. We stopped being wary, and it bit us . . ." He trailed off. He began to take in what had happened. He glanced at Richard's body, but he couldn't keep his eyes on it.

Albert approached the last living savage. The savage frothed at the mouth. His eyes were a luminous green. They all managed, with considerable struggle, to tie him up and then put him face down on the ground. He squirmed and strained against the ropes until they cut into him.

After what felt like hours, Sister Clare tore through a thick cluster of brush. "What's happened here?" she asked.

"They were too fast. We didn't hear them until they were on us," Albert said. "They killed Brother Richard."

On hearing this, Clare straightened and took on a stance that seemed to indicate determined listening. She quickly turned to where Richard's body lay, and went to it. She fell to her knees. "You had a job, to protect us from what was in the forest." Albert couldn't tell if she was saying this to

Richard, or to him. Her voice didn't sound angry, just tired and disappointed. She stood and walked back to Albert.

"I failed," Albert said to her.

"Yes." Clare paused. "But this was a difficult task. This is the forest." She turned to the bound Baixan and kneeled beside him.

She turned the Baixan over on his back. He writhed and tried to bite at Clare at first, but she put a hand on him and made him still. A moment of quiet extended for several minutes.

The wild tension that inhabited the Baixan suddenly left him. His body relaxed. His eyes changed, becoming a dull brown. When she stepped away, he was calm and nearly asleep.

"Was he under some kind of spell?" Albert asked.

"Close enough. He was in thrall. Take him into camp. Keep watch over him, but take care of him as well. This wasn't his fault."

"So whose fault is it, then? Someone is controlling them? Something?"

Clare paused again. Albert could see her study the interior of her mind, cribbing together the right thing to say. "We'll stay put for a while and bring in reinforcements." She then walked back to Richard and gently lifted his mangled body. She started to walk back to camp. With her back to Albert, she said, "It's not your fault, either."

"Are you saying that to convince me, or yourself?"

She turned, carrying Richard, and looked directly at Albert. "He wanted to patrol. We never wanted someone as valuable as Richard to be put in such a risky position. But he insisted. He said he wanted to watch the forest with you."

+ + +

They stayed in place for several days. Every day, another pack of enthralled Baixans attacked. Each day put more weight on Albert's shoulders: the weight of the forest, the weight of the threat around them. Albert calculated how many soldiers were needed to protect the camp and put double that number around the perimeter. He had plenty of bored, scared troops who wanted something to do. The Adepts told the soldiers to treat the attackers humanely. Once the savages were broken of their spell, they had no memory of their actions. To a one, they proclaimed themselves peaceful forest-dwellers and showed fear and meekness at the sight of the approaching army. None of them ever showed signs of reversion to savagery. They were kept in camp as briefly as possible.

Aengus met the pause with worry and impatience. "I don't like just sitting here. It feels like we're a target."

"You don't like it when we're moving in, and you don't like it when we're staying still," Albert said. "This is as good as it gets, Aengus. The only other direction is retreat, and if we're moved to that, then things will be much worse."

Twelve days after the first attack, a group from the Green Island arrived. Twenty more soldiers, all of whom looked older, stouter, and more grizzled than any soldiers Albert had ever seen. And two Old People: two women, one who was taller than Richard had been, and one who was much shorter. The Old People were accompanied by Niall.

Albert first saw Niall on the horse-cart as it drove toward the camp. They approached from the northwest. Niall sat up front with one of the soldiers, laughing loudly and thumping the soldier on the back. Niall's robes weren't different materially from any other Adept's, but they looked simpler for some reason. They were certainly wrinkled. He wore them loose to accommodate his prodigious belly. He talked to the soldier like he owned the world. He reminded Albert of the laughing Buddha from the sutras back in school.

The cart pulled up to the perimeter; Niall had caught Albert's eye about fifty feet back. Niall jumped off the cart and approached Albert directly. His head and face were covered with stubble, black as pitch. Albert had never seen eyes like his. They were blue and silver, like full midday sun trapped in ice.

"Do they have children in command?" he asked Albert. "Are you the child in command of this world-changing effort? Tell me who you are, and where the important people are staying."

Albert said nothing. He met Niall's eye and held his gaze.

Niall returned it, and they stared for a few moments. Then Niall laughed. "I like you," he said. He walked off.

The Old People in the group were Richard's sisters. The first sister, Lucy, had wild hair and patchwork robes, nervous tics and desperate, craving eyes. She grieved loudly and heavily, wailing constantly: she could be heard throughout the camp. Susan, the second sister, was quiet, formal, and grave. Her hair hung to the middle of her neck and terminated in a perfectly straight horizontal line. She didn't look much like Lucy, and neither of them looked much like Richard. She wore an immaculate robe, like Richard had. She alone seemed to keep Lucy in control. At one point, Albert watched Lucy work herself into a fever, barking and shaking, only to be suddenly and totally calmed by just a touch from Susan. They were always together.

Albert patrolled constantly now. He vowed to miss nothing, to meet any savage or animal that came from the woods. Even more Baixans came now, swarms of them, and especially at night. They glowed all over at times, as if the green energy in them had filled to bursting. They came forth from the brush with screams and wails. They seemed not only hungry and desperate, but also possessed with their own mourning. *Maybe they mourn the coming death of Terra Baixa*, Albert thought. They seemed like grief itself, which infuriated Albert. He held his grief and guilt as precious, and hated the thought that these things could also suffer.

Whenever they patrolled with an Adept, Albert would follow her lead and would let the Baixans be sedated and bound. "It's ridiculous, though. They'll just come back," he said to Aengus.

The Adepts had much to occupy them with the death of Richard and were often absent from the patrols. When he patrolled alone with the other troops, Albert ordered all Baixans put to death.

Richard was wrapped from head to toe in a shroud and placed in state, in a glade just adjacent to the camp. He rested there for weeks, but his body didn't change, and no animals came for him, nor did any savages.

Finally, they held a ceremony. Richard's family and the Adepts sat with him for a full day and night. The next morning, everyone in camp joined them.

Sister Clare said some words. "Few of you really knew Richard. He was the eldest of the Old People, and he was first to lead us in the ways of the Adept. The Islands are what they are because of what he gave to us. He gave us civilization."

At that point, Lucy burst out. The Adepts reacted as if this were unexpected, which made Albert wonder if they had been paying attention. "We're not supposed to be here. We were never supposed to be here. But Richard decided he loved all of . . . *you*. He stopped trying to fix what happened to us, and started trying to turn you all into giant, new versions of us. And here's where it all ended up, isn't it? This great legacy."

"Stop it, Lucy," Susan said.

"This is supposed to be the time when we speak about our brother, isn't it?" Lucy said with indignation, her voice rising to a scream. "Right? This is a funeral. So I'm speaking. Funerals are for the living." She then broke down again in sobs.

There was silence for a little while, and then Susan said, "Thank you for remembering Richard with us." Niall took Richard's body. He, the Old Sisters, and the rest of the Adepts marched solemnly into the forest until they were out of sight.

They stayed in place for another day. With Richard's death, Brother Niall became the Adept in charge of the effort. Albert met with him to discuss resuming the march. Niall tried to bait him a couple of times, calling him "boy," but Albert met him darkly. They soon turned to business.

"What did his sister Lucy mean, that Richard wanted to make us like the Old People?" Albert asked.

Niall said, "They showed us how to become Adepts. Adepts exist because of the Old People. And everything that followed: agriculture, education, commerce, towns. It all started with the Old People, with Richard. Without him, we would still be like the Baixans are: chaotic, primitive, disorganized, desperate."

"She said they weren't supposed to be here. What did that mean?"

Niall, after a short silence: "She was very upset. I'm sure it didn't mean anything."

Albert held his tongue for a moment, but only a moment. "Clare, the day Richard died. She said the Baixans were in thrall. What is that, 'thrall'? Is that what the green glow is about?"

"We call it the Dragon," Niall said. "It's an intelligence that controls the Baixans. It turns them against us. It's more complex than what we should discuss now. Trust me that we're taking care of it."

"But what is it? Are they diseased? Is it some kind of forest spirit? Is it an Adept thing? You know it well enough to cure it, don't you?"

"It's called the Dragon," Niall repeated, testily, "and it's dangerous when you see signs of it. That's all you need to know." Then, with cold cynicism: "Why are you asking, anyway? What good does it do you to know? If you know, then you'll have to think about your responsibility for what's happening. I know what you children do on patrol."

Albert looked at him with rage.

"I know everything, boy," Niall murmured. "Weren't you in school, next to one of us every day, for a decade? You know, you know it in your bones. I can see you. I can see all of you."

After a long silence, Albert said, shaking, "I don't care what you can see. They killed my parents." Then, with indignation, he said, "And they killed Richard. He was the same as your parent, wasn't he? You would be out there killing with me, if you cared, if you loved anything. You should thank me."

Niall pursed his lips for a moment, then put on a false smile and said, with brassy sarcasm: "It's fine, boy. It's what we're here for, right? This is the progress of civilization. We're going to kill a lot more trees and Baixans before this is all over.

"You've asked enough questions. I'll ask you questions for a change. Tell me how we are going to march your troops forward."

The next morning, the sisters left with a few soldiers. The troops packed up and set out again, wearier than before they made camp.

It should have been only a day or two more to get to

their destination: Lutetia, the Old City of the Baixans. It took longer. There were fewer attacks from Baixans under thrall, but still four or five a day, with up to twenty in each attack. The enthralled Baixans attacked viciously, breaking limbs and wounding soldiers, but they had lost their ability to surprise. The troops had learned to put a phalanx around the Adepts quickly, to separate the savages from each other, to hold them down and tie them together, to leave them tied in the forest.

"Do you think they'll starve?" Aengus asked.

"I don't care. I hope so. Why? Are you worried about them?"

"No, of course not," Aengus said. "I'm tired of this, though. They're trying to wear us down."

"I don't know, I think they're actually doing us a favor. We're getting better at this, aren't we? You can feel when they're coming, can't you?"

Aengus paused for a second. "I can. They make sounds well before they get here. A distinctive rustle, back in the woods. I can hear them earlier and earlier."

"Exactly. We've learned to be on our guard. We've learned how to work together. We know how to subdue them and win without using more energy than we have to. We're learning to be less afraid and more at home with this, aren't we? It's not wearing us down, just letting us practice. Warming us up."

Aengus gave a little smile to Albert. He looked more relaxed than he had in a while.

Albert smiled back for a moment, and then said to Aengus, "We're ready. We're ready to wipe them off the face of the fucking world."

Aengus stared at him in shock, then turned away. "We should stay alert," he said.

They had gotten so deeply into the forest that everywhere

was just the forest, all around them and forever, as deep as it was going to get. They hacked through brush up to their chests. The canopy above covered them for miles and miles. No one had seen the sun for weeks now.

During the day, Albert and Aengus didn't look at each other, didn't talk. At night, they grabbed and gnawed at each other with desperation. Their tent was like a small burning box where everything they felt and feared each day could burst out. In this container they could only damage each other. Albert clung to Aengus with every nerve, and Aengus to him. They desperately needed to be like everything around them, vast and chaotic, cruel and seething with life.

They finished. Aengus pushed himself away from Albert. "I don't want to feel like this anymore." He broke into sobs. "I want to go home."

"I don't understand. What did I do?" Albert said, and then, as an afterthought, "I'm sorry."

"You're different now. Don't you feel it, the difference? You used to be tender. You used to need me. Now all you need is to feel like a soldier, and a citizen. And you want to kill. You *crave* it, when did you start *craving* it? I miss you. You're right here, but I miss you. You don't have to be like this."

"You aren't making any sense. This is me. What do you want? Do you want me to pretend that we're still farm boys, or in school? I act like a soldier because we're soldiers. I act like I do because we're surrounded by thousands of Baixans, who kill us as soon as we drop our guard. Did you manage to notice that? I'm acting how we have to act. We have a mission."

"*You* have a mission! *You* do. You want to chop your way through all this. I don't have a mission. I don't know what any of this is for. Deep down, I don't think you do either.

I think you just want to become some sort of war hero and impress everyone, so that you can go home and make Thomas love you."

Albert just glared at him.

"Because you love him, and you're always going to, and . . ." Aengus stared at the top of the tent, at his comfort spot, tears running down his face. ". . . and I knew. I knew that very first night. I knew this was a stupid decision, and I kept right on making it."

Albert didn't know what to say. Aengus was wrong, he thought. Thomas had barely occurred to him in the past weeks. His mind had reduced itself to two recurring thoughts: the memory of Baixans tearing Richard apart, and his fantasies of revenge, his dreams of expiating his guilt and sadness on the bodies of Baixans, piled in the streets of their Old City. These thoughts ran through his mind over and over, constantly, like a wheel. But he couldn't share something so terrible with Aengus. He couldn't stand seeing him suffer. He drew Aengus close. "I didn't mean to hurt you."

"I just want to go home," Aengus shuddered.

The fourth day after they buried Richard, not long after sunrise, they found themselves at the top of a hill that looked down into the Old City of the Baixans.

Neither Albert nor Aengus had ever been to London. They had never seen an Old City. It was vast, starting where they were and spilling down for miles into the valley below them. The city consisted of ruins, metal and stone, as far as the eye could see. It was a skeleton, a mammoth body almost fully decayed. Trees interrupted the ruins, growing through them. A river flowed in the distance, through the middle of the city. Around it, and in pockets beyond, the Baixans had built new villages, many of them resting on the more solid bits of the ruins, topping the old stone with ramshackle arrays of hovels. Albert could see some smoke coming from fires down along the river. The villages were sleepily coming to in the quiet morning. It looked less like a battleground, and more like just an old place where people lived.

They found some spots in the nearby ruins to camp. They had grown up among ruins and found them familiar. The Old City was simply more of it, melting into the ground a century at a time, smooth to the touch, pockmarked with grasses, and heavy in places with trees. These outskirts felt like a weird variegated space, not forest, but not really city either. They leaned against some walls that rose out of soft, thin grass and moss. They put down the tents again. Albert hammered in the tent posts solidly, as if for the last time. Troops gathered wood and water. The Adepts set up some different tents this time. They were longer, and had more beds inside them. Albert knew what these were for, but said nothing to Aengus.

It took hours to establish camp. The sun began to set. A crowd began to gather in the center of the camp. Everyone knew, on some level, what was about to happen. No one wanted to be alone. Soldiers stared at the fires, poked at them, whispered in one another's ears.

"Do you think we're too visible?" Aengus asked Albert.

"I get the feeling it doesn't matter if we're visible or not," Albert said. He then saw Sister Clare across the way, sitting quietly and unusually separated from her fellow Adepts. Clare held a box and was staring intently at it. Albert approached her.

"Hello," he said.

"Hello, Albert," Clare said.

He took a seat, cross-legged, near her. They sat quietly for a while.

"There's shame in what we do here," she said.

He didn't know what to say. He didn't agree with her,

not after Richard. He wanted to burn the trees and raze the villages before them. But Clare had been his teacher, and he hated to see her sadness. He reached out and put his hand on her shoulder.

She reacted, pulling away. "It's all right, Albert," she said. "I'm fine."

He had focused on her intently, and it took him a moment to realize that they weren't alone. He looked up to see Niall, all belly and chest, staring down at them. "Clare, are you all right?" Niall asked. "There's a man-boy here, just thought you might want to be aware."

"I'm fine, Niall," Clare said. She rose and walked away.

Albert stood as well, and looked at Niall. "What are you on about?" he asked. He felt a bit like a fight.

Niall shrugged. "I was just saying hello, boy," he said, and walked away.

The night was empty of any Baixans or monsters. It contained only the terror of the troops of the Islands.

In the morning they rose, bleary. Few had slept. They left the tents where they were. Half of the Adepts would go forward, and the others would stay behind with a small retinue of troops. The rest began to march. They marched quietly, in an order and rhythm that was now ingrained.

They wound through the ruins, using the old remnants of buildings to give them cover. The terrain grew more difficult as they advanced, and they spread out more and more. Gradually, it became less a march and more a broad flow of furtive troops. They tried to surround the enemy as much as they could, mutating from a solid column to a broad fan.

Aengus kept with Albert, as did Sister Clare, one of the few Adepts who moved forward with troops in the front lines. They marched with Heather, who was from Overtown and a year older than Albert, and Holden, a blond with big arms, freckles, and a sneer. Holden took nothing seriously, and he and Aengus got into joking banter readily. Holden would offer a remark; Aengus would smile warmly; Holden would blow out a raucous laugh. Albert watched them and saw the old Aengus, the Aengus from Eden-town. *If they end up together, fine,* he thought. *Aengus deserves to be happier than I can make him.*

They had been walking for several miles, settling into an automatic pattern, moving as one body, unthinking, lost in movement and perception. Then Aengus pointed ahead, and they all followed his arm and gaze. They saw a strange, jagged tower of iron in the distance, across the river. They drew closer, more mindfully now. Albert started to make out details of the tower, its latticework structure and the places where it was broken.

The dark masses that surrounded the tower began to come into view as well. Albert could now count the camps of people, hundreds of people, scattered about in groups of tents, milling about fires. From a quick and admittedly nervous assessment, Albert figured it was nearly double their troop count.

"This might be tough," he said under his breath.

Aengus looked at him, then said, "These aren't military camps, though. These are just villages, aren't they?" He paused, then said in shock, "There might be children. What if there are children?"

"Hush," Albert said. "The children here are just Baixans. We've had to kill them before."

Aengus stared at him in creeping, horrified recognition. Albert felt a swell of contempt, but let it pass, and said, with as much compassion as he could muster: "You didn't notice, did you? It's always just a bunch of wild things with terrible eyes. You didn't notice." He put his hand on Aengus's shoulder. "I'm so sorry we're here, Aengus. I just want you to survive."

Aengus said, "I won't do it. I won't do any more of this."

"I thought you'd kill a thousand Baixans for what they did to me," Albert said. "Do you remember that?" It was the worst thing he could say, the most effective means of destroying anything Aengus and he might have held for one another. *I'm good at that, at least,* Albert thought. *I'm good at killing things.*

"Look," he said, "Terra Baixa attacked us, and they will attack us again, don't you get that? Didn't all this time marching through this chaos impress that on you? Until this world is civilized, we aren't safe. That's why we're here."

Albert could feel air between them, the chasm between him and Aengus. He turned away and started checking on the other troops.

They waited. Albert had to tell Holden to shut up exactly once. Finally, Sister Clare locked eyes with Albert. "Everyone is ready. Here comes the signal."

From behind them came a flare from the Adepts, signaling the attack. Holden let out a shout; Heather echoed him. Other voices joined in. They ran through something that used to be a door, or a window. Right now it was their gateway to war.

Albert shot out toward the camp before him, sword drawn. He wanted to fight. He wanted to kill everything, to claim all this violence for himself, to change everything around him.

He ran toward a group of four Baixans gathered around a fire topped by a pot hung on a cast-iron frame. They didn't notice him; they were staring at the Adepts' flare. By the time they registered his presence, it was too late. He slashed across one on his left and kicked the pot over onto two others, splashing its scalding contents over them. Albert turned to the one on his right while the scalded ones screamed.

He saw a young man screaming at the sight of his father's death. Albert noticed that the scalded two were likely the mother and a sister. He had just attacked a family making their meal. The young man scrambled across the fire, surely burning himself in the process, and dove to cover the rest of his family, to protect them, but also just to hold them. Albert looked into his eyes. They were just eyes.

He remembered his mother saying: *I guess you could call it 'soldier'? We didn't have a word like that. It's different from what we have here. We were just a bunch of people with weapons and a goal.* And he imagined his father saying: *What is 'warfare'? We didn't have 'warfare.'* He let himself see what was happening, the world that was going on outside the veil of his anger, and he let himself see the horror of himself within it all.

The scalded ones were trying to compose themselves. The one who took the bulk of the cauldron was doing better than the one who got the glancing splash; that one still stared at her legs and panted as if they had been cut off. The young man grabbed a burning log and swung it at Albert to keep him away. Albert pitched back a few steps, almost losing his footing, and then sat down firmly on the ground. He bowed his head down and said, "I deserve to die. Just do it." He managed to say it in Baixan.

The young man could have easily cracked the limb across Albert's head and ended it, but he didn't. When Albert looked up, he saw him and his family stumbling into the distance.

He looked around. Some ways off, in the air, he saw a wave of Baixans flying, as if swept up and thrown by an invisible hand. He saw ahead of him many rows of tents, more stove fires, more slaughter. He heard a shout and saw Aengus and Holden rushing forward, to his left, about two hundred yards away, meeting three Baixans at the next set of tents. He leaned over, hunched on his knees. He looked at the ground and it spun.

Albert yelled to them, "Stop! We have to stop." No one heard him. There was too much distance and noise between them. He tried to stand, but felt too dizzy. He tried to listen to his breath and compose himself. Every nerve shouted at him, every fear stood between him and his breath. He remembered a refrain Sister Alice taught them—*I am on fire, I am calm*—and he repeated it to himself.

After a minute or two, he found the calm to stand and run forward. Someone had started setting the Baixan tents aflame. It hadn't rained for several days, and the tents went up quickly. The first few had lost their inhabitants already. Two cats leapt from one just as Albert passed. Both of them looked at Albert with annoyance and scurried away, sure of their footing and direction in all of this human confusion. He could still hear Aengus and Holden, and he could see Sister Clare and Heather a short distance away. The magic box Sister Clare held shone a bright gold. She appeared to be immobilizing Baixans so that Heather could easily disembowel them.

He started to call to them, but interrupted himself with a racking cough from the smoke spewing from the tents. Then, out of the smoky fog, the nearest burning tent put forth a big and clearly unhappy human.

The man was enormous. Albert stood ten feet tall, and he barely came to the top of this one's chest. The man wore a dirty, half-torn tunic and muddy breeches. The breeches bunched up and surrendered all hope of coverage before even reaching his calves. Patchwork hair of all colors peppered his face, his beard roughly the same length as the hair on his head, none of it enough to be called anything more than unshavenness. He hunched over with the weight of his own body, and with what seemed to be an overwhelming disorientation and fatigue. His eyes glowed the weird green of the savages, but not as livid; the glow was dirty and faded. He burst from the tent with a confused roar. Albert jumped back to give him room and prepared to strike, then stopped. The big man stopped with the roar and appeared to be nodding off.

They stood for what seemed like a very long time, in silence, as the sounds of battle seemed to drift away from them. Albert eased his stance and looked at the man, who panted and murmured. The man struggled to stay awake, like someone drunk past looseness into blind stupor. In his delirium, he had changed from a threat to someone soft and vulnerable, his mouth open, his eyes wavering and sad, his swaying body in need of a catch. Albert felt an overwhelming need to protect him. *Who is driving them?* he thought. *The Dragon isn't a forest sickness. It's an Adept trick, but it killed Richard. Is Niall doing it? Are they all doing it? Why would they do it?*

After a few moments, Albert tried to rouse the big man gently. "Hallo, sir? All right?"

The man moved his lips, murmuring, with a bare deep purring coming out. His eyes were closed now.

"All right, buddy? What's your name, buddy? I'm Albert."

"My name's Cas," the man mumbled, in Baixan. Then his eyes snapped open with a new green intensity. "Drop your weapon, boy!" he screamed. "I'm going to slice you from your neck to your cock and rip the hole open wide and eat you out from the inside, you little pecker. I'm going to cut off your head and use it to, to piss . . . piss and, and spew in . . ." He lost most of his intensity mid-sentence, and his eyes darted about in confusion. But his eyes stayed open, and he said, half whimpering, "Drop your weapon. Drop it, so I can cut you with my sword." Cas held a limb, about a foot and a half long and about three inches in diameter. *This is the miracle of civilization*, Albert thought. *Deluded by our masters and knocking each other with sticks.*

Albert wouldn't hurt Cas. He wouldn't hurt anyone ever again. "Sure, buddy. Whatever you say." He dropped his sword to the ground. "Maybe you could gut me in a little while, sir. Maybe we could sleep for a bit first? It's all right if you want to." He took a tentative step toward Cas, and another once he noticed that Cas had nodded off again. With each step he took without consequence, he drew a little closer, with a little more speed, until finally he stood at Cas's chest.

The giant chest heaved with the work of staying upright in the midst of all that confusion. Cas smelled a bit, but not as bad as Albert had feared: unwashed, rank mostly with his own sweat. They were close enough that Albert could hear his breath. Albert admitted to himself, with shame, that he wanted him, more than a little. He knew he was making stupid decisions and went right on making them.

"It's all right, Cas. You don't have to keep fighting," he said, and put his hand against the unshaven, red face.

Cas's eyes snapped open and green again. He yelled and swung his limb at Albert, who tried to evade it, but still caught it on his shoulder. Albert's right arm went numb, and he staggered back. Cas went for another blow to his head. His second strike was broad and clumsy, and Albert dodged it easily.

Cas roared and rushed for Albert, who grabbed a handful of dirt and pebbles and threw them in his face. Cas not only reared back in surprise, but dropped his limb altogether. Albert picked it up and bashed it into the big man's gut, hoping to be forceful enough to take him out, but not so harsh as to damage him. He bent over, and Albert made a second tentative blow to his head. That knocked him out.

Albert turned Cas over on his side, cautiously, in case

he went green again. When he remained still, Albert came down to a resting kneel. Albert's shoulders hunched forward. He rested his head on Cas's shoulder. He could wake up Cas and save him, Albert thought. They could head to the forest and sleep in a tent. They would live a life with their own minds for themselves, and a love that was uncomplicated: a life where everything wasn't ruined.

He kissed Cas on the head. "I'll come back," he said.

He stood and oriented himself again. He couldn't hear any of his troops. He saw something bearing toward him, a soldier on a mount. The mount wasn't a horse. He ran to it.

It was a soldier from the Green Island, broad and redfaced, riding a boar. Albert had seen big boars before, but none of them as big as this one: it stretched at least twenty feet from the head to the tail. It had been groomed, which somehow made it look far more awful. It had a harness and a saddle, and the rider wore full armor and acted as if riding a boar into battle were something completely normal.

Albert kept his sword in his sheath, but took the bow from his back. He yelled at the soldier. "Stop! This isn't a battle, this is a slaughter. This is wrong. We have to stop."

The mounted soldier stared at him for a moment, dumbfounded. He then growled and began charging. Albert began to nock an arrow, but realized the boar and rider were too fast. Albert put away his bow, swallowed, and realized he had to be ready. Everything needed to happen smoothly.

As the boar came down upon him, he dove to the left side, opposite the soldier's sword arm. He didn't fall, which pleased him. He lunged for the back of the saddle, hoping to pull himself onto the boar.

He caught the saddle with a firm grip, but failed to sweep himself up as elegantly as he'd imagined. The running boar dragged him alongside for several feet, while the soldier attempted to strike at Albert. He took a couple of angry swipes with his shield arm at Albert. Albert was lucky: his awkward angle alongside the boar made him difficult to strike.

Albert's arms burned with the weight of his dragging body and the effort of pulling himself onto the boar. He threw his legs up a couple of times without luck but finally hooked his foot on the boar's flanks. As he climbed up, the soldier threw his shield in frustration, hoping to maneuver himself better against Albert.

Albert pulled himself snug to the soldier and tugged at the soldier's helmet. As Albert had hoped, it lacked a buckle and came right off. He could see the soldier's tangled hair and reddened neck. The collar of his chest armor rode low on his neck. Albert wanted to try to talk him down, one last time, but all he could get out was "Stop."

The soldier raised his sword and poked randomly behind his head with it, hoping to stab Albert. Albert grabbed the arm. He bent the wrist back from the arm until he thought he would snap it right off, like the limb off a boiled chicken. The soldier screamed and dropped the sword. Then Albert pushed him off the boar, trying to get him away without hurting him.

He failed. When the soldier slid to the left, his foot stuck in the stirrup, and head connected to ground with a crack. The boar caught the now-dead soldier underfoot, stumbled, and lurched forward, its flanks bucking up and throwing Albert several yards.

Albert landed on his back. The flying fall knocked the breath out of him, and he lay immobile. He could hear the boar braying and hoped it was still off its feet as well. He'd been knocked flat plenty of times before, and he knew to let the breath come back to him.

During the long few seconds, he stared at the sky. He saw smoke to his right, at the periphery. He heard fighting around him, metal on metal and screams and howls. He thought of how he'd lost his troops. He lost them today by going wild and breaking ranks, but he'd been losing them for weeks, bringing nothing but terror and killing to them. He located the feeling of all the shame and disgust and dejection in his body: a cold melody in the minor key on his left side, starting where his ear met his jaw and resonating all the way to his thigh.

He drifted from there to thoughts and feelings about Richard: *I loved him; it was my fault; it was Richard's fault; it was all Richard's fault; fuck Brother Richard, he is a fucking liar and should have never given me this responsibility in the first place; I loved him, though; he never killed, only I did; it's my fault.* Then he noticed that he heard less of the boar. Then his lungs decided to operate again.

He sat up with a gasp. He saw the boar fleeing from the battlefield, dead soldier still in tow. There was a strange quiet in the land around him, nothing but a wordless rush of Baixans in the distance, streaming toward the ruined steel tower. Albert was now close enough to the tower to make out details. Four wide feet grounded it, and stairways rose from those feet up into the tower itself, winding metal that could be climbed. Baixans had gathered on its landings. But instead of trying to mount some defense from the landings, the Baixans rushed them, crowded them, climbed over one another to escape the soldiers of the Islands. They scrambled and clawed at each other. They threw one another from the landings. Between Albert and the chaos at the tower were some Island soldiers floating in air, gently, over the river, sent across by the magic winds of the Adepts.

Albert searched the distance for his troops. He could see the soldiers move toward the tower in an amorphous scatter, starting a few hundred yards ahead of him and extending several hundred yards beyond. He studied the crowd, trying to discern some grouping or pattern to it, finding none. Some soldiers struggled with one another, or wandered aimlessly, unsure what to do with the screaming innocents around them. Some tried to tend to the Baixans, others to control the crowds. There were sporadic groups of wild Baixans, small perturbations of whirling, green-eyed banshees that would emerge and attack anything nearby. He saw a few explosions in the distance, past the troops, and more flying bodies. The Adepts did most of the work of conquest, he thought, leaving the soldiers to clean up.

He looked around him. He realized that he lagged behind nearly everyone. The huts, tents, and fires around him were still freshly abandoned, food still cooking. A cat came up and rubbed up against his shin. He scratched it gently behind the ears. He heard the noise of the massacre drift away from him.

Suddenly, a group of five wild Baixans rushed forward, their eyes greener than he had seen since the raids just after Richard's death. They looked in many directions, but moved as one, like a many-headed beast in composite. Albert went to his sword by instinct, but then took his hand away from the hilt, dropped his arms, and stood there, ready to let them sweep over him.

They focused on him and ran at him full-tilt. All the wild packs he had seen in the past had emerged suddenly from the trees: here, in the open, they were less startling but still remarkably fast. He breathed in and thought for a moment about what it would feel like to be torn apart. He thought of his parents and began quieting his mind for death, stilling himself to his breath and body, focusing on what moved directly before him.

The pack kept up its speed until only a few feet from him, then stopped abruptly. They crept forward, snarling and barking, but with a strange air that Albert read as curiosity.

The forward-facing Baixan crept up to Albert, sniffing, and Albert could smell them, too. The green permeated them; it sat on their clothes, on their very breath.

"You smell different," the green ones said in unison.

A calm settled over Albert. He let go of the tension and reaction he had learned from weeks of fighting the wild Baixans. He didn't feel safe, but he didn't care any longer.

"Different from what?" he asked.

"I don't know," the chorus said. "Different." It smelled, looked around some more. "You were with him. Richard," it said.

"When you killed him? It was you, wasn't it?"

The chorus wailed and spun about. Some of the Baixans dropped and pounded the ground, while others tore at their clothes and skin. "It was an accident!" they screamed. "It was an accident." After a few minutes, the green ones settled down. A new one presented its face to Albert.

"They call you the Dragon," Albert said.

"They do. That's what I am. I am the Dragon."

"In all this mess, I'm glad of one thing," Albert said. "We're hurting you. We'll turn this into a city, and we'll feed and clothe and teach these people. We'll make up for what we did. And, when civilization is here, then we'll be rid of you."

The chorus laughed at him. "Hurting? *Hurting?* Not at all, I feel wonderful! I wanted this. I wanted this to happen from the very start."

The chorus broke apart then from its circle, and re-formed itself around Albert. All five stared at him, green and burning. Albert stared at the one before him, locking eyes. "I'm not afraid of you," Albert said.

The face laughed again, loudly and joylessly, another bark. Something crept up from Albert's sternum and began to flush his cheeks. He burned green. A fire spread through him. He closed his eyes and saw the green burning behind his eyelids, looking into his body and mind. Then, abruptly, he felt the green waver, then immediately disappear. He had a moment of cool black relief before losing consciousness.

+ + +

Albert dreamed of the people in the forest again. It felt earlier than the dreams before. He saw two women there, a wise woman and a quick woman. The smart man was sick.

The wise woman said to them, "We can change the forest."

The strong man, healthy, ruddy, and full of hope, said, "Tell me what I can do." And she told him to begin cutting down trees.

The smart man, wan but determined, said, "Tell me what I can do." And she told him to measure a place, a square, where they could grow crops.

The quick woman asked, "What are you doing?" And the wise woman told her to go into the forest and tell the forest what they were doing.

They made a clearing and put vegetables in it. The vegetables got the whole of the sun, because the strong man had cleared away the trees. They made a small house and were happy.

+ + +

Albert woke up staring at the sky, which glowed with diffuse purples and pinks and comforting light. He sat up slowly, a tinny ringing in his ears, and looked around. It was dusk; he had slept a long time. He looked up again at the layers and layers of color streaming through the wispy clouds, finding it hard to separate the clouds from their brilliant surroundings. He had never seen a more beautiful sunset.

He looked out toward the tower. Plumes of smoke drifted lazily from and around it. He could make out some scattered, tired activity. Island soldiers milled about the tower in a loose circle, an accidental orbit. Defeated Baixans funneled out of the tower in orderly rows. When they arrived on the ground, they sat down in place to wait, knowing instinctively some pattern of subjugation. The Island soldiers guided them one by one into circles, taking breathtaking care, showing incomprehensible gentleness. In the circles, the Baixans crossed their legs and closed their eyes. Adepts roamed around the circles, free elements that drew toward and connected with every circle, even if they never actually became a part. The Adepts were teaching the Baixans already.

Still figures pockmarked the ground for acres and acres. The figures posed randomly, crookedly, in positions no one living would take.

Albert sat for a long time and stared at the bodies, living and dead. He noticed some idle soldiers begin to approach the dead. They struggled to move the bodies into dignified positions. They straightened splayed legs, crossed arms over torsos. Then they began to line the bodies up, one after another in tidy rows along the riverside. So gentle, treating the bodies like family, so kind, so sickeningly gentle.

When he couldn't look at it any more, he went back down the hill from where they'd come. He went back to where Cas had been. The camp still burned and smoldered in places. The smoke was heavy. They had covered all of Baixa in smoke, he thought.

He found the place, he knew that it was the place, but no one was there. "Cas?" he shouted. "Cas, come back, buddy, please come back." He waited, but heard no response and saw nothing.

He shouted again. He ran into a tent to try to find Cas,

but there was nothing inside but smoke. He stared in vain into the smoke. He was sure he could find Cas, that Cas was waiting for him, that Cas was ready to forgive and embrace him, somewhere beyond this mess, this smoke. He tried another tent, and another. His eyes filled with burning, sooty tears. His chest was full of ash. His very breath burned. He fell, coughing, out of the fifth tent. He sat down in the middle of the smoldering tents, everything about him acrid and hot.

Sister Clare found him, hours later, ranting and immobile, burned from trying to put out tent fires, still calling for Cas.

+ + +

Clare led him back to the camp on the edge of town. He stared at the ground, every few minutes catching a bit of stone hiding within the grasses. The stone bore the marks of human hands, their touch echoing in the stones still. He remembered the stories that Sister Alice had told him, stories of before the end, when the Old Cities were still living cities. The ancient cities once erected towers that reached tall into the sky, tall as trees, trees with their innards full of people, trees made of metal and stone. The ground of the cities was once blanketed in stone. In the ancient stone cities, the trees had been dwarves, bred and manicured things, tiny, gathered into small groups, spaced rows, a garden.

He looked up and saw white canvas in front of him. One of the long tents they had set up, the tents for healing and medicine. He noticed his calm and realized that Clare had taken charge of his decisions for the walk. He didn't mind. She was a better person than he was, he thought. He wanted her to stay with him, to guide him forever, even though he knew that was how they had all gotten into this mess in the first place. He looked for her inside his mind and said *hello* to her.

She stopped suddenly and stood still. "You heard me," she whispered. It was several moments before she started leading him again. He spent the time listening to her breath, feeling the heat that crossed her cheeks and brow.

She walked in front of him and he followed. He stared at the backs of her feet, the leather sandals that she wore, that everyone wore. Always the gray wool, always the leather sandals, he thought. Simple.

The leather sandals stopped beside a cot. She suggested to Albert's mind that he sleep. *Thank you*, he said. If his words shocked her again, she didn't show it.

He felt the fabric of the cot against him, and then he slept. The dreams didn't have figures, or places, or communication. Just heat and noise, cacophony and headaches, the sound of blood in ears, and colors. Colors shaded with blood.

When he woke, he was hungry and needed to piss. It was dark. He could hear everyone around him. Most were Baixan, he realized. All were in pain. He stumbled outside and pissed in the first grass he saw. "You're welcome," he said to the grass. He curled up there on the ground. When he opened his eyes again, though, he was back in the cot. He heard himself wheeze, felt the smoke in his lungs.

There was some light coming through the canvas now, early morning light. He looked around him. To his left was a half-burned face, darkened and pockmarked. He looked away from the face, to his right, and saw Aengus. There was something different about him. Albert stared at Aengus for a while until he noticed the absence, the flatness under the wool blanket where his left arm should have been.

Albert was drawn to the empty space, the strange

absence of something natural. He reached out to touch it before he realized that he was reaching toward nothing. He looked at Aengus's face, then, sweet and placid, lips barely parted in what looked like a smile. Albert hadn't seen him sleep like that since they had left Eden-town. *He's going to be all right*, Albert thought, his heart feeling lighter for the first time he could remember. *I didn't destroy him.* He watched Aengus sleep for a while and wished that his face was the only thing that occupied his mind.

After a while, Aengus woke. He looked at Albert. "All right, Al?" he said.

Albert smiled. "Hallo, Aengus," he said.

Aengus grinned back. He shifted, looked at the place where his arm had been, and shifted again, away from the place, giving the place a gentle berth. "Sister Clare turned off some parts of my mind that feel pain, just for a while," Aengus said. "So it won't hurt as much."

"What happened?" Albert asked.

"You would have been proud of us. Holden was brave, and I was, too. There was a man with an axe. I don't think he was a fighter, not by practice. Maybe just a lumberjack. Seemed to hold his axe like a lumberjack, at least to me. I wondered about it when I saw him, actually. Funny what you think about, isn't it? Me, wondering whether he was a lumberjack as he went for my arm." Aengus paused. "It felt different than I expected. Just something slamming against me, and then my arm felt wrong, like it was a thing I was carrying. It wasn't mine any more.

"Holden jumped at the lumberjack. He swung a sword at him, but the lumberjack swung too. He caught . . . he caught Holden in the stomach. Holden shouted, and I wanted to help but I couldn't. I sat down instead. I fell asleep. When I woke up, I was here." Aengus's mouth hung slack for a moment, his head occupied in a conversation with his mind, an attempt to construct reason from pain. "Holden died, they said. The lumberjack died, too. I asked."

"I'm sorry, Aengus," Albert said. "I'm so sorry. I'm sorry for everything."

Aengus smiled wide at Albert. His eyes were wet. He didn't say anything.

Albert imagined climbing into bed with Aengus, to hold and comfort him and help him heal. He would upset the wound if he did that, though. He would just make Aengus worse.

+ + +

Someone brought food to them three times a day. There was a place behind the tent where they could clean themselves, in a cistern that the Adepts and soldiers had made. As the other patients got better, they took more trips down to the river to bathe and ventured out to eat. Albert stayed in the tent. When they were all healthy, he thought, he could then be alone, and he was glad of that.

He stood naked at the cistern and poured cold water on himself. There was a fire that could be stoked to warm the water, but he didn't use it. He wanted to be uncomfortable. He wanted to hurt himself, really, but he refused himself that. It would hurt Aengus, and he had promised himself to stop hurting Aengus. He would wait until Aengus felt better, until Aengus went away.

As he stood there, shivering, prolonging his small mortification, he noticed a limb. The limb was still attached to a tree, but he could see what it was going to be. He stumbled into the trees, naked, and broke the limb off.

Sister Clare visited them once a day, always at the same time, early evening, about an hour after their supper. She spent most of her time by Aengus's bedside, checking his wounds, putting her hand on his brow and speaking gently. She always said hello to Albert, and asked briefly after his health, just before she left.

That night, when she asked, Albert had a different answer. "I'm well, but I'd like some thread," Albert said. "May I have some thread? Please?"

He saw something soften in her gaze. He wanted to connect to her, to hear her, but he realized the wounds between them were just starting to heal. He didn't want to tear them open. "Of course," she said.

She brought some thread the next day. Two spools, two colors. She brought some nails and a hammer for his loom, and a knife to whittle his shuttle, as well, even though he had forgotten to ask.

He put the frame together from the broken pieces of limb. The threads were white and green. He did a simple pattern, one of the first ones Mama Lini had taught him. It was a pattern from Viru, she had told him, a pattern that she had learned from her mother, and her mother from her mother's mother, and so on.

In Viru, Mama Lini and Arto lived in huts made of mud and grass, round ones. They had told him stories about their village. They lived in huts by a river, for generations. They were happy there, until the raiders came.

He rested inside the pattern he wove, inside the threads alternating and interlocking. The same actions, over and over, the small atomic interactions, the relationships between the threads, regular, repeated, graduating into the fabric, a system of switching and turning and pulling. *My hands*, he thought. *Me.* He was trying to become familiar with them again, his terrible, killing hands. He was trying to use them to do something precise and helpful and kind.

He finished the first piece after a few days. A small, simple square of fabric, not quite a cloth. He kept it for himself, underneath his shirt and against his skin. When Aengus asked what had happened to the piece, Albert shrugged and promised him a bracelet.

He finished five bracelets for Aengus and four bracelets for Sister Clare. He didn't know how long he spent weaving. One day, mid-morning, he looked up from the loom and noticed that the weather had started to cool. He decided to try leaving the tent.

The Old City was down the valley from the tent; he could see all the new structures as he headed toward it. The Adepts and troops had already finished a couple of wooden structures: a house of government and a school. He walked to the school and looked through the door. He saw a circle, again, with Baixans sitting in contemplation, Adepts strolling around them. It was different from the schools at home. No one was speaking. The room was so peaceful. It was like nothing had happened.

He strolled around the square and then sat outside the house of government for a while. He saw a small group of soldiers he knew, but they avoided his eye. There were many Islanders around that he didn't recognize. He saw two young men in Administrators' robes, like the ones Thomas and Lady Newton would wear.

"The bank," one said to the other, pointing to an empty, grassy space nearby. "We'll take our time introducing banking, of course, but they may pick it up briskly." The other Administrator mentioned that building would begin on the clock tower next week. Four dozen Baixans were to work on it.

On the way back to the tent, Albert saw Heather training troops in a militia exercise. He wondered why he found them all unfamiliar, then realized they were Baixans.

Sister Clare visited that evening, at her usual time.

She sat at the foot of his bed. He felt something on the

edge of her and said the first thing that came to mind. "There aren't any attacks any more, are there?" he asked. "No green eyes. No Dragon."

She shook her head. There was pain in her expression.

"You all had a plan for this, right?" he asked her. "Adepts. You knew exactly what would happen. You had a plan all along."

Clare looked at him, incensed. "They . . ." But then she sighed. "No, I'm a part of it, too. I'm responsible, too. Yes, we did. Of course we did. I think it's wrong."

"You just followed Niall's orders," he said. "We all did."

"Did you only follow Niall's orders?" Clare asked. "We all share the guilt. Niall was following orders, too." She stood up and backed away a couple of steps.

"I'm sorry," he said. He looked at the place at the bed where she used to sit. "You're right. I didn't mean to—"

Clare deflated, sighed. "Of course you didn't," she said. "I shouldn't take offense. It's all right." He knew he had reopened the wound between them, though.

He looked over to Aengus after she left. He wanted to look Aengus in the eyes. He remembered Aengus's eyes on the farm, before all this happened. He wanted to see how much of those eyes he had left. Aengus was asleep, though, his face soft with that same smile.

The tent was close to the road that stretched from the Old City all the way to the beach. Each morning, the sound of the road grew a little louder. Carts, horses, shouts from Islanders. The shouts were always from Islanders; sometimes, they would hear a little bit of Baixan in mumbled, muted, blank tones. On the other side of the tent, people were starting to farm. Albert could see them clearing the land from his perch in the back, at the cistern. One day, the Baixans working the land noticed him. They tried not to stare.

"It's all right, it's just a big, naked Islander," he called, in Baixan. "Nothing to worry about." He meant to mock himself, to take a small mortification, but regretted it as soon as he said it. It was a small violence.

He wrapped wool around himself and went out into the woods. He lay flat there and listened to the forest. He listened to the road from there, as well. He listened to the Island voices in their commerce. He wondered if he would hear Thomas's voice from the road.

That night, Sister Clare came to Aengus with a smile. "The supply road is finished enough, now," she said. "We can travel back on it. They can take you back." She sat on the side of Aengus that was whole and held his hand. "There's a big wagon. We'll take you back to shore on it."

"I can march," Aengus said. "I lost an arm, not a leg." He looked at Albert. Albert knew Aengus hoped for a smile, and wanted desperately to give one back to him. He did the best he could.

+   +   +

On the morning of his departure, Aengus whistled and cleaned the space around his cot, his small kit packed and sitting at the foot edge.

He stopped whistling when he saw Albert. "Where's your stuff?" he asked.

"I'm not going," Albert said. "I should have told you, Aengus. I'm sorry. You were so happy, though."

There was a long silence between them. Aengus flushed red. The floor spun underneath Albert. "Don't," Albert said. "Don't be upset. I didn't want to hurt you."

Aengus shook. "I'm not staying here!" he shouted. "I can't stay here! I'm going home! We're going home!"

"I'm not going home," Albert said. He didn't know how

to put any comfort into what he was saying, so he gave up. "I don't have a home. I'm not going back. That's the only thing I know. I'm not going back. You need to go, Aengus. You need to go home. I'm sorry. I'm so sorry."

Aengus rushed him. He ran into Albert with his right side, his whole side. He knocked Albert flat on his back.

"You're always sorry," Aengus cried. "But you never do anything about it."

Albert lay there and stared at the white canvas of the tent, perpendicular lines that came together at a point. He stared at them until he was sure Aengus was gone. Everyone was gone, now. The tent was his.

He stood and walked to the threshold. The carts and the people gathered to travel back to the shore, to home. He found Aengus in the crowd, talking to Sister Clare. Sister Clare gave Aengus a strong hug and a kiss on the cheek. Albert had never seen that kind of affection from an Adept, for anyone. Sister Clare whispered something into Aengus's ear, something Albert couldn't hear. Aengus wiped his eyes and nodded.

Albert went back into the tent. He paced for a few minutes, then took off his clothes and walked to the cistern. He scratched at his head wildly as he walked, like he was trying to wake it up. He took some soap and a blade and scraped the beard off his face. Then he cut the hair from his head, then scraped his scalp clean as well. There was blood on his hands from his head and face. He washed it off, then washed the rest of himself.

He went to the cistern and climbed into it head-first. He immersed himself from his head to his waist. It was dark inside the cistern; he couldn't see anything before him. He stayed in the water as the pressure built in his head and as his lungs grew hungry. He thought about all the green Baixans that he killed. He tried to imagine green energy pulsing through him. He tried to imagine something wild in him, something that would make him guiltless and violent and easy to kill.

He wondered what it felt like when the world ended. He always had thought of the fire; that was how Sister Alice described the apocalypse to them. But surely some people lived after the fire was done. Some of them died of sickness from the tainted ground, he imagined. Some killed each other in delusion and rage. Some kept going for a long time. And surely some, having survived long after the fire, decided to stop. Maybe they just put themselves in the water and let it fill their lungs until they gave in to the water. Maybe they just went out into the woods and sat until they ended. He was going to end now, here in the water, here by the woods.

He didn't, though. Something within him pulled him out. Maybe it was his lungs, or maybe his mind, or maybe something he didn't know. Maybe it was the Dragon, or an Adept in his mind. Whatever it was, it made decisions for him. It put him on the ground, beside the cistern, coughing out water and gasping.

It took him a long time to catch his breath. When he sat up, he felt her eyes, looking at him from the tent. He turned to face her, but Sister Clare was already gone.

He returned to the tent. A book sat on his cot, a thick one with a strong binding. He picked it up and flipped it open. An inscription, a picture, lay just inside the cover. An Adept had drawn it, in the way only Adepts knew how to draw: so precise and detailed that it looked real, like a window into another real world.

It was a picture of Aengus and him. It must have been early in the campaign. They sat next to one another, talking, before a fire. Aengus had his hand on Albert's shoulder, his eyes closed in a bright laugh. Albert smiled and gazed at

Aengus. Albert thought to himself, *those boys were happy,* then realized he had thought that instead of *we were happy.*

Beneath the picture, the words:

Forgive yourself.

The next page also had a picture: Thomas and Albert studying at their desks, at the school. The Albert in the picture quietly focused on the book before him, and Thomas pointed to a page, explaining something to Albert. Sister Clare watched them in the background. Beneath the picture, the words:

Don't forget.

The book's pages smelled of school when he flipped through it. He saw some familiar sutras, and some new stories. Nothing military. No physics.

He found a pack and put the book in it. He reached under the bed and got his loom. He wrapped it gently with cloth and put it in the pack, along with the rest of his thread. He had a cup he liked: that, too.

His armor was in a wicker chest nearby. He took it out, put it on the bed, turned to leave it, then reconsidered and put it on. He found a knife, his hammer, an axe, his sword, a bow. He didn't bother with food. Hunting would be good.

Albert walked across the city and started heading the opposite direction from the road and the coast. He walked out of town, farther into the forest. After more than a mile of new clearings and farmland, he finally reached a point where the forest opened ahead of him. He looked out at it. The field and rubble of the Old City began to thicken into low brush, then the reach of saplings, thicker and thicker.

He pulled out the small square, the fabric he kept against him. He squinted at the repeated pattern of the weave. He lost himself in the pattern for a few moments, then looked into the woods and tried to find the pattern. He tried.

3

The new trip into Baixa began exactly where Niall had started the first trip into Baixa. He faced the same entry into the continent: a continuation of sand beyond the shore into a space between two brushy dunes. The tents to either side of it were peopled differently, but they were the same tents. He tried to picture it all—the coast, the dunes, the entry into the forest—as it had been then, and then he tried to picture it as it had been thousands of years ago. Perhaps some small houses at the shore, he thought, and perhaps a wall where eroded old stones stood now. Perhaps it would look like that again, he thought. Or perhaps not: perhaps it would look like this in a hundred years, except for the tents.

His driver, a Green Islander, had the confidence of all Green Islanders: the confidence that comes of being the first to receive civilization. Two horses pulled the cart laden with metal wares for cooking, making garments, and building houses and structures of government. Niall brought a bag of coins he had been asked to shepherd to the Baixan city. The driver let Niall load it onto the cart himself.

The road cut a swath through the forest now, twenty feet

wide. Adepts and troops appeared before them regularly, keeping the road clear and free of the worst of the forest. The traffic was heavy here at the head of the road but eased a little as they moved along it.

Merchants had set up carts every few hundred yards, selling provisions for horses and humans. Niall saw one cart owner arguing with a soldier over whether the cart was too close to the road. As they passed, Niall gave a cheery wave to the merchant. The merchant stood still, then fell to his face in supplication.

"The Baixans, they do that in front of Adepts," the driver said. "The merchants, at least. They're trying to impress you."

"They've been through much," Niall said. "It'll take some time to convince them that we don't mean harm. That this will better them."

"They're savages," the driver said. "I've been driving this cart for months now, and I know. They're a lower form of life than we are."

"Well, then, that's the lovely thing about civilization, isn't it?" Niall said. "Everyone used to be a lower form of life, but bit by bit we all get to be something better. How about your grandparents? Did they drive a nice cart?"

The driver grunted and went silent. Niall waved at two more merchants, then stopped when he realized it would inevitably lead to prostration.

The first march into Baixa had taken months: this trip took just over three weeks. They slept in the cart most nights, though they found a few tent villages along the road where they could sleep more comfortably. The driver insisted on giving the Adept the best bedding. The driver was initially a snorer, but Niall had learned a trick a long time ago, a little adjustment of the sinuses that made the breathing quiet.

The road began to feel like a long, strange city of its own

to Niall, a civilization in itself, with its own community and commerce. He particularly felt its scope, its complexity, at the point where it opened up to the ruins of the Old City. They came to the end of the road on a sunny morning, with the mist beginning to burn off and the ground beginning to warm. The buildings and carts there rivaled the bustle of the city center itself.

"So nice to travel with you," Niall said to the driver. The driver snorted and put Niall's bag of coins on the ground with a heavy clink.

He approached the river. The main square had risen up on the near bank. There were dozens of new wood buildings: houses, taverns, a hall of government. Not far away, Baixans cleared out fields of ruins and tilled the ground to farm. Niall liked the farms; they had a point.

The ancient metal tower stood across the river, near the square, but opposite it. There was a wide clearance around the tower. The Adepts had begun teaching that it was consecrated ground, to be set apart.

Niall found two Administrators inside the bank. One was adding curlicues and finials to a book of blank pages. The other was sweeping. Niall dropped the coins on the table, waved, and left before they had a chance to react.

Niall visited the school first. Two Adepts presided there, teaching a large group of adults and children alike. Everyone sat on the ground, silently, their eyes closed. They were using a new technique, developed just before the attack: wordless programming and instruction, to save time.

It seems to be going well, Niall thought, and one of the instructors thought back to him: *Yes.*

Why have you come? We weren't expecting you, one of the others thought.

No plan, just to see our progress, he responded. *Just to admire.*

He sat down with them, connected with them. He listened to the learning for a while. The adult students learned about agriculture. The younger students learned about market economics.

Niall relaxed in the murmur of the shared mind until a voice emerged from it. Esther, one of his fellow Adepts. *Brian is getting closer. He'll be there soon.*

Will he? Niall replied. *I've stopped listening.*

The casualness, the apathy you perform, Esther said. *It's sad.*

Everything is sad, Niall said.

Disconnected, disaffected, snide, Esther said. *You know why they went silent? Because of attitudes like yours. They gave up on us because Adepts like you were too petty to commit to an ontology of boundlessness.*

For someone who is committed to an ontology of boundlessness, you use a lot of pronouns, Niall replied.

Another voice came up to consciousness. *Brian is close to the castle, now,* it said breathlessly. *He's close to the Old People.*

They had always been able to hear the Old People. When Richard died, they all knew right away. Then Susan and Lucy came to Baixa and became so quiet then. It was disconcerting, but the Adepts understood. They knew Susan was in mourning, and they could feel her there, still. It was the feeling of being in a room with someone silent, a soundless presence. They took comfort in that, in feeling her there, even though she was quiet for a long time.

Susan never spoke to them again. One morning, months later, the Adepts felt her leave altogether. They chattered about it for a long time, speculating, worrying, trying to understand how to make it right, how to restore sense to the world-mind. They weren't used to acting without explicit instruction from them. They didn't know what to do.

After days of silence, Brian decided to leave Niall and

the other Adepts in London and head across the sea to the Green Island, to the home of the Old People.

"They lost their brother," Niall said to Brian. "Give them some time to mourn."

"We're their family, too," Brian said, as if it were simple. Brian was big and charming and stupid and always said things as if they were simple. He had headed out with a great fanfare from the Old City, broadcasting everything he experienced to everyone. That same day, Niall decided to return to Baixa.

Pay attention, Esther said to Niall. *Brian is there, now. This is important.* Niall scanned the world-mind and found Brian. He connected to him and was transported to the Green Island.

Brian was approaching the ancient castle that was etched in every Adept's mind: the crumbling stone, the cloudless sky, the treeless green crags. He was moving quickly, flying. *I can sense them, I think,* Brian said. *I believe they are here.* He rushed toward one of the towers. There were two figures standing upon it, still too far away to be distinguishable. *I see them,* Brian said. *I see them.*

Niall then felt a sick dropping away as Brian suddenly went silent, disconnected. He heard Esther moan in nausea and pain across the schoolroom, then tremors of disturbance as the connections with the Baixans in the room began to quaver.

Get a hold of yourself, Niall said to Esther, and lent his focus to the connections. The crops and their seasons. Supply and demand.

+   +   +

Once they were able to close out the lessons, they sat weary in the back of the schoolhouse.

"What do we do now?" Esther said. "What do we do?"

"We'll figure it out," Niall said. "We're enlightened creatures. We didn't spend all this time and effort just to act like children when they aren't available."

"It hurts," Esther said. "It hurts when we aren't in concert. It hurts when we are alone. We have been hurting for months now."

"We deserve to hurt," Niall said. "The things we've done."

"Spare me," Esther said. "You were at the forefront of the bloodshed, and now you're at the forefront of the self-torture. No one believes in war any more, Niall. You aren't saying anything interesting."

"Everyone is pretending that we've learned all our lessons," Niall said. "But they're already planning the next stages in London. They want to go into Viru, into the Southern Lands. They're desperate without Richard. And they call it something kinder now, but it's the same project, just with more stupidity. It's going to be bloodier than this was."

"You just can't admit that someone other than you might have a better plan for civilization," Esther said.

Niall took a long breath, evenly inhaling and exhaling, and watched his rage at Esther travel across his mind. "You're probably right, Esther," he said. "I should step away and let progress move forward."

"Why are you here, really?" Esther asked.

"I told you already," Niall replied.

They sat silent.

Remember what Richard said about him, the boy? Esther said. *He said that his energy had a strange and subtle smell. Pronounced and bright, like a potential Adept's, but with a sourness to it. It was the smell of entropy, the smell of the forest.*

I have no idea what you're talking about, Niall said, then laughed, aloud, in the physical world. *Richard loved him, I know that.*

Does that make him less dangerous? Esther asked. *Or more?*

I'm just here to see our progress, Niall said.

+   +   +

After he left the school, Niall spent some time along the river, watching the fishers catch the big salmon that the river bore. Most of the fishers tried to ignore him, but one approached.

"Holy," the fisher said in Baixan.

"No," Niall responded, also in Baixan. "Remember that. We aren't special. You are as holy."

The fisher shrugged. "You look Baixan," he said to Niall.

Niall laughed. "So do you," he said. And then: "My parents were Baixan."

"This is all fine, all right? Whatever they like. You tell them that. Do it for your parents," the fisher said. "No more killing, all right? We'll live like this if you want. No more killing. You tell them that."

+   +   +

The Adepts had taught Niall to identify every memory he held. He could remember the sensations of life all the way back to his infancy. The smell of London, of the Dark River. The smell of his mother and father, musk, the smell of brewing beer. The warmth of them. His mother making food on the fire outside. The heavy smell of oregano, an herb the Islanders never used in their foods. The heavy smell of Baixan cooking.

He and his mother sat at the fire. He played with Bird, a piece of cloth stuffed with feathers and decorated with them as well. His mother had put eyes on Bird, small woven bits of black and white. He remembered her putting them on Bird. "These are helpful, but so tiny," she said, holding up the metal needle she used to put on the eyes. "I keep losing it until someone steps on it." He loved Bird, and he loved his mother for making Bird. He kept Bird from the fire: it was warm, but he had hurt himself on it once. He kept his distance.

"The wind is better for me here," Mother said. She smiled at him. "The wind is better for my breath." She breathed deeply. He breathed in deeply to match her. He took in the smell of oregano. Mother pulled him a little closer. The Adepts took him away from her not long after that.

Niall saw a new wooden longhouse built close to the river, but well away from the Islanders' construction. It used the same fresh beech as the buildings on the square, but round logs, not hewn, and not squared, but extending long from the corners. They were filled in with river mud, had a sod roof with grass already green enough to glow in the high twilight. It was a Baixan building. There was a fire to the side of the building with food cooking. He could smell the oregano, and mustard, too. He remembered the mustard now.

He closed his eyes as he walked closer to the building, taking in the smell. When he reopened them, he saw a large man tending to a pot of food. It was a bird stew, full of quail and dove meat, with onions and beets as well. He was about to put some peas in. The man was remarkably large, with hair and beard cut short to his head, in an array of dirty colors, somewhat piebald. He was cooking food in a cast-iron pot with a look of worry on his face.

"You're a big one," Niall called to him, in Baixan. "You're bigger than the biggest boy I know."

The man grunted without looking up, concentrating on the pot. "We got this thing from an Islander," the man said. "I don't like it. It's too hot. The clay pots cook better." Then the man looked at Niall and stiffened. "Why are you dressed like one of their priests?"

"Because I'm one of their priests," Niall said. "Relax. I'm just here to eat, if that's all right."

The man stared at the pot. "Evi decides," he said. "If Evi says it's all right, it is."

"Evi's inside?" Niall asked. The man nodded. He didn't look at Niall. Niall went inside.

The tavern was packed with Baixans eating and drinking. There were many families with children running around and babies on their parents' knees. There were newcomers to the city, and those damaged by the battle, all quiet, traumatized, taking shelter in the corners, focused on their bowls and glasses. A rent boy and girl, sitting with two strong, gruff, self-important Baixan men, the boy and girl more interested in each other than the men, the men more interested in each other than the boy and girl. There were groups of young people, speaking loudly, failing to hold their liquor.

He felt a moment of pause, or maybe the moment before; the room noticing the difference in Niall, but not yet turning that difference into an idea. He decided to do something, then. He sent out a counter-feeling from his mind, not a thought so much as a sense of calm. *Nothing's wrong*, he projected, *nothing is unusual*. And, with that, the moment never happened. Just the tavern going about its business, with Niall noiseless in the middle of it.

There was a table at the far wall, long and sturdy, with pots of food, bowls, and cups. There were barrels of drink on either side of the table. A woman was there, serving food, stone-faced, young, with a color about her, florid and compelling. She pulled back long black hair and wore a plain canvas hat over it. There were several hats in the room, some with feathers, some with leaves or bones attached, some colored in dyes. A new fashion of the city. The woman wore colorful tattoos on her face and neck, which indicated a proud warrior family. *What's her story?* Niall wondered. *Is she a village leader down on her luck? Or is she adapting, trying to assimilate?* He thought about looking into her mind to find out, but chose to leave it a question.

He erred on the side of politeness and greeted her with honorific Baixan. "By your mercy, a cup of ale for me." She filled the glass with a businesslike air, but her response as she set it on the bar—"My mercy is yours"—showed the gesture was appreciated.

He stayed there, waiting for her to notice him. She was checking some food, and it took a minute. Eventually, though, she looked up. "You're one of the Island priests," she said.

"I am. You're Evi? I would like to sit for a while, to eat and drink. Is that all right?"

"You? Really?" she asked. Before he could respond, though, she shrugged and pointed to a corner. "Sit there," she said.

It was a seat on the edge of a bench, against a wall, with a good view. Niall took one of the seats, one hand clutching the cup and another scratching his belly. When he took the seat, he was noticed by the other people nearby. They sat quietly but found other seats when they had the chance, and he let them.

He fidgeted for a while, shifting from side to side and surveying the room. After a while, he slowed down and focused on Evi. He watched her work: broad focus, subtle and balanced attention to the food and drink and people and needs that awaited her.

After a while, she caught his gaze and locked to it. Not a passing glance but a fixed stare. Niall looked into her eyes, took in all of her, and then managed to communicate approval with just his eyes. She didn't reciprocate, but she didn't look away, either.

She approached him with a bowl of food. "Do you need another drink?" she asked.

He decided to go for it and downed his ale with a gulp. "Yes." He grinned.

She smiled curtly and drew another cup for him. He leaned in when she brought it. He knew how to take in subtle scents from years of training, and picked up the smell of her. She smelled of work and smoke and soap and malt and the herbs that Baixans wore to scent themselves.

He thought for a moment that he might introduce himself. But then she was away again. The rhythm of the bar didn't give him much time to deliberate.

He let it go and took a short meditation. He followed the smells, froth, and flavors of the ale. He sat with the patterns of his breath as he drank.

She came back around after a while. In his reverie he must have looked a bit strange. "You good, holy man? All right?"

"I am. Thank you, Evi," he said.

She didn't warm to the intimacy. He beamed at her anyway. He couldn't help it. "Adepts aren't holy or different, really," he said. "We've just learned things."

"I don't know from Adepts. We didn't have Adepts before," she said, her voice trailing off at the end.

His smile turned sad and grim. "I'm just a man. Nothing special. Don't worry about it. Thank you for the ale." He went back to contemplating his cup.

She paused for a moment, then reached forward and picked his chin up. She looked at his cup. "I think you're all right for ale."

"For now," he said.

She stared directly at him. The last time he was here, he'd adjusted to Baixan interaction: its ease, its directness, its lack of boundaries. He realized that he would have to get used to it again.

"What's your name?" she asked.

"I'm Niall."

She smiled. "You have pretty eyes, Niall." She returned to the rhythm of her tavern.

+   +   +

He stayed in his seat. It didn't feel like long, even though it was hours. She kept her rhythm in the business of the evening and then tapered off when the night drew late. She had a few long and laughing chats with customers at the bar. She talked down the cook from outside, who grew very drunk as the evening went on. Every warm, precise moment of the conversation made it obvious that she had done this many, many times before. When she showed him the door, the drunk cook seemed almost comforted.

After a while, most of the patrons took the door. Finally, it was down to him and a couple of people in the corner. He had put down several more ales by then, and he felt them. He knew techniques to clear his mind, to counteract the effects of the ale. He liked the feeling, though, and wanted to stay with it. *That's kind of the point,* he thought.

Evi sat with the people in the corner, talking. He took in the dynamic she shared with the other Baixans, their interaction and laughter and familiarity. He kept staring for a bit, realizing the awkwardness of that and not caring.

Finally, she caught his eye. He smiled at her, and she smiled back. She turned away and went back to her conversation.

Eventually, she showed the couple out. She stood, took up their cups, started walking back to the bar. "We're closing up now, Niall."

"You remember my name. I'm flattered," he smiled.

"Of course I remember. You just told me a couple of hours ago. Shouldn't you be in bed, or in contemplation or something?"

"I tend to stay out later than most Adepts." He drew his finger around the lip of his cup.

"Yeah, it seems like you are different from most priests in a lot of ways." She let the moment drag out. The fired clay cups in her hand knocked gently together. "Like I said, I'm closing. It's no difference to me if you want to sit around while I clean up."

"I'd like that."

She turned to some shelves on the wall, behind the table of food, and drew a bottle from the back. She took out two cups, put them on the bar, and pushed one to him. "I make this myself," she said as she poured. "I gather herbs and berries from the forest." She filled the cups halfway with the liquor, then finished them with water from a jug on the bar.

He took a hearty drink of it. It was floral, citric, and not too sweet. He noticed a taste like pine at the end. "It's lovely," he said.

"I don't pull that off the shelf for just anybody. Appreciate it." She wiped down the bar, the cask, washed the glasses.

"Do you want some help?" he asked as she moved to clean the last few tables.

"No. I prefer it to be done a certain way."

They talked as she cleaned up. "So, there is the closer island, where the polite ones are from, and the farther islands, where the strange ones are from. Which are you? You're polite, but you're also strange."

"All Adepts spend some time in the farther islands. We train Adepts there. But I grew up on the closer island, the White Island. And you? Where are you from?" he said, half joking.

She grinned. "I'm from here, idiot. Like everyone else, except the Adepts and the soldiers."

He blushed again. He had never been called an idiot before, and it amused him. "So, you come from the woods."

"Yes. We lived in the forest, my family. My aunt, she led our tribe. So my family were leaders, but not really. We were the relatives of leaders. My father didn't work. He thought it was beneath him. But Aunt didn't give him anything. So we were the poorest, even though my father thought we were special. Everyone in the tribe laughed at us.

"My father grew tired of it, of the mockery and the hunger. One day, he said, 'We will go now to the Old City.' And we said, 'No, it is cursed.' But he made us. He had the green eyes of a demon. He took us through the woods." She trailed off then, for a while, then resumed: "And then we came here. There was no food, and everyone got sick. And then all of you came here and attacked us. And many died. You know this part.

"It was terrible. I wanted to fight you all, fight until I died. But it all ended too soon. We just gave up, all of us. It still saddens me. But now there is plenty of food, and less sickness. So, I don't know." She shrugged.

"Your family is still here?"

"My brother died on the way here." She trailed off again. "Then, two sisters, they got sick and died before you came here. And then my mother, and my last brother and sister, they died when you came here."

Niall was quiet. He didn't want to say anything. But Evi kept her silence better than he did, until he couldn't take it anymore. He filled the silence with, "So there's no one? Your father?"

"I hate my father. I don't talk about him."

She clearly meant it. Niall let another pause rest between them. "This is your tavern?" he said after the pause.

"With someone I know. He built it, and I do all the work. I like it. I stay up late, but I never went to sleep when my family did, anyway. And I like money. Money is great. Thank you, Islands, for money! I can get food, and ale, and wine, and baths, and oil, and clothes . . . all I want. Money, it's a good idea."

"So this is better to you? This is better than the forest?"

Evi paused for a second. "I like it. All the people we see, and the money, and the friends. It's good. But I miss the forest sometimes. Here, it's always place to place to place, no time to stop and listen to the woods and the birds and the wind. I miss that." She paused again. "But there's no money in the forest."

She put down a glass, reached across the bar, and stroked the hair on his forearm. He watched her fingers. He put his hand on hers and said, "This might not go the way you prefer tonight."

She shrugged. "I don't know what you mean."

He smiled at her in silence.

"What's wrong? So the Adepts, you don't have sex?" she asked. "I thought you weren't different or special. You don't want it?"

He smiled. "You're right, we aren't different or special. Sex becomes surplus to requirements in a lot of ways, but it's important. I take the opportunity whenever it's appropriate."

She slapped him on the arm. "Well, I am appropriate, and I don't feel like sleeping alone tonight." She paused for a minute. "What, you want someone else, a boy? What have you been sticking around here for, then?"

"Boys are fine. I don't seek them out." He traced a shape on the back of her hand. "I like you very much."

"Yeah, of course you do. You boys from the Islands. It's all you want. Maybe you are a little strange about it, you pretty Adept. The rest of you are mad for it, though. You all say there is sex in the Islands, but I don't believe you. You all act like it's something new."

She looked into her glass, empty of liquor, then turned it over. "Done." She took her hand away from his arm and began rubbing his neck. He smiled again, blushing deeper, and sat a little more stiffly.

"You have beautiful eyes," she said. "And the way you look at me. You look big and simple like all the Island boys, but when you look at me, I think you see me, and not all the things you want, all the thrill and rest and happiness that boys want. You're looking at me."

"You look amazing," Niall said. "I like thinking about what you want, not what I want."

She smiled and sat quiet for a moment. Niall looked at his own glass, half full, and passed it over to her. She drank it.

Finally, she said, "Let's go into my room and you can think about what I want."

+   +   +

They woke later than he had expected. The sun was high by the time they left the bed. Evi warmed some bread, cooked pheasant eggs, and brewed tea. He went out by the fire and sat beside her while she cooked. When she was finished, she put the food in bowls and they ate together, outside, before the fire.

"I'm happy," Evi said. She smiled. "Thank you."

"I'm glad. I'm really glad," Niall said.

She sat close to him and scratched his back as he ate. "Beautiful boy," she murmured. "Who makes you feel good?"

"You do," he said. "You did. I love to see you happy. Thank you."

She sat for a minute, pensive, then traced a finger across his stubbly hair, just above the ear. "You know what I mean," she said, her hand on his shoulder. Then she shook herself out of it and said, more formally, "So, you have to go into the woods?"

"I do. I have to go today. I'm already late."

"When you come back, you come back here, to me. Do you hear me?"

He made a face of mock surprise and laughed. "Without question!"

She smiled back. "Good."

He finished his bowl. She took it from him, then handed the rest of her eggs over to him. "You eat these for me. You have to eat so you can be strong for the forest."

+   +   +

He put on some clothes that would work better than robes in the forest: breeches, boots, and a decently sturdy shirt. He said good-bye to Evi and headed to the edge of town. A couple of farmers were turning soil there. They looked at him as he passed. They waved their arms at him and pointed in the opposite direction, sure he was going the wrong way. He smiled and gave them a thumbs-up.

He ventured into the wilderness, the land beyond. It was free of roads and of any trails he could follow, but he had a clear destination. His path hung obviously in the air, as if marked with rope.

He was able to manage the first mile or so well, and he let himself get confident. Before long, though, he noticed that brush surrounded him up to his waist, for as far around as he could see. *This is why we have soldiers*, he sighed. He drew the machete: he had hoped, irrationally, that he wouldn't need it. His arm started to feel tired even before he started chopping. He preferred it to the exhaustion of clearing brush with his mind, though.

He hated the forest. *I don't hate it*, he told himself. *I love it, of course, like we all should, system or no system, it's what the world is before we interfere with it, it's what we all come from. It's what I come from.* He thought these words with his official mind, his Adept orthodoxy that celebrated the forest even as it planned how to wipe it out.

His informal, human mind, on the other hand, noticed the humidity and lack of useful landmarks and dwelled on the biting insects and big animals it might encounter. Also, it was bored. It daydreamed of London, his library, his comfortable rooms, a nice warm lunch from a kitchen, a well-kept bottle of wine.

His home city was a pattern drawn on his nervous system, a map he could navigate without effort, a union of landscape and atmosphere and mind. Here, though, every step forced another moment of awareness, a study of the mud and roots and brush that would trip and scratch. Every step reminded him of his mission, of his path, and of the current situation, which might lead to the end of the world as he knew it. There was pain in every bit, every second of the reality around him. He took a moment to wipe his brow, close his eyes, let the pain wash across. Then he went back to hacking at the forest.

And it was just hours of it, hours of him and the green and the knife, chopping and clearing. Even the forest around him, the knife in his hand, became invisible; it became one moment of chopping and clearing, the same moment over and over again.

He started to slow down in the subtle changes of early sunset. The light still accommodated him, and would for a couple of hours more, but he was tired. He finally came to a clearing, an auspicious spot where the pine trees had grown hundreds of feet, the ground beneath them a soft blanket of needles. He made camp, built a small fire, and took out some of his provisions. The food was basic: some bean cakes, dried fruit, and a little wine from the skin he had brought. He wasn't so much satisfied after eating as less hungry.

He sat still for a while. He let himself fall away. He relaxed the matrix of needs and preferences and insistences and regrets that was "Niall." He let himself just be experience for a while: the coolness and quiet of the clearing in dusk, the depth and vastness of the forest, the moisture of the life and decay around him.

With surprise, he realized his own happiness. He realized that, after the struggle of the brush and in the exhaustion of his own body, he had joy in being here.

A vision came to him. The clearing became a village, a set of longhouses nestled in the trees, warmth and smoke from cooking fires, the smell of peat. A bigger fire burned at the edge of the village, where the clearing met the trees. The fire burned in a holy place, a space surrounded by stones, deliberately arranged in a circle, with decorated limbs at the cardinal points. A dozen villagers sat within the circle, parents and children listening rapt to a shaman telling a story.

Niall knew that his face lay beneath the tattooed runes that adorned the shaman's face, that he was himself the shaman. His Adept robes were gone; he wore animal skins. His face and body were softer, his arms bare of their coats of hair. He spoke with a different voice, a more imposing tone. This Niall was practiced at telling stories. He was in the middle of a story, and he spoke these words:

The wise woman went into the forest to talk to it. She went to the oldest and largest tree and put her hand to it.

"Why are you here? What have you come to ask of me?" asked the forest.

"When we live with you, we get sick. When we live away from you, we get sick. You turned my sister into a dragon. What are you doing to us? Why is this happening?"

"I don't understand your questions. I am the forest. This is what happens."

"What is the purpose of all this? What do you want us to do?"

"Want? I don't want, I don't need. I am patient and vast. I am complete. I do not care. Your questions are all about what you want, and what your people want."

The wise woman struck the tree. "I'm tired of this, of you. I just want a world I can understand. Do you hear me? I want to understand."

The forest was silent.

The vision popped like a bubble. He sat alone in the clearing again, feeling the atmosphere, and his breath. He felt the tension and coldness and stomachache of the truth: that this was exactly where he was supposed to be, where they were all supposed to be; that, despite all their machinations, they would all eventually return here, to the vastness and silence of the forest.

+   +   +

He woke the next morning, cooked some bacon over the fire, and brewed some tea from a sachet of herbs he had brought all the way from London, his favorite blend.

As he drank his tea, a fox came into view, approaching the clearing from the forest. He looked at Niall tentatively, then back to the woods, then back at Niall. He held his left foreleg in midair, ready to launch an escape. Niall smiled, then, on an impulse, tried reaching out and connecting to the fox's mind. He picked up some flashes of sensation, strong smells, the taste of blood, textures touching the bottoms of his paws. Then the connection broke, and the fox fled.

Niall shrugged. He knew it wouldn't really work. It never did. He drank from his tea and began to break camp to head out again. He took his time. It wasn't terribly far.

He set out. He walked for about a half hour through the big canopies of trees before coming to the village.

It was a small village, with a longhouse in the center of it and some smaller cabins around. There was a big pit for cooking, some skins hanging from lines. *Was this the village in my dream?* Niall wondered. He looked on impulse for a holy circle. He saw a clear spot, a couple of stones, not enough to establish a pattern. Their holiness had gone, or was kept secret.

He made himself deliberately noisy. "I am a traveler," he said in Baixan. He saw a couple of faces peek out from the door of the longhouse, then dart back into darkness.

A long pause followed, blanketed in the sounds of bird and breeze, and of frogs and nature rutting. A bird cried something that sounded like despair, and a breeze kicked up. Niall spoke again. "Peace. I wish to change nothing."

A man emerged from the longhouse door. He was as wide as it. His head was shaved closely, and he carried a sword. He wore armor. It was White Island armor, of high quality. Niall recognized it.

"If you wish to change nothing, then you should leave now," the man said. "We know your agenda. We know you came from the Islands to desecrate the ancient place. We're staying here. The boy shaman has come to us and told us. He told us what you are doing. We're staying here."

Niall considered addressing each point in series, but thought better of it, and skipped to: "I'm a friend of the boy shaman. I just want to talk to him."

"You leave us alone. He's a part of us now. Go away."

"I'm asking with courtesy because I'm not eager to fight."

"Leave us alone. There's no green here, no reason. Go back to the ancient place and keep on with your blasphemy. You don't need us."

Niall felt the stones at the clear spot behind him. He connected to them, lifted them, brought them to him. They orbited around him: concurrent, irregular orbits, with a small but constant increment of acceleration.

"I'm a shaman, too," Niall said.

"I know this already," the man replied.

"I just want to talk to him. I don't want trouble. No one wants trouble. Right?"

The man struck his sword against the side of the door and cursed floridly in Baixan. Niall was impressed.

"Follow me," the man said.

They walked to the far edge of the forest and into the brush. The path was subtle, but the man knew it and followed it easily. He fidgeted with brush that wasn't in his way.

"I'm not going to hurt him," Niall said in Baixan to the man. "It's going to be all right."

The man struck a branch with his sword.

They came to a clearing after about ten minutes of traveling. Some large trees had been felled and reduced to logs and mulch. Some sunlight shone through the opening in the canopy. Greens and tubers grew in a small patch of land. A tiny cabin sat near the patch, covered in dyes.

"Hallo!" Niall hollered to the cabin. The man brandished his sword and snarled at Niall. Niall raised his hands and took a step back. "Sorry," he said.

The man left him and went into the cabin. Niall admitted to himself that he was tired, and leaned against a tree.

After a few moments, Niall spoke again, still audibly, but

more softly this time. "Hallo, Albert? It's Niall." And then a little bit louder, "I know you remember me, Albert! You hate me."

Not long after, a figure appeared at the doorway, leaner than he was before, but still as big a presence. He wore a red beard across his face, but still a boy's beard. His hair had been cut close. It looked like he was keeping it with a knife. None of it was enough to be called anything more than unshavenness. "I don't hate you," Albert said. "I don't hate anyone. Go away." The man stood near Albert, sheltering him.

Niall smiled to himself and took a few steps closer. "All right, Al? May I come over?"

Albert turned away from Niall to the man and spoke to him in hushed tones. The man spoke with a disproportionate intensity: Niall felt the agitation pulse out from him. The man and Albert spoke in whispers for a while. Finally, the man put his head against Albert's shoulder for exactly five breaths, then walked out from the way they had come. He didn't look at Niall.

"I just want to talk," Niall said.

Albert shrugged.

"I brought some food. It's town food, from the Old City. Would you like some?"

"I'm fine for food," Albert said. "I guess it would be nice to have a change." He started back into the house. "Are you coming in?" Niall followed him into the house.

Niall came as far as the doorway. "You look terrible. I guess you haven't managed to make any soap yet."

Albert stared at him and didn't look away.

Niall paused for a second. "I'll stop. Sometimes I find it makes things easier. We're all uncomfortable, always. Sometimes a little stupidity helps."

"You want to talk?" Albert said in a monotone, nodding

toward a bench for Niall to sit. "Go ahead. Hurry up, so you can leave before the sun falls."

"I thought you might offer me some tea first," Niall said.

"I guess you would need a break, wouldn't you? I'm surprised that you could make it all the way here, the shape you're in."

"I did fine. We can't all be strapping child behemoths," Niall said, more testily than he intended. He realized his reactions, took a breath and relaxed. "I suppose I could use a sit."

"Do it, then."

Niall sat on the bench. Albert stood and stared at him, and Niall stared back. "I wasn't kidding about the tea," Niall said.

Albert shrugged and went outside.

Niall looked around the house. It had a simple wood frame and a roof shingled in bark. A decent number of furnishings decorated the house. A hammock stretched across one corner, and a table and bench occupied another. A book sat on the table, as did a couple of earthen cups, which looked to be from the old Baixan city, and a simple wooden bowl and fork, whittled. The cabin was clean, and more civilized than he had imagined it would be. A handmade broom sat by the door, and some weavings decorated the walls. They were new. Niall knew the handiwork, the traditions of Viru.

Albert came back in with a pot. "Here's your tea," he said.

Niall pushed both cups toward him. "It's our tea," he said. "It's pine tea, isn't it? I can smell it."

"I never run out of pine." Albert poured it and they drank silently for a while.

"Do you want to know how I found you?" Niall said to break the silence.

"I don't have to ask," Albert said. "I know already. You know everything. You see inside me, right?"

"There's plenty I don't know," Niall said, adding, "boy shaman" in Baixan.

"I don't know what that's about. They call me that," Albert said. "I think maybe they haven't seen many people like me. Red hair."

"There's plenty I don't know, but I'm not stupid," Niall said, and then let Albert connect. *You can hear,* he said silently to Albert. *You can hear this.*

You have dreams, right? Alien dreams, with sensations and emotions you can't imagine? Dreams of a forest, like this one, but not this one. It feels like the parent of this forest, if such a thing could exist, doesn't it? And you can hear the forest always, waking or sleeping, right? You hear it talking to you, but you know that can't be possible. You think you're going mad, because you don't want to accept the things right in front of you. Am I wrong? Is that how you are?

Albert pushed back from the table and stood. He held himself and stared at Niall. Then he ran out of the room.

Niall stayed in place for a moment, sipping his tea. He stared at the doorway, at the space where Albert had been and left. He listened to the forest, the breeze through the leaves, gentle enough. It was a nice day. He felt the murmurs of birds and of tree frogs.

Then he rose and walked out of the doorway, behind the cabin, through a cluster of trees to a clearing, cool and shaded, a bed of pine needles making a soft floor. Albert lay there, flat on his back, staring up at the sky.

Niall sat down, cross-legged, next to Albert. He didn't say anything. After a few moments, he took his hand and ran it over the stubble on Albert's head. Albert recoiled in surprise, then cautiously and stiffly let Niall touch him. They stayed like that for several minutes before Albert turned onto his side, facing Niall, and curled up in a ball.

I'll tell you how I am, Albert said. *I hunt, and I hear the forest talking to me when I hunt. When I listen, I know everything, and hunting is easy, but there's something terrifying. I eat what I hunt, and I read, and I talk to myself. Then I sleep, and I dream about the forest, and I dream about the people in the forest. I dream about the people from the forest that I killed. I don't know how long I've been here anymore.*

They sat there in silence for a little while, connected, present to one another.

Then, Albert said: *I deserve it. I deserve to die out here, alone and mad.*

Why do you deserve that?

You deserve it, too, Albert said, and then let the thought sit for a while. *I deserve it most of all, though. You killed because you had a plan. Most of the soldiers killed because they didn't know. But I knew. I knew it was wrong, and I did it anyway. I knew but wouldn't admit it. I was angry, and I didn't know what to do, and I was good at killing. I've been learning to kill since I was a baby.*

You're still a baby, Niall said. And then: *What if we changed everything, you and I? What if we stopped the killing and changed civilization? Would that feel like penance to you?*

Albert got up and walked toward the cabin.

Niall waited a moment. He looked out again, toward the forest. He thought, his own private thought, *I could go now, just go. It would be kinder.* But, when he rose, he walked toward the cabin as well.

From the doorway he saw Albert in his hammock, laying back, eyes closed.

"Are you all right?" Niall said aloud.

"I'm trying to center myself. That's what you always

taught us, right? You tell us to be stillness and the sound of breathing. So shut up and let me be stillness."

Niall smirked. "Fine." Albert grew quiet and so did Niall. He sat, stilled himself and experienced himself, the room, Albert, himself with all of it. When he spoke, it was for Albert.

The core of the universe has no order, just collision and vibration, decay and regeneration, churning. Somehow this resolves into the universe. We struggle to understand how.

"What's that all about?" Albert said aloud.

"It's part of the doctrine we recite to initiates. To those becoming Adepts."

Albert curled up on the hammock, turning his back to Niall. "I don't want to do that. The last thing I want to do is be an Adept."

You want to know, though, don't you? You want to understand.

Niall then walked to the door, which was slightly ajar, and opened it entirely. A breeze blew through, and the light of the sun-dappled forest shone in. He walked back toward Albert, circled the hammock. He took a chair beside the hammock.

You want to be able to speak back to the forest, to understand it. You want the dreams to make sense. If you are initiated, you'll understand, Niall said. *I can't promise anything else, but I promise you'll understand everything.*

Albert flipped around and stared silently into Niall's eyes. He reached out and started stroking Niall's hand and forearm.

He'll do it just to share it with me, Niall thought. *He just wants to be with somebody.* This was a poor decision on so many levels, but it was a decision he went on making.

He took the index finger of his right hand and touched it

to Albert's forehead, just above the eyes and between the eyebrows. "There," he said.

+   +   +

Suddenly Albert flew away. He landed in a different place. It wasn't clear whether time had passed. The place surrounded and shrouded him in gray. The gray felt close. Albert tried to reach out and touch it, but it was different from fog. He tried to squint through it, and thought he could make out shapes. He wasn't sure where they were relative to him, whether they were big things far away, or smaller things near to him. After a while, he decided that they were trees, and that he was near a forest. He started walking toward the trees. He walked for a while before he realized they weren't getting any closer.

This is it, he thought. *This is initiation.* With nowhere to go, he sat down and listened to his breathing. It sounded vast: it was the only sound he could find. He counted a hundred breaths. He thought he heard the rush of wind, but realized it was his imagination. He counted three hundred more breaths. His ears started to ring. He counted five hundred more before the ringing faded.

He swam in a trance for six hundred breaths before his mind rejected the whole enterprise, called Niall a liar, called himself a fool, and despaired. He sat still and counted a thousand more.

"Are you showing up, Niall?" He shouted. It didn't echo. The space felt small. "I imagine you're going to show up eventually. Any time now." He waited and then shouted, "Niall!" It was as muffled as before.

He returned to his quiet and stayed still. A thousand breaths more.

He began to feel pine needles and brush beneath him.

He opened his eyes and could see trees in their detail. He was in a clearing. The forest had a peculiar green glow.

It was the clearing where he had made his home in Baixa. He could see his cabin. And then it wasn't his home, wasn't his cabin, was just somewhere much like it. Other people lived here. He saw Baixans helping one another with their chores, bringing in food from the forest, cooking, bathing one another, taking midday naps.

A priest was making rounds there, talking closely to a woman with a baby. The woman seemed concerned, as if the baby might be in danger, or sick. The priest spoke matter-of-factly but calmly to the woman for a few moments, then looked to the baby and put a hand to the baby's brow. The baby stopped its crying. The mother spoke again, affirming what the priest had told her. She kissed the priest on the cheek.

It can't be Niall, he thought, *but it is.* He stared intently at the priest.

And then he heard Niall in his ear. *Don't try so hard. You can just relax and look. You don't try to look at things with your eyes, right? You just look.*

You're cross, Albert said. *You're a man but you can bear a child.*

Did your parents teach you that word? Niall asked.

When I was a boy, there was a cross at our school. She was a girl, but her body was a boy's. The Adepts realized it. They took her and her parents to the Old City, to London. We talked about it a lot. Everyone was very excited. Albert remembered that it was a great moment, something remarkable. Her parents were so proud. Albert remembered wanting to be cross when he saw how special it was.

That's right, Niall said, *Adria is from the north. I should have remembered that.*

Niall stared at the tableau, the village, his other self,

before speaking again. *My parents and brother were from Terra Baixa. They fled from here on a boat. They were hungry and sick, and they wanted to be somewhere safer and better. They went to London, and I was born there. My parents knew; they always knew.*

When I was four, the Adepts came for me. My parents were content with letting me go. They still live in the city. I haven't seen them since I was four years old. I grew up with the Adepts. Albert noticed a surprising hint of bitterness in the last sentence.

You have a man's body, Albert said. It was partially a question, partially just an observation.

The Old People taught me as a child how to grow as a man, Niall said. *Our strength, our height, our bodies are just codes and chemicals, bits that we organize into a system. Adepts are experts in what these codes all mean. We can control the systems of our bodies. That's much of how we heal people.*

It's not just about bodies, though, Niall said. *'Man' is just a word for how we act in this world.* He paused. *It was different in Baixa, before. My body would be different if my parents had stayed in Baixa, or if we lived before the Old People. The Old People gave us different words for our bodies, to organize us. They changed what our bodies meant.*

What is this place? Is this real? Albert asked. *Why didn't you come when I called?*

You needed to sit a little longer. This is a place. You'll learn that there's something subjective about 'real.'

When does the initiation start?

It's started already. Niall leaned in closely to Albert, as if for a kiss. But Niall just put his finger at Albert's third eye again.

And then there was a moment, and Albert didn't know when it was. Niall was above him; Albert could feel Niall's weight on him. And then he was wrapped around Niall: it hurt, but Albert also wanted it, he wanted to feel Niall. He felt the free fall of Niall in control; he gave in to it and then fell apart. It became a crystal prism of moments: Niall was inside him, he was inside Niall, in a moment that might have happened right now, or a long time ago, or was maybe something he dreamed. They were somewhere else; Niall lay back, naked, scratched his belly, looked at Albert, and said, "C'mon." And then he was pinned beneath Niall again, staring at him helplessly, losing himself in Niall's indomitable, impenetrable, calm, relentless, laughing eyes. He could hear Niall's words in his mind again, unsure if he was hearing them just from his mind or from Niall himself, those words from before: *You want to know, don't you? You want to understand. What if we changed everything, you and I?*

And then they were done for a moment, again maybe this moment, or maybe the past, or perhaps something Albert was anticipating. Albert was spooned against Niall now, staring at the black stubble of his neck. He nestled against it and smelled him and said *I love you*, and Niall said: *I love you, too. It happens as a part of this. It's beautiful and very frightening the way we fall in love with each other.*

Niall rolled around to face Albert. He grasped Albert's chin again and took him into his eyes. And for a moment, for just a moment, Niall let the act drop and let Albert see the fear and machination in his eyes. A surge of adrenaline pulsed through Albert: he tried to label it as either terror or excitement. The difference was too subtle, so he stopped trying to give it a name, but he knew he wanted more.

Niall was gone, though. Albert woke up in the forest, or else they had been here the whole time. He remembered the pine needles against his back, the humid slight breeze on his flesh, bits of mud striped on Niall's thigh, on Niall's furry chest and shoulders.

He sat up, dressed. As he looked around the clearing, a

feeling of vague familiarity crystallized into realization. He stood and walked directly across to the far side of the clearing. That was the way back to the farm.

He emerged from the forest and walked the boundary of the pasture, around the fence. There were no animals in the pasture. Beyond the pasture sat the gardens, where they grew vegetables for the house. The season was the same as Baixa; the late summer vegetables were full. The garden looked well-tended. He saw the wooden markers that Lini had used to label the rows.

He went into the house. He could smell dough rising. A fire burned; through an open window in the kitchen, a breeze dried dishes on a wooden rack. The house was as he remembered it, before his parents died, before he left, but no one was there. He went through the rooms, looking and finding no one. He combed the house for dogs or cats. Nothing lived here.

He sat in a chair. He watched the fire for a while. He listened to the sounds of outside from the open front door and the open window. He started crying a little, and let himself. He would cry and then stop, and then sit calmly, and then cry again. Little wells of emotion. With each well of emotion, he felt a color creep into his peripheral vision, a grassy green. His view got greener and greener.

After a while he said to the fire, "You killed my parents. You bastards killed my parents."

Richard was there, by the fire. He drank a cup of tea. He said, "It was an accident, but yes."

They're all dead, Albert thought. *Everything good is gone. We'll never get it back. And it's him, and his stupid plans, their plans for civilization. They don't care about the people. They don't care whom they hurt.*

There was a flood of thoughts, green thoughts. Albert pictured filling Richard's chest with arrows, chopping off

Richard's head, running a sword through Richard's gut, slowly. And then he dreamed of doing the same to others. Sister Alice. The little, terrible Old Sisters. Every green, sick savage in Terra Baixa. Even Niall, who manipulated him without giving him enough credit to think he might realize it. All of them.

He would bathe in the screams and stomp on their spilling viscera. He could do it. He was better at it than anyone. He could do it forever. He could ride all of it like a wave, a warm safe wave of the cries and dying exhalations and misery of others, all the others that put him where he was.

He swam in that place for a while. It felt good, and he started to think of making it happen for real, or as real as this place was. He had a sword and a fist and he took it toward Richard. He imagined putting a fist in Richard's face. He could feel it. It was so close. All he had to do was let it happen. Richard stared at him, his stare unwavering. "Do it," he said.

Albert stopped. "No." He felt the heat and weight and tension detach from him, and with a rush move through him. He swam beneath the wave and felt its power finish itself above, around, away from him.

Richard shifted his posture. "You're supposed to smack me now."

"Shut up," Albert said.

Richard smiled.

"I don't want to hurt you," Albert said. "I love you. I don't want to kill anybody. And if that's what it means to be initiated, it's a terrible plan and it's not going to work."

Richard smiled. "You're not being initiated. None of this is an initiation. This is something different. I love you, too."

Albert looked down. "I killed parents, too. I killed parents and children." He collapsed in on himself, spine curving around his heart, and began shaking. "I killed, too. I did,

I did, I did." He watched himself say I *did* over and over, like it was breathing. He watched himself shaking and heard the sound of his own anguish.

After a while, his shaking settled, and he looked up at Richard, or the ghost of Richard, or whatever it was. It smiled upon him kindly, warmly, but it never touched him. "I don't want to do that, never again. I never want to kill again," he said to it. The two of them were quiet for a very long time. Albert listened to his breath, relaxed in the wake of his grief. He tried to listen to Richard's, but he heard nothing.

"But I will, won't I?" Albert asked.

"Yes," Richard said.

With that, Albert fell away. He tumbled, deeper and deeper, into himself and away from himself, and he spun, and a voice said, "It's all right. You can let go. It's all right to let go," and he didn't know if the voice was himself, or Richard, or his papa, or someone else. He collapsed and let himself go. He fell, and fell apart. Everything fell apart: his home, Richard, the light through the window. He fell, and there wasn't anything.

+   +   +

There were four of them. Four in a faraway place, in the mountains, in a series of rooms, rooms that were white and smoother than any stone he knew. They called it a "laboratory." One called himself a monk. The monk was a teacher, who knew his mind and how to be calm, and knew the sutras. He was older than Albert, but he looked like Albert. It was confusing; Albert wasn't sure if he was himself, or if he was the monk.

Susan was here. She could map the mind from outside, just as he—he and the monk were the same here, he decided—could map the mind from experience. Lucy was here: she was a doctor, who could mix elixirs to change the mind. And Richard was here, with his understanding of the stories of forces and particles and spaces of being: the physicist.

It was a clean place, a bubble, isolated from the chaos of the world. Here, they could remove variables. Their method was to consider themselves both observers and subjects. They had decided this was the best way to make their discoveries. Richard and Susan provided the theory, an idea of perception and its effect on physical space. He and Lucy created the conditions: elixirs to alter the preconditions of the mind, practice to sharpen and calm and expand and open the mind as it was, to make it something sharp and of use, a sword, an earth-mover, a key. They were there, the four of them, in the most intimate of conditions, for ten years. Naturally, they would grow to love one another deeply, or hate one another desperately, or both.

It began with a lot of talking, and diagrams, and conceptual models: chemical formulae and enumerations of the relevant objects, maps, proofs, protocols, classifications of data, goals, all of which, over the course of months and years, dropped away, became meaningless. In the second year, they determined they had no more use for the drugs and medicines. In the third year, they had mastered the practice and chosen to let it fall away. For years after that, it was simply the four, in the room, sitting. Taking exercise together four times a day, in perfect synchrony. Eating four small meals, their preparation and consumption and cleaning like a dance. Sleeping on cots immediately adjacent to their sitting pillows, all of them attentive to the sleep as well, engaged in the real-time study of their dreams.

They didn't speak: they heard each other completely, first in movement and disruptions of air, in breaths and shifts of posture, then later in the spaces before those actions. They knew each other in the moment, and they knew each other in the seconds before; they could read one another's minds in the anticipatory possibility of space before thought and action. And then, after a while, *before* and *after* and *myself* and *you* became meaningless, and they were all the same mind, the same thing. And that thing began letting itself hear more deeply, to read the microscopy and transcendence that underlay everything, and that thing began knowing all the cosmos as well, began making that cosmos intimate to it.

They began to feel cosmos as a pool they floated on, a fluid state with a pattern of waves. The waves rocked them and soothed them. The waves loved them. And, after a long time, they began to understand the waves deeply, to know the tides and the patterns, to anticipate the waves as well, to surf on them. Then there was a moment when the wave was obvious to them: where it came from, where it went, how it worked. The machinery of the universe was an engine they could tinker with, a schematic where the inputs and outputs and processes were breathtakingly simple.

And, in that moment, they asked a question: "What if we . . ."

And then replied, "Relax. Leave it alone."

And then justified, "But we'd just . . ."

And then insisted, "Why? Why is that necessary?"

And then conceded, "Fine, whatever. Fine."

But then asked again, "But surely if we just did this . . ."

They made a shift, the subtlest, most trivial shift. It was all there, so obvious, so simple. Surely, it was meant to be changed like this. Just to see.

They saw it approaching and then happening, a white burning and an uncontrollable shaking, through them, through everything. The wave crashed across them and through them, over and over again, a cyclone, until there was nothing but the crashing, beyond duration or direction. They screamed. It was broken. It was all broken.

+   +   +

Albert felt something, heat and coolness. No sounds, no light or things to see, no sense of where he was, or what kind of space surrounded him. Just heat, coolness. Like the feeling of the pillow as you sleep; there is warmth, and then you flip to the other side, and it is cool. Not painful or uncomfortable. Just temperature.

After a while, he started to see color. If pressed, he couldn't really guarantee that it was sight as he knew it. There was nothing here to make out, no point of reference, only darkness. But there was a color in the darkness, vague, maybe red, maybe green or brown. The darkness itself had a color, some colors. He didn't know whether this was external to him, or just changes he saw on the insides of his eyelids.

Then, somehow, the color organized itself, demarcated itself into multiple colors, hot and cool colors, as if the color had reached an accord with the temperature. There was a golden color that felt bright and crisp and fresh, and a hot iridescent green, and each of them had a pull. *Adept energies and Dragon energies*, he thought. He had the ability to make a choice.

He stayed still, giving in to neither of them. He observed them, felt their color and temperature. He could feel what was behind them, the Adepts' energy organizing into a structured world-mind, the Dragon's energy enslaving scared and disorganized minds into a swarming, undulating mass. It was possible to stand outside the Dragon and look at it. One could dance with it, dodge it when it rushed forward, point it in directions, surf on it, and use its energy as one's own. It wasn't a bad thing, really.

He kept his place and watched for a while longer. It wasn't really possible to say how long. Finally, he could understand where he was, where he sat relative to the color and temperature.

He was in the forest, the deepest forest of all, with every tree spidering out of the ground, and into the other trees. When he looked above, there was no sun, only dim light through the canopy. There were pine needles on the floor where he sat. There were no birdsongs, but he could feel the humming of life around him. He thought: *The forest is what we try to control, but it is bigger than any of us.*

He could see the pattern of every tree inside the leaves, and he knew that the pattern of the forest was the same as the pattern of the tree. He was in it so deeply that he didn't know where he was, or how to get out. He was inside a thicket, and it felt like shelter.

And then the shadow came over him. He couldn't see the shadow, but he could feel that the shadow was warm, and wanted Albert, and Albert wanted it back. And when he buried his face into the shadow, feeling its pulse and skin and warmth, he was the shadow, too, and they were the forest, too.

He couldn't say how long they were there, he and the forest, holding and being held, warm, timeless, and endless. After a while, he started to feel colder and wetter. Water seeped up against his body and started to cover him.

He found himself washed on a rocky shore. It was cold, so cold, and the rock and sand scraped against him. He was being covered in it, and in the surf, and he cried to himself, *no, please, you're washing him off, you're washing him off and I'll forget him, I'll never have him back.* Then he collapsed into unconsciousness.

+ + +

He woke in a warm bed covered in blankets. He could hear the surf. He could feel a little breeze through an open window and sunlight through it as well. Morning.

He looked around. It was a small cabin, one room. Two cats purred around a butcher block. Sister Clare was at the butcher block, taking apart a chicken. He reached out to her with his mind. *Where are we?*

Clare's face pinched in pain. "Stop connecting like that. You've been doing that all while you slept. Stop it, stop," she said. "I can hear you, but you aren't a part of us. What are you? What the hell happened to you?" She said the last words loudly, nervously, clearly upset.

He stopped and stayed silent.

After a moment she said, "This is the Green Island, Albert. This is where we come once the initiation is over. You went through the initiation, correct?"

He wasn't sure he had, but he nodded nonetheless.

"What happened? How do you feel right now?" she asked.

"I'm not . . . Albert anymore, am I? Not in the way that I was. I let go of him."

"That's what happens in initiations, normal ones. I suppose it happened to you."

"I don't think I realized that would happen. I . . . I miss him."

"Yes," Clare said. For a moment, she let go of her fear and confusion about what he had become, and focused on comforting him. They just looked at each other for a moment.

"Would you do anything different, now that you know what happens?" she asked.

He stared at her, helplessly.

She stared down at the chicken, working a leg from the body with her knife. "I guess now we're both enlightened."

4

When Clare was very young, she lived with her grand-mother. Her parents were dead; no one would ever tell her how, or why. Clare's grandmother was the oldest person on the Green Island, save the Old People themselves. Grand-mother remembered the time before, and what happened when the Old People came, and she told those stories to Clare.

"We lived in caves and huts in the forest," Grandmother said. "We always fought with the other tribes. Sometimes we would ally with a tribe to fight another tribe, then we would fight the tribe that had been our ally. I could never tell our allies from those we hated. I just attacked any-one I didn't know. We would usually figure it out before I killed them.

"If there was a problem in the tribe, we had to work it out or we would be tainted," Grandmother said. "The people with the problem would go out in the woods and fight each other, or fuck each other. Either way, it was settled in body and blood.

"Some nights, we would all gather around the fire to

roast the boar, and sing, and pass around the drink," Grandmother said. "We drank until we were blind, and then we would all go out in the woods and work out our problems. Those nights it was more fucking than fighting. You would grab the person next to you, after you were finished with the drink and the boar, and have a go. Those were the happy nights."

Clare's grandmother had three brothers and two sisters. The brothers had died, and the sisters had both become Adepts, some of the first Adepts. Clare's grandmother had stopped talking to them a long time ago.

"We're all enslaved to the little people, but they are worse, because they volunteered. They wanted to be slaves. They pretend like it was always happy. Everyone pretends like it was all kind and happy. The thin one and the bald one pretended, too. They would show us all their teeth, and sing their light songs to us. But then, when someone from the tribe would fight them, the littlest one would take them into the woods and turn them inside out. She settled it in blood."

Clare listened to her grandmother. The little people were monsters, and her aunts were fools. Then her grandmother died, and she went to live with her aunts, and eventually she became an Adept. She chose to stop believing the stories her grandmother told. She never forgot them, though.

+ + +

Niall would be there within a month, he said. She and Albert were to wait.

She decided to ignore the fact that Albert terrified her. She decided to organize things. He wanted to stay in bed, even after waking, with his back to her and to everything. She got him out of bed, sent him out to chop firewood and harvest vegetables. She remembered he could make bread, and put him to that.

"Does everyone wash up on the shore like that, when they become an Adept?" he asked her. They were making lunch. He was looking out the open window at the cliffs.

"Yes. It's where the Old People first arrived. There's always an Adept here, to meet initiates."

"The Old People didn't build the columns, though," Albert said. "They are very old. It was just the rock and the water, working together. Molten rock came from the sea and turned into the columns."

"Yes, that's right. The patterns of nature can be complex, Albert," she said, then noticed her tone. "You know all that already."

Albert nodded and smiled. "It's all right. I like it when you act like you're still my teacher."

There was something on the edges of Albert. She was trying to let herself understand. "The forest has a life and a pattern that we can't comprehend. It's too much impulse and color and sound. It's too much. You sound like that to me now. That's why I can't hear you properly, and why it's . . . upsetting. You're like the forest."

Albert kneaded the dough.

After hesitating, Clare finally let herself say, "Do you want to talk about it?"

"Albert's—I—I'm still trying to figure it out," he said. "It's very big. It loves me, but it's bigger than its love for me. I mean, it *is* me, and I'm Albert, too, and I . . . I'm not making sense." His knuckles were white.

"Relax. You'll toughen up the dough too much," Clare said. She put her hand on his. "Put your arms to the side. Hold still for a moment. Breathe in and out. Your center, your breath: it's still available to you, right? You can find some comfort there."

Albert nodded, his eyes desperately closed. Clare guided him a little longer. She could see the boy he used to be and didn't have to pretend any more.

+   +   +

The world-mind used to be musical, but now it was chattering and noise. Esther was shouting at her.

Alice says that Niall is a traitor, that he deserves exile or perhaps even death. She says that you are a traitor as well, an accomplice. Why did you go there, to the Green Island, if not to aid in this?

I had no idea that this was going to happen, Clare said. *I came back here because it's my home. I came here because I had participated in an atrocity, and I'd earned the right to step back.*

See? It's exactly this, Esther said. *You and Niall have been two of the biggest malcontents since Baixa. And you just happen to be right by the shore to harvest Niall's little insurrection. It's awfully convenient.*

Clare started to respond—*Coincidence is not causation, Esther, what an obvious*—but then stopped. *Actually, fuck you, Esther,* Clare said. *If you or anyone else has a problem, you come here and work it out with me. I've noticed no one has managed to do that, to come up here and confront me, or Albert. Because you're all afraid, right?*

She could feel Esther's shock and anger, but Esther said nothing.

Come here to the shore, if you have such a care, Clare said. *Come here and we'll settle it, in body or blood.*

Her ears rung and her face flushed. She filtered Esther out. More and more, she found it easier to filter out the world-mind. Many Adepts had started to filter it, or to become quiet. Niall spoke only to her at this point.

She took her sketchbook outside and went to the edge of the cliffs. She sketched the sea and the cliffs for a while. Art had always been part of her practice. Albert sat not far from her, a few hundred yards, in contemplation. She started working him into her sketch. The grasses around him were longer than anywhere else on shore. They seemed to be growing taller by the moment. She drew for a while longer, then approached him. She sat beside him for a while until he roused himself.

"Are the visualizations working?" she said. Training a young Adept was usually seamless: everyone just shared a mind. This work had been awkward, but Clare liked the challenge.

"I've had to change them a little, but yes. Thank you."

"I should be thanking you," Clare said. "Maybe this is for the best, for all of us. The forest can be a nurturer, a mother. We thought of it as an enemy in Baixa because we were doing it violence, and it just responded."

"Maybe. I don't know. I'm still figuring it out," Albert said. "I'm not—it. It's not cruel, but it can do terrible things. It loves you, but it's not your friend."

"I don't understand, what do you—"

"I really need to sit quietly now," Albert said, squinting, as if fighting off a headache. He closed his eyes again, sat up straight, and relaxed his face.

She wanted to touch him. It wasn't an erotic feeling. She told herself it came from a desire to comfort him, but it wasn't. He was strange to her, something unknown, and she just wanted to know what he felt like to the touch. But she left him alone. She walked down the cliff trail to stare at the sea.

+ + +

Niall finally arrived, sailing a small dinghy from down-coast. They saw Niall from the shore, and they watched him climb the cliff. They were standing on the mossy, breezy top of the cliff, but the way up was made of dark, irregular wet rock. By the time he reached the top, Niall was huffing a little.

Albert ran toward Niall and embraced him, nestling his head in Niall's shoulder. Niall reciprocated, stiffly. They leaned back and looked at each other for a moment, then Niall dropped his gaze and walked toward Clare.

"I hear you've been fighting with Esther," he said.

She ignored him. "Albert, are you all right?"

Niall made a thin smile. "Even the most normal initiation leaves some unresolved feelings, Clare, and what we've been through was far from normal. We'll work it out. Won't we, Albert?"

"Right, sure, work it out. Tame it. Organize it into a system," Albert said, and walked away, descending the cliff that Niall had just climbed.

Niall stared blankly at Clare.

"What are you doing?" Clare said. "Go after him. He's your acolyte."

"It's complicated," Niall said. "It was a very different initiation. One of the ego loss phases manifested as intimacy. Strong intimacy."

"Oh," Clare said.

"In retrospect, I should have managed it better. There's a lot to work out now."

"But that wasn't a surprise, was it? He's eighteen years old, a young man. He's almost entirely lust and rage and fear right now, and you took him into an initiation ritual."

Niall didn't say anything.

"Unbelievable," Clare said. She kicked dirt on his foot.

"Have you ever tried to initiate an adult, Clare? Have you?" Niall said. "Do you have any grounds whatsoever on which to judge me?"

"I haven't initiated an adult, and I wouldn't," Clare said. "But, if I had to, I would have had a fucking plan for what to do when sexual cathexis happens, as it inevitably would between two adults in an initiation."

"When did you become so crude?" Niall said.

"I get it from my grandmother. I think my language is the least of our fucking concerns right now."

She let Albert sit quietly on the beach for a half hour, and then took some tea down to him.

"Niall's very good at ideas and systems. He's not very good at people," she said.

"He forgets that God is in the details," Albert said.

Clare furrowed her brow and looked at him. "That's a way to put it, I guess."

They sat in silence for a little while.

"Everyone falls in love with their mentor, Albert. It always happens. I fell in love with mine. Usually we're children when it happens, and it's not as painful or complicated."

"Thank you for the tea," Albert said, and managed a small smile. "I'm just going to sit a little longer."

She left him and went back to the house. She had killed and plucked a chicken, and she got it to roasting. Niall had brought some gin and had a drink. He started to pour another when Clare told him to chop some onions.

Albert came in after the sun had set. "I'm sorry, I didn't help with supper," he said.

"It's fine," Clare said. "Niall helped. We're all ready."

"I know it's hard, Albert," Niall said. "But we're going to get through this. This is an exciting opportunity. I've been thinking a lot about how you're now connected to the primordial chaos, and I've thought of some exercises—"

"Shut up, Niall," Clare said. "Just shut up and pour Albert a drink. We're having supper. The primordial chaos can wait."

+ + +

"Albert, I think you've had enough to drink. *Niall*," she said, as Niall poured Albert another glass. They both ignored her. Niall had a plan, and he was electric with its potential. Albert had had too much gin. He nodded with his eyes hooded.

Niall wanted to go back to Baixa. He wanted to return to the woods beyond the Baixan Old City and start a new civilization. They would take the dinghy downcoast, travel east by land, and take a larger boat back to the continent.

"When you feel ready, Albert," Niall said. "Not until you feel up to it." Albert nodded. Niall felt like they could start over. He believed that the Baixans would easily follow "what Albert has become," as Niall put it.

"Just Albert," Albert slurred, stopping his rhythmic nodding.

"Beg pardon, Albert?" Niall asked. "What's that?"

"My name is Albert. It's not 'What Albert Has Become.' I'm just Albert."

"Of course you are, Albert. I just meant that—"

"No, I get it. Albert's not really that interesting, is he? Certainly not as good as What Albert Has Become." He gave Clare a miserable stare, then looked back into his glass. Then he put his hand on Niall's thigh and leaned in to caress Niall's back. "I could be What Albert Has Become if you would kiss me. How about that? Would you, Niall? Would you sleep with What Albert Has Become?" He slurred the last words into Niall's ear.

Niall held himself still for a moment. He took Albert's hand away from his thigh and held it in both his hands.

"We're going to work this out, all right?" Niall said. "I've thought of some exercises."

Albert pulled away and curled into himself. "I wish I'd never done any of this. I wish I'd never met you," he murmured, eyes welling. "I love you. It hurts."

"You've had too much to drink, Albert," Clare said, rising up from the table to go to him. "Here, let's put you to bed. We'll go ahead and clean up—"

"Clare, would you give us a moment?" Niall interrupted.

Clare stared at him and then sat down again. "You get a moment," she said. "One."

Niall took Albert outside for a walk. Clare connected to Niall and followed them. She felt the intensity of Albert's emotions and Niall's attempts to control the situation. At some point, Niall's control eroded, and they moved into a relationship of energy that was best kept private.

Clare disconnected. She stood from her stool and kicked it across the room. She poured herself a glass of gin, then another.

When Niall came back in his robe hung off the edges of his shoulders. His legs were spattered with mud.

She walked up to him and hit him, a left hook across the jaw. She had never hit anybody before. Her fist glanced awkwardly off his chin.

She grabbed her hand. "That hurts!" Her voice was plaintive. "That really hurts."

Niall clutched his chin. "*Why?* Why would you do that?" he cried through his hands.

"You fucking know why," she said. "Why would *you* do that? What are you doing to him?"

Niall connected with her. *He's an adult, Clare*, he said. *He's also an unprecedented being. He and I talked about it. We came to an understanding that it would be better to work with the feelings than repress them. It isn't a mentor-acolyte relationship. It's something more complex, not least because of what Albert has become.*

Stop it. Stop calling him that. He hates it. And I hate it, too.

I'm just describing phenomena. I'm just saying what we all know, whether we want to acknowledge it or not.

You keep acting like you have a plan, Clare said. *Like you know. You have no fucking plan. You came up with all that Baixan civilization bullshit spontaneously. I could see it in your face. Sister Alice talks about your plots like you're some sort of revolutionary mastermind. They have no idea. The world's at stake and you're experimenting.*

What else can we do? Niall asked. *It's over, Clare. Everything relied on a narrative the Old People produced. We're pretending like there's still a narrative, that we know what's next. We don't. It's gone. Maybe that's for the best.*

Just then, Clare noticed something different in Niall: a change in texture. *You're different.* She focused on it for a moment, then looked at him in the physical world and said, "You aren't controlling your body any more. You aren't controlling how it expresses."

"I'm experimenting, Clare," Niall said. "I'm tired of the narrative. I'm experimenting with not knowing what's next."

She looked at him for a long time.

"We're not going to Baixa," Clare said. "There's no way you're taking him back there."

"Fine," Niall said. "We'll stay here for a while. We'll settle in and try to let Albert grow into what he has—"

"Don't. Don't say it."

Niall sighed. "We'll help Albert adjust."

"We don't have time for that. You hear the others as well as I do. They won't stay afraid of us for long. They'll get a gang together and come for us."

Niall groaned, placed a glass loudly in front of him and

poured a finger of gin. "What would you suggest we do then, Clare?"

"We're going to the Old People. We're going to talk to them."

"There are no more Old People."

"There are. You know there are," Clare said. "They're as traumatized as we are, and they need a reason to engage again. This is the reason."

"Why would we even want to do that? They'll attack him, try to imprison or brainwash him."

"That's a terrible lie. Susan would study Albert and work with him. She would come up with a plan and communicate with us about it. Stop pretending you don't know who Susan is. Stop pretending you don't remember what she means to us."

"Maybe we're both deceiving ourselves," Niall said. "I thought you were taking after your grandmother now, anyway. The old wild woman—"

"My grandmother hit me whenever her capacity for language was inadequate for conversation," Clare said. "My grandmother died because she decided to paint herself with sigils and fight the cat demons in her body instead of accepting medicine. I loved my grandmother, but we have very different opinions of the value of civilization. I knew what I was doing when I became an Adept. I believed in civilization. I still believe in it."

Albert had come in a few moments earlier. He sat on a stool.

"Clare wants us to go talk to the Old People," Niall said.

"Yes. That's what's we do," Albert said.

"It's up to you, Albert," Niall said. "No one's forcing you."

Albert shook his head. "It doesn't matter what I want to do. That's what is going to happen. We're going to visit the Old People. We leave in three days."

+ + +

In three days they set east.

The dinghy was just at the next beach from where Albert had washed ashore. It was small but sufficient. They set off in the morning and sailed all day, only putting down anchor when there was no more light to guide them. Clare and Niall were both strong sailors, and they let themselves connect and coordinate and work like a unit.

Clare sat by Albert while Niall manned the tiller. Albert had a faraway look in his eyes. "What's wrong?" she asked.

"You're all family," Albert said. "The Old People are your parents, and you're the children, and you're all connected. When you and Niall get going, you're like the same body."

"We'll talk to them, to Susan," Clare said. "They'll help. You'll understand. You'll experience this, too."

"No, I won't," Albert said. "I never will."

They sailed for another day along the coast. Finally, they landed at a place where the sea met the river. They pulled the dinghy up the beach above the tideline. They started walking inland. They had only one pack, with bare provisions, and Albert volunteered to carry it.

They walked inland along a clear path by the river. After the better part of a day, Clare stopped at the foot of a tall hill. "We're here," she said.

"Where do they live?" Albert asked. Clare and Niall pointed up the hill, at the same time.

There was a place, here at the foot of the river, with a few stones, some cover, places to sit. The sun was setting.

"Let's make camp for the night," Niall said. "We can approach the castle fresh in the morning."

"We're very close," Clare said. "You're not backing out of the plan, are you?"

"I just want to be ready," Niall said. He took out some

food and began preparing them a supper: he passed around some cheese and hard sausage and bread that Albert had made.

Niall took a teapot from the pack and filled it with river water. "We can clean and heat this, Albert, can't we?" he asked.

He and Albert worked with the nature of the water, filtering it, agitating its molecules. When it was hot, Niall put in a sachet of tea.

"A fire would have been easier," Clare said.

They ate for a while quietly. Niall broke the silence with: "They chose this place for the lines and auras of force permeating the earth around it. Can you see them, Albert?" Albert nodded.

Clare stared into the trees at the foot of the hill. She hadn't been there for years, not since she was an acolyte. The Old People lived in a square stone castle at the top of the hill, and the acolytes lived nearby, in what the Old People called the megalith. The megalith had been ancient in the days of the Old People: one of the oldest structures ever built. Its builders meant it to be a tomb.

The supper was simple but good. Niall had brought a wineskin, and they passed that around as well. Niall asked if they should do some more exercises with Albert, in order to understand his forest mind. Clare said, "A good exercise would be to just sit and see what happens."

They sat for a while in silence. Once Clare grew very quiet, she noticed something she hadn't before, a tension all along her left side: her aversion and fear of Albert. She let it go, and a flood of noise and color and activity covered her. She let it buzz and burn across her in waves. In the wake of it, she looked at Albert.

"You're alone. You really are," she said to him.

"It's all right. I know," he said.

"I'm sorry, I'm so sorry," she said. She put her hands on his hand and squeezed it. "We'll . . . we'll talk to Susan. We'll fix this."

"It won't work out like you expect, or like you hope," Albert said.

"How do you know that?" Clare asked him.

"It's all right, don't be sad," Albert said. "It happens soon. I'll be alone. I'll have a good conversation with Susan. Then something terrible happens."

"I know you think that this is all beyond our control," Clare said. "That we are just marching to something inevitable. I don't believe that, do you hear me? I believe we have a choice." She considered her next statement, and then: "We can walk away. We can walk away right now."

"It's not chaos," Albert said. "Just patterns you don't understand. And 'choice' is part of the pattern, too."

Albert smiled at her. He stood up. He stepped toward Niall, lifted Niall up, and nuzzled him. "I love your body," he said to Niall. "It's beautiful. I love the smell of you. I'm glad you're going to try letting yourself be different, though." He kissed Niall. "It's all about to happen, and that's all right."

Suddenly, there was a painful tug from the top of the hill, from the castle. Clare found herself in the air, flying toward it. The wind around them was loud and rapid and cold with their speed. She looked around and saw Albert and Niall floating with him. They flew toward the top of the tower, a roof of stone.

They landed there gently. She looked to Albert, who seemed to find this all commonplace. Albert pointed to a wooden door that was ajar, a stairwell past it. They walked across the roof, their heels touching the slick moss and smoothness of stone worn for thousands of years. They went down the stairs.

The circular stairwell was dark and tight, the only light

from an occasional opening in the side of the turret. Clare led, looking back to make sure Niall and Albert were following suit. Clare had to focus on the stairs at the end, as they were worn and treacherous. When she reached the landing, Clare saw a hallway with three doors and stairs continuing down at the end of the hall. She looked back to find only Niall descending the last step.

"Where's Albert?" Clare asked.

Niall looked behind her as if expecting to see him, and then looked back at Clare in shock. "Where? He . . . I don't know."

+   +   +

Albert looked to the stone wall of the staircase and squinted at the sunlight coming through a small opening. He could see everything through the opening: He could see the cliffs where they had departed, far to the north, and the shore. He saw a moment that wasn't the moment he occupied. It was many years ago. The smart man was there, lying in the water on a rocky shore. The wise woman and the quick woman sat before him. The quick woman glanced around wildly, her eyes blank and her mouth wide open. They were surrounded on all sides by outcroppings of rock. The cold sea breeze stung. The wise woman was looking at the smart man. She smiled when he woke.

"What happened? Where are we?"

"Somewhere else. We don't know yet."

The smart man looked around. "I think it's Ireland."

The wise woman pursed her lips in thoughtful surprise, and looked about herself. "You think so? Maybe."

"Where have you been?" he asked. "It's been ages."

The wise woman looked at the quick woman. "We fought for a while. Then we came to an understanding. Isn't that right, Lucy?" The quick woman looked at her with a helpless shrug.

The smart man studied them for a while, then breathed in deeply through his nostrils. The air was so fresh here. The air was so fresh that it burned his nostrils. Suddenly, he noticed something about himself. "I'm hungry," he said. "I can't remember the last time I was hungry. What are we going to eat?"

The moment disappeared, and Albert saw the staircase around him again. Clare passed from sight in a turn of the staircase. She was gone. When he finished descending the staircase, he came to an open room. Openings in the walls let in light and a breeze.

At the far wall, a small, thin woman sat in one of two chairs at a sturdy wooden desk, her back to Albert. Albert had seen her before. "Hello there," she said.

"Hello," Albert said.

She stood and walked toward Albert briskly, politely, joylessly. "I'm Susan," she said, extending her hand.

Albert took her hand, her tiny hand, and shook it. "I know. And you know who I am already," he said. It felt rude to say, but it felt worse to pretend.

"Yes," Susan said, dusting the front of her robe a bit. She gestured to the chairs. "Sit down, if you like." They walked over and took their seats.

They sat for a moment, just looking at each other.

"Clare thinks that we'll work some things out," Albert said.

"I imagine you know better than I do how this will resolve," Susan said.

"I guess I do," Albert said. He paused. "I saw what . . . the four of you did." For a moment he had wanted to say *what we did*. "I saw your plan with mind and the fundamental forces. I understand a little."

Susan smiled, but it wasn't a smile. "We were very young, and very intelligent. We believed in our practice and in our science. We were going to change everything. We assumed that letting go of our underlying mental models would be necessary to get us where we needed to be," she said. "This was an assumption from our old spiritual traditions. You know, of course. You've read the sutras."

"Yes."

"We realized, eventually, that the reality was more nuanced. That, to an extent, a narrative was necessary for what we were doing, a world story. It gave us a trajectory to travel, among other things."

"You needed a story to know where to go?" Albert said.

"You could say so. Our ancestors had a practice, *vajray-ana*, which worked in some sympathetic ways. We decided to contemplate a story, as their practitioners would con-template a deity. We decided to apply that contemplative perspective to the observation of fundamental physical phenomena. Do you understand?"

Albert smiled. "I feel like part of me does, or should. But no, not really."

"We tried to control our world by creating a story of the world. It worked. I suppose I should say it had an effect, rather. It didn't do the things we thought it might."

"That's when it all happened to you," Albert said. "The apocalypse."

Susan closed her eyes. When she began speaking, it was as if the words were coming through her. The two of them were alone, but if someone had observed them, they would have noticed that Albert was murmuring the words in unison.

+ + +

A long time ago, the last world ended, with the cities collapsing, and everything becoming forest. The forest had always been there, waiting for the end of the world. It was patient, and vast, and it did not care.

Four people survived the end of the world. One was a wise woman, and one was a smart man, and one was a quick woman, and one was a strong man.

The forest brought them difficulty: bugs, and animals, and sickness.

They lived in the forest for many years. The smart man grew sick. And the wise woman said, "I believe we can change this. We can change the forest."

The strong man said, "Tell me what I can do." And she told him to begin cutting down trees.

The smart man said, "Tell me what I can do." And she told him to measure a place, a square, where they could grow crops.

The quick woman asked, "What are you doing?" And the wise woman told her to go into the forest, and to tell the forest what they were doing.

They made a clearing and put vegetables in it. The vegetables got the whole of the sun, because the strong man had cleared away the trees. They made a small house and were happy.

One day the quick woman returned. She had become a giant, fearsome dragon. She growled, "You left me there. You left me in the forest. It was dark and loud and terrible, and I didn't know who I was. So I became a dragon to be strong."

The wise woman said, "You cannot stay with us."

The dragon laughed. "Why would I want to stay with you? I hate you. I will burn you." And the dragon flew away.

They were alone. The smart man grew well again in the clearing. But the strong man grew sick.

The smart man held the strong man and asked, "What is happening? Why are you sick?"

"I had a place in the forest, a purpose," the strong man said. "What do I do now that we live here?"

The wise woman went into the forest to talk to it. She went to the oldest and largest tree and put her hand to it.

"Why are you here? What have you come to ask of me?" asked the forest.

"When we live with you, we get sick. When we live away from you, we get sick. You turned my sister into a dragon. What are you doing to us? Why is this happening?"

"I don't understand your questions. I am the forest. This is what happens."

"What is the purpose of all this? What do you want us to do?"

"Want? I don't want, I don't need. I am patient and vast. I am complete. I do not care. Your questions are all about what you want, and what your people want."

The wise woman struck the tree. "I'm tired of this, of you. I just want a world I can understand. Do you hear me? I want to understand."

The forest was silent.

The wise woman came back to the clearing. The crops were big and green in the sunlight. She walked into their cabin. The strong man was sicker, and the smart man held him in his arms.

"He's worse. What did the forest say?" the smart man asked.

"Nothing. The forest has nothing to say." And the wise woman came to the edge of the clearing with an axe and a torch. She burned everything she saw and cut everything that would not catch. She cut and burned until her eyes watered and her arms tired and tears ran down her cheeks. "I hate you, I hate you," she cried.

Her cutting and burning brought the dragon. The dragon said, "What are you doing? This is madness." The dragon didn't care for the forest, but she hated the people for all that had happened. She attacked the wise woman, but the wise woman was

strong and fought her. The dragon clenched the wise woman in
her jaws, and the wise woman set her mouth afire. They flew
away, thrashing and burning.

The smart man knew they were alone now. He tended to the
strong man. He brought him clean water, and food, and cool
cloths to soothe the strong man's hot brow. "I should be well, I
should be well," the strong man groaned.

"Just rest. I'll take care of you," the smart man said.

The smart man did everything he knew to do. He made poul-
tices and potions; he made the strong man's bed cool and warm;
he fed him broth and water, and porridge with herbs. None of it
worked, and the strong man grew weaker and weaker.

At the end, the strong man leaned his head against the smart
man's chest. "Thank you. I'm dying, but these last days have
been my happiest. Thank you for taking care of me. I love you."

The smart man wailed, "I love you, I can't lose you. Why is
this happening?"

The strong man kissed his cheek. "This is the forest still. This
is what happens."

The strong man died that night, and the smart man buried
him near the clearing. Each morning, the smart man would
visit the strong man's grave. Each day, he would grow crops
and clear trees and gather the harvest. Each night, he would
dream of killing the forest.

+ + +

They sat for a long while in silence.

"Obviously," Susan said, "we weren't in an entirely rational place. We suffered for what felt like millennia, inde-
scribable suffering. After a while, we weren't sure what part
of it was observation, and what part was just story. We lost
ourselves.

"So, when we arrived here, we began experimenting with

stories again. But it was completely different. No patience, no contemplation, no integration or nuance, just clumsy experiments in social manipulation. We had different tools before, powerful tools to engineer the fabric of what was real. Now all we could engineer was a little primitive handful, barely a society, children becoming adults. We tried our best to start a new story of civilization."

"But the war—how is that civilization? To fabricate a war."

Susan paused. "It made more sense in context. In our old cultures, the ones we had come from, every civilization grew through colonization, conquest. It was a good story, and it was a way to organize the people and land, as well. There was a tidiness to it." She paused. "The violence was regrettable," she said.

She paused again. "And, yes, of course, we wanted to tame it, to hurt it, the thousands of acres of it, right across the water, never leaving us alone, putting out all its noise and disorder. We had suffered so long with it, and it wouldn't stop. We wanted to make it stop—I guess *you* are it, now, on some level. Like I said, it wasn't rational. It was what we felt."

"It's not me," Albert said. "You were upset. I can understand that much, I suppose. I'm not angry, anyway."

"We used to be so perceptive, so powerful," Susan said. "We had everything at our fingertips; bodies and forces and meaning itself were subject to our subtle control. And then we ruined it all and ended up here, weakened and mad. But we immediately tried the same thing we had tried before, even with all our weakness. We tried control.

"We started from all the wrong premises. We thought you needed to look at the universe from a given vantage point. We thought the 'noise' of nature itself was something that you have to tame or reduce or yoke. That it's 'chaos,' and that there's something different between that chaos and what you're actually trying to understand."

Susan put her head in her hands. The movement was controlled and elegant, as Albert expected. In this position, she exhaled several times. When she brought her face back from her hands, it was sad and gray.

"I should be dead. I felt the pain of destroying the world, and then I came here and started destroying it all over again. I'm foolish, and I'm tired. I'm tired of stories. I'm tired of control. It's all right to let it fall apart. It's all right for the world to start over without us."

She looked at Albert. "I wish this hadn't happened to you. It's all because you reminded Richard of someone. You remind me of him, too." She paused, unsure if she could say what she meant to. "If you need to hate us for this, it's all right. Do you understand me? It's all right, if that's what it takes to keep you going." She took his face in her hands. "Just don't stop. I can't bear the thought of you wasting away again. I'm begging you. You have to promise."

He felt very far away, that there were layers and layers between him and the world. From his faraway place, he could hear himself say, "There's no Albert anymore. I'm foolish and terrible, too. I've killed innocents, and now I'm this thing. There's nothing to save."

Susan took that in sadly, but her response was skeptical. "Stop it. There's a 'you' down there, still. It's just not the 'you' that you thought it would be, and you aren't being creative. Don't stop because of this. Hold on to what's simple and real, not a story. Who loves you? Whom do you love?"

That question stirred something in him, and he was Albert again, saying plaintively: "I love him, I love Niall, but he doesn't care, he just needed an instrument—"

Susan interrupted him. "I didn't ask toward whom you had complicated, ambivalent feelings. Focus. Whom do you love? Who loves you?"

Albert thought of home and of Thomas. He hadn't looked at that part of himself for a long time. "I want to go home," he said.

"Go home, then." She took his hand in her small hands.

A wail came from far below them, deep within the castle. Susan, with a look of despair, said, "We need to talk about Lucy." She smiled, that kind of smile that tries to hide or mitigate grief.

"We may not have long," Susan said, but continued with her speech as it was: deliberate, unhurried. "She's never been the same. There are days when she is amazing, when she's like the old Lucy, sharp, clever . . . She actually made most of the theoretical leaps that led us here. Did you know that? She was the smartest of us." Susan was quiet for a long while after that. "But then she gets into the green moods. We knew about her and the green in the forest. We always knew. We hoped she would be better once we had started to tame the forest, once we had taken the Old City of Terra Baixa."

Her eyes had drifted away in reverie, but she brought them back to Albert. "She's family. There were only three of us, three of us left in the world. It probably seems clear-cut to you, but it wasn't to us."

At that moment, there was a great cracking as a hole ripped in the wall. Albert noted that, as raw and violent as the action was, the hole it created was mathematically symmetrical. In the middle of it floated Lucy, her wild hair coruscating with a green glow. She breathed out the same bioluminescence from her lips, an exhalation of shimmering algae, airy bits of her soul.

"My sister was trying to keep you from me," Lucy said, "but I know, I know everything. I can hear all of you."

"Lucy, no!" Susan cried. "Why does it always have to be a fight? Will you please just calm down and talk to us?"

"Shut up," Lucy said to Susan. And then, turning to Albert: "We got here and you . . . things, living in the trees, eating the ground, fucking your sisters and brothers and parents, anything, eating anything, you were like apes, do you understand?" she cried. "Apes! And we taught you, we made you human. We made you more than human! We made you special! And now you all have the temerity to come here because you feel *compromised*, you feel that this doesn't fit in with your *ethical model*, when you were consuming each other indiscriminately like bugs not a century ago.

"And you: abomination. You dove back into it. You don't care what chaos you bring forward, as long as it stops your little-boy hurting. You want to turn it back around. I can't even imagine that kind of perversion. I'm sick of you. I'll choke all of you."

"I'm sorry, Lucy," Albert said, and then looked to Susan. "We have to start over. We all do."

Lucy shrieked at that, in rage. The green extended tentacles and feelers across the space between her and the castle before her; across the space to Albert. The green crept to him, began touching him, began to try to consume him. Then, with a start, the green recoiled from him and flew back toward Lucy. She stared at Albert in awe and horror, understanding a little of what he felt, what he saw.

"He's sorry," Albert said. And with that, a rumbling began from deep beneath them, deep under the castle.

Lucy snarled and flew toward Albert, her skin beginning to wrinkle and desiccate, molded puffs of green exhaling from her. Susan leapt forward into Lucy's path, grappling with her.

"Stop this, Lucy. You're sick," Susan said.

"I hate you. I'll burn you," Lucy cried.

+   +   +

Niall heard the rumbling from the hallway, and heard a voice that was Albert's but that seemed to come from everywhere at once. *Run. Get out.*

He and Clare ran to climb the narrow stairs, which were surprisingly moist. Moss was forming rapidly on the walls. The rumbling increased, and they could feel the walls shaking.

Then the walls collapsed around them, only seconds after Niall noticed them beginning to crumble. "Defenses, Clare! Your defenses," he shouted. Niall imagined his breath as a stream, an open stream, and his body as supple stone. He rode the stones as they fell around him.

Light emerged, and he realized the top of the castle had fallen away around them. He and Clare were next to one another on the now-exposed stairs. Their defenses had kept them from the worst damage, but not all of it. He could feel wetness from his nose and ears and knew it was blood.

He reached out to Clare, and she reached back. Connected, they lifted one another into the air and began flight back to where camp and supper had been. They looked behind them to see the rest of the castle dissolving into rubble, with a mass of trees growing from the ground, through the tower, consuming it and breaking it apart. As they drifted closer to the ground, the westernmost side crumbled, and then the bulk of it fell into itself.

With that they fell about six feet, landing clumsily on the ground.

Niall had the wind knocked out of him, but as he regained his breath, he realized that wasn't why Clare's mind, the system, everything Adept had suddenly and completely gone silent.

He struggled to still himself and listen to his body, but he could detect nothing beyond. All he could perceive, with his clumsy senses, was Clare, curled up in a ball with her hands at her ears, screaming: "I can't hear, I can't hear."

He realized that the castle, the Old People, everything that made an Adept an Adept lay in the rubble of a newly grown grove of trees. His first thought to himself was, *This wasn't supposed to happen*, but there was a vision beneath that thought. It reminded him that it indeed was supposed to happen, that there was a Niall in a village, in a dream, in another world, a Niall that needed to be.

He was filled with guilt and satisfaction and fear and excitement all at once, a blur of pulsing impulses and emotions that made him ashamed. He feared that his blasphemous thoughts would proclaim themselves to the Adept world-mind for all to see. The worry was a reflex and unnecessary; he heard nothing, and no one heard him.

5

Thomas was inconsolable the morning after Albert went to war. He kept his misery in silence as he ate the breakfast Mister Ewan made him, and as he watched Mister Ewan pack his things, and as Mister Ewan drove him and his mother to Over-town, where they were to see the Kelvins.

Thomas and Cynthia had last met over a decade before, when they were children. They spent most of that meeting staring tentatively at one another and then got into a short but vicious fight just before the Newtons returned to Eden-town. In retrospect, everyone chose to describe the meeting as auspicious.

The Kelvins met them at the door of their house. Cynthia introduced herself with a joke about the fight. "I promised them I'd behave better this time," she said. They shared a polite laugh. She had chestnut hair and color on her lips, Thomas noted: they were red and matched the embroidery on her robes.

She took Thomas for a tour of the town. It was smaller than Eden-town but had an energy about it. He heard people talking about construction and progress, some in skeptical tones, which was surprising to him.

They passed by the bank, crowded with people doing business and chatting. Thomas noticed a set of totems in front of the bank. "What are those?" he asked.

Cynthia looked at him with some disbelief. "What? They're the old gods," she said, with an implied *obviously*.

"You mean . . . from before?" Sister Alice forbade any mention of the gods, the ones before the Old People came. He remembered a time that his mother had said the names in conversation; he had never seen Sister Alice so angry.

"The people like to worship here," she said. "They worship at the bank, then they use the bank. It helps us with the adoption of commerce. We'll phase the gods out eventually, of course."

To a one, the people of Over-town greeted Cynthia with an enthusiasm Thomas envied, and when she greeted them in turn, she knew each one by name.

They took lunch at a tavern not far from the river. Over-town's river was called the Clyde Water, and the tavern was called that, too. They sat at benches outside and enjoyed Over-town in spring. A few canoes drifted by; their inhabitants waved at Cynthia, and she waved back.

They had mutton and cheese and a drink Thomas had never tried, ale mixed with apple juice. Cynthia called it a shandy. She told a couple of stories, and Thomas laughed at them without having to pretend. He stopped worrying. It was all going to be fine.

At first he had planned to tell her nothing about Albert, but after the afternoon he decided it would be good for him—for *them*, really—if he shared it all. On the way back to her parents' house, he asked if they could sit and chat. They sat under a fruit tree.

"I miss him," he told her. "Terra Baixa is so far away."

"It's not that far away, really," she said.

"And . . . you're all right with this? I imagine how it must sound to you," he said.

"It's fine, it's all right," she said, quickly. "This is a strange arrangement for us. I wouldn't expect us to just fall in love by coincidence." She paused. "I just want to be happy. I want us to be happy. To make a nice family."

"I do, too, I really do."

"If he comes back, I'd love to meet him. I'm sure he's nice. We'll work it out." She smiled at Thomas, briefly, then focused on smoothing out her robes.

"You're wonderful, you know that? Thank you for understanding."

"Of course." She stood and walked ahead of him along the bank of the Clyde Water.

Later in the evening, they took a stroll alone in the courtyard of her house. Thomas kissed her once. She smelled nice.

"That went well," Lady Newton said on the way home.

"They allow the people to worship the old gods in Overtown. Did you know that?"

Lady Newton flushed. "We don't talk about that. Do you understand?" she said.

Thomas made a face. "Fine," he said. "It seems like a good idea, though. Their bank gets a lot more use."

"Thomas," Lady Newton said, loudly.

He shrugged. He didn't talk to her much any longer. When he did, this tended to happen.

When they returned to Eden-town, Sister Alice was waiting for him. "We are going to begin a new round of education for you," she said. "Something appropriate to the next generation of Administration."

Sister Alice accompanied him to his quarters, where they had a cup of tea. She told him that he had to sleep for the kind of travel they were about to do. He did, on his bed, right in front of her.

When he woke up, she was there, but they were in a different room, with different light and different smells. They were somewhere else, now, in the White Island's Old City.

Sister Alice began his new lessons the next day. The future was in conquest and warfare, she said. This effort required soldiers, but also Administrators. Administrators would keep the law, and manage the resources of towns, and inspire the people in these newly civilized lands to be a part of the enlightened world.

Thomas stayed in the Old City for months. He learned about how to keep the law and adjudicate differences. He learned how to raise and discipline a militia, how to grant and manage property, and how to keep a bank. The more he studied the concepts of banking, the less he understood. The mechanics themselves were simple mathematics, but the core concept was emptiness itself.

"Banks only have value because we say they do," he said to Sister Alice.

"Is that a statement, or a question?" she replied. "Commerce is crucial for what we are building. The Adepts, the Old People, all of our society values the bank."

About a month after he arrived in the city, Sister Alice drew him and other Administrators together. "We're going on a trip," Alice said. "The first troops are heading to Terra Baixa. I want you to see them off with me."

They went to the Abyss. Thomas had heard stories of it since he was tiny, but he had never thought it actually existed. They rode two days, along the river. When they got there, they saw the holes—the dark, ancient holes to hell.

"They're just an old structure from before the apocalypse. There is no hell," Sister Alice said.

"And . . . you're sure of this? Conclusively?" Thomas asked. Sister Alice stared at him, and he shut up.

There were hundreds of soldiers there. Thomas was certain Albert was, too. He tried to gaze into the crowd to see him, but there were too many soldiers. They stretched out for leagues, a wave of heads and arms and movement.

Then they all started screaming, a scream of anger and fear. Thomas started in shock. Every cell in him wanted to run. He closed his eyes and found his breath, scanned his body, found his stillness. It was difficult. Albert had always been better at this. He tried to listen to his breath, but all he could hear was the screaming.

"That was awful," he said to Alice later. "Why did they do that?"

"They are leaving here, to go to a land they have never seen before, a land that is hostile. They are going there to confront the unknown and kill people. Wouldn't that idea make you want to scream as well?"

"Are we doing the right thing? Is this really the best way to advance civilization, to take an army into an unknown land and kill?"

"Warfare is the advancement of nobler ends through organized violence," Alice said. "That's the point of all this." She was gone the next day.

Thomas got to know another Administrator named Matthew. Matthew was a few years older than Thomas and lived in the Old City. He helped the Adepts with development and plans. Many nobles lived in the Old City, preparing to take and administer land in Terra Baixa. When Matthew spoke of Terra Baixa, he always impressed Thomas with his enthusiasm, his energy. "It's going to be amazing—wild and full of life. An opportunity to make a mark in a place that hasn't seen civilization for thousands of years."

Matthew showed Thomas all around the Old City. It was

even bigger than Thomas had imagined, but Matthew could navigate it without missing a beat. The town was built along both sides of the Dark River. Most people took boats to get across. The river was filled with them going back and forth as well as the boats that traveled between the city and the coast. Thomas stayed on the north bank, where the Adept schools and banks and government were established. The south end was full of taverns, and entertainment, and common people.

On Midsummer's Night, Matthew found them a boat to the south side. They took in a play about the days before the Old People arrived. The characters ran about naked and crouched in trees. They hit each other and pretended to rut and defecate, and everyone laughed. Then the actors playing the Old People came in wearing bright robes. The parts of the Old People were played by children. Thomas had seen one of the Old People, from a distance, at the Abyss. He was so small. The audience was raucous at the play, but Thomas found himself sad for a reason he couldn't pinpoint.

They went to a tavern after that. Thomas had too much to drink, far too much. He ended up going home with Matthew and passing out next to him. He didn't remember much of the night. He was mortified the next morning, but Matthew just laughed.

The next week, Matthew left for Terra Baixa. "Wish me luck. I'll try to find Albert and send him your regards." Thomas never heard from Matthew again.

Thomas lost track of the days. The summer whiled away with work and reading and the sights of the city. He learned about the next five years the Adepts had planned. Before long, Eden-town would trade goods with the Baixans. Everything would be connected.

Each evening, he would walk down to the bank and watch the oranges and reds and purples of the setting sun.

He would watch the evening descend into gray, watch the color disappear into the water of the Dark River. He thought about going across the river to see another play. He approached a boat, once, but turned away when the owner greeted him. Matthew had always done it before.

He returned from his walk one night to find an Adept waiting outside his door.

"There is a message for you," the Adept said.

"Thank you. What is it?"

"Open the door," the Adept said. "Give me a sheet of parchment and a stylus."

Thomas did, and showed the Adept to a desk. The Adept closed his eyes and sat perfectly still for several seconds. Then he started to write. When he was finished, he produced a letter in Albert's handwriting.

"That's lovely," Thomas said. "It's from Albert. Albert is a school chum," he said to the Adept.

"This came to me from Richard, of the Old People," the Adept said. That seemed like a happy thing to Thomas, but the Adept didn't seem happy.

Thomas read the letter. "He's a bit homesick, I think. Poor thing. I hope he doesn't have to stay too long. I've heard a range of estimates on the military presence, but I choose to remain optimistic." He smiled to the Adept.

The Adept snorted at him. It was a very uncommon thing for an Adept to do. Thomas opened his mouth, then shut it. "Are you all right? Shall I fetch you a glass of water?" he asked. The Adept simply stood and left, without another word.

Thomas stayed in the Old City until the equinox, when the training was concluded. He went home the old way, on a horse, northbound up the coast.

When he arrived home, Lady Newton told him it was time. The Kelvins and their Adepts took the trip to

Eden-town. Thomas and Cynthia married in Lady Newton's study, a quiet and official ceremony. They had a nice supper in their house; Mister Ewan made a pudding. Then the Kelvins all left, except for Cynthia.

+ + +

"We . . . usually noble couples have a child within the first year or so. We might . . . want to start trying," she said. She had been in Eden-town over a month.

"I'm just so nervous. I don't even know what to do," he said.

That night, Cynthia ordered a light supper brought to their quarters, some cured pork and cheese with a salad. Mister Ewan also brought a bottle each of wine and gin. Thomas knew the clear liquid on sight, though he'd never drunk more than a sip himself. Lady Newton always had a small glass at the end of the night.

"Thank you, Ewan," Cynthia said.

"We're having gin? With supper?"

"It calms the nerves. You said you were nervous."

"I guess you want to start trying."

"Whatever it takes."

They both had their fair share, Thomas a little more than Cynthia. The drink made him dizzy, dizzier than wine, and it made him feel warm. He opened the window, loosened his robe to the waist. He and Cynthia told funny stories, and then Cynthia told a bawdy story. Thomas told one as well, but it was one about Albert and him. With the gin, he was halfway through before he realized that it was a bad idea. "I guess you didn't want to hear that," he said.

Cynthia laughed. "It's fine, I don't care anymore. Look, you can fuck Albert as much as you want, as long as you fuck me, too, and we have babies." As soon as the words

[185]

left her mouth, she widened her eyes, covered her mouth, and gasped in horror. Then she began laughing hysterically, and Thomas did, too. They fell over each other and lost their breath.

That night was blurry and clumsy, but Thomas would remember it fondly. It was different, and kind of curious, but wonderful, too. With Albert it had been intense and rushed, with a desperation that exceeded both of them. With Cynthia, it was slower, rife with smiling and giggling pauses, softer, more a hike than a race. Neither of them needed it to be more than exactly what it was.

The next morning, Mister Ewan brought them breakfast. They spent a little time in bed, nursing hangovers and telling each other jokes. They took supper in their quarters for the next month. A month after that, Cynthia announced she was expecting.

+ + +

Sister Alice checked in once a week during the pregnancy. She would focus on Cynthia, observe the rhythms of her body and the baby, the balance of her body's chemicals and energies.

"Everything is going wonderfully. The baby is healthy."

"Do you know if it is a boy or a girl?" Thomas asked.

Sister Alice paused. "I do. But you know that it is terrible fortune and poor form to tell you. Focus on your child's happiness and not its gender."

Thomas shrugged. "Fine," he said, annoyed.

Cynthia would sing and hum warm, old songs as she moved around the house. Thomas would sing, as well. They would read together by the fire. Thomas thought he might be falling in love with Cynthia. Even Lady Newton was in a good mood. They all took more meals together, and Thomas and Lady Newton had whole conversations without disagreement.

Thomas began to take on more of the mayoral duties in his mother's stead. He led a ceremony that fall celebrating the first troops to come back from the war in Baixa. He wore his formal robes and carried a stylus that his mother had given him. Everyone stood in the middle of the square, and Thomas read the names of the two soldiers who had died in the battle: Paul Henry, Malcolm Abbe. He then read the names of the soldiers who had returned and gave each of them an honor, a certificate that the children had made in the school.

After the ceremony concluded, he found himself close to Aengus from school. "Hello, Aengus," he said. "I'm so sorry. We're very proud of you." He looked at Aengus's missing arm, then chided himself for doing that, then chided himself for his awkwardness.

"What? Oh, sure." Aengus shrugged. He looked at his feet, then at something behind Thomas.

"I haven't forgotten how you helped Albert after the terrible business with his parents. I appreciate that, as well." Aengus stared away from Thomas at something else, now. *He seems so upset*, Thomas thought, and remembered Sister Alice's words about the advancement of nobler ends. He tried to feel noble about it all.

"You traveled with Albert on the way to Baixa, didn't you? Do you have any news back from him? I've asked Sister Alice, but she doesn't know."

Aengus shook his head. "He's still there, I know that. He didn't come back with us."

"It's helpful just to know that, Aengus. Thank you. We're making such good progress that I'm sure he'll be home soon." Thomas reached forward to pat Aengus on the shoulder, then realized he was heading for the missing arm's shoulder. He pulled back, began to reach for the other shoulder, then gave up. "Thank you, Aengus," he said again. Aengus said nothing, so Thomas just left.

"I'm proud of you," his mother said after the ceremony concluded. "You're becoming a leader and starting a legacy. Eden-town is in good hands. Thank you."

"Of course, you're welcome," he said, not saying what he truly felt. He had decided this was all for Albert. If Albert could leave his home, just after losing his parents, and venture across the sea to face homesickness and war, just to make himself worthy of Thomas, the least Thomas could do for him was keep a place, an Eden-town, that was ready to welcome him back. Surely Albert regretted his words the last time they spoke, the madness about the woods. There was no reason they couldn't make it work here. He and Cynthia and Albert could make it work together.

Early in the spring, Sister Alice came to the house accompanied by a short, thin woman wearing the simplest of wool clothing, gray and naked of embroidery. She had enormous eyes that never made contact with Thomas's. "This is Anya," Sister Alice said to Cynthia and Thomas. "She'll begin work as your nurse. I've discussed this with Lady Newton."

Anya nodded at them, shyly.

"I've been working with her on our language. She knows enough to do the work."

"She's not from the Islands?"

"She's from Terra Baixa. She was displaced by the war."

"Displaced?" Cynthia asked.

"She can speak—ask her," Sister Alice said.

Cynthia did. "How did you come to be here with us, Anya?"

Anya paused and then spoke hesitatingly. "My family, we lived in the woods with our tribe. A green sickness came over us, and we left our village. We fought the Islanders. I'm sorry to fight you. It was sickness. Then we were prisoners in your camp. And now I am here."

Thomas, taken aback, stayed silent. He had heard some discussions of the war and its effects, and had worried about Albert, but it had all been abstract and far away. The war was here, in the room.

Cynthia met eyes with Anya and smiled sadly. "I'm sorry for your misfortune. Did you have children in Terra Baixa?"

"My children fell to the sickness. I nursed them. I can be a nurse for you."

Cynthia took Anya's hand, her eyes welling. "Thank you. We will try to make a good home for you." Anya looked back at her blankly.

+ + +

Summer came, and Cynthia was big with child. "I hope it doesn't get warm too soon," she said. That morning she had an appointment with Sister Alice.

"Let's ask her today if she knows how soon the baby will come," Thomas said.

The hour came, but there was no knock on the door from Sister Alice.

"What's happened? You should go and see if she's all right," Cynthia said.

"I'm sure she's fine," Thomas said. "She's just running a bit late."

"Is she?" Cynthia asked. "Has she ever run late, ever? Have you ever known an Adept to run late?"

Thomas started to open his mouth to respond, but knew that Cynthia was right. He got up, put on his jacket, and crossed the square to the school and Alice's quarters.

It was early in the morning: Sister Alice made her rounds before and after school. Her modest apartment was just behind the school. Thomas approached the door and gave it a brief knock. "Sister Alice? So sorry to trouble you, it's Thomas Newton." No answer. He waited for several moments, shuffling his feet, whistling, hands in pockets. He knocked again, with a little more force, but still well within the boundaries of deference and politeness.

It was silent still. Thomas began to suspect she was away on another visit and had gotten held up. *Adepts are never late, and never forget,* he thought, *but if they are helping someone and the time gets away from them, surely they would tend to the matter at hand. That's all that's happened.* It was early, though, the beginning of the day. And Thomas felt something, something on the edges of his perception. He had a feeling Sister Alice was there.

He knocked once again, with strength but without impatience. It was a knock that communicated a brisk and forceful concern, a good knock. "Sister Alice, this is Thomas still. I'm worried something might be wrong. I'm going to open your door and come in. I hope that's all right. Please speak up if you're there and would rather I stay outside." He knew what Sister Alice had the power to do, and preferred to act deliberately and with great transparency. He waited another couple of moments. "Trying the doorknob, Sister Alice!" he said with nervous cheer.

The doorknob turned; the door was unlocked. Thomas paused for another moment before moving forward. He had never entered or really seen the interior of an Adept's quarters before. He worried that it was sacrosanct, or full of dangers. "Sister Alice?" he called, tentatively.

There was a small and simple kitchen with a table. There was a book on the table, some clean paper for writing, and what looked to be a stack of student assignments. There was a hearth at the wall next to the kitchen, with a modest pile of wood. The hearth was cold. Beyond that was a doorway. Thomas saw a cat peer from the doorway, then disappear once it was detected. A low moan came from the doorway.

"Sister Alice, are you unwell?" There was no response. He walked to the doorway.

She lay sprawled on the bed. Her hair, usually tied back and up, fell loose around her, across her face and nightgown and across the bed. Thomas was struck by how long her hair actually was, and how much gray it had. She had an arm over her face, and her jaw was slack. She groaned again.

"Oh, you are ill. Sister Alice, is there anything I can get you?"

Sister Alice moaned again, an angry, desperate moan.

Thomas wasn't sure what to do. She was breathing and seemed to be reacting to things, but this didn't seem like just a headache. If this were anyone else, he would call Sister Alice to tend to them.

"I'll bring Muriel over." Muriel was an elder who retained some of the healing practices of the old ways. "I know it's not the same, but maybe she will be able to help a little. And then we can call the Brother over from Over-town right away."

"No," Sister Alice shouted.

Thomas, stunned at that, blurted, "Sister Alice, what do you want me to do?"

"No Adepts! I don't want an Adept to see me like this." She then began to sob. "I don't think there are any more Adepts."

Thomas didn't know what that meant. "Look, I'll bring Muriel over, and we'll figure out what to do after that. Having Muriel over can't hurt."

"I don't want any of you to touch me. I don't want to be touched by apes." She sobbed quietly. "I'm like an ape now, too. I'm an ape again."

"You're not yourself," Thomas said.

"Get out! Get out of my house, you . . . you *pet*, you pampered, simpering animal."

Thomas flushed at her curses. "I'll leave you to collect yourself," he said. "I'll come back when you have your composure back."

"Get the hell out of my house," Sister Alice shouted.

He left. Several strides away from the house, he realized he'd left the door open, thought about going back to close it, then let it be. *To hell with her*, he thought.

Some students were beginning to collect in front of the school. "The school is usually open by now," one of them said to Thomas. "Where's Sister Alice?"

"School is cancelled today. Sister Alice is ill." He dismissed the children. He crossed the street to the house, went to his mother's chamber, and related the incident to her. Lady Newton was incredulous and went to Sister Alice's to see for herself. While she did so, Thomas composed a sign for the door of the school and posted it. He then returned to Cynthia, who was having a cup of tea with Anya at this point, and told her. As he was finishing the story, Lady Newton came back.

"So?" Thomas asked.

"She called me a deluded old hag."

"She's very ill."

"Let's send a letter to Cynthia's family and see if they can spare Brother Benedict for a day or two. He should be able to get to the bottom of this. She seems to have some sort of brain fever."

"Is it a mistake to leave her alone?"

"She just seems to get agitated when we are there. Let's leave her be and check in every once in a while."

Lady Newton sent a horse messenger to the Kelvins. They let Alice have the day in solitude; the next morning, both Lady Newton and Thomas went to her door, knocked stiffly, and let themselves in when there was no response. They found some drawers pulled open and empty, the cat curled up in one of them. Sister Alice was gone.

Two days later, they received word back from Over-town. Brother Benedict had been found in his room the same day Sister Alice took ill. He had hung himself.

"She said to me that she didn't think there were any more Adepts. That morning," Thomas said. "I thought that she was just talking nonsense. But something has happened."

"Of course there are still Adepts. How could there not be?" Lady Newton said. "How would one stop being an Adept? That makes no sense. Certainly, something happened, and two Adepts took ill. That's troubling, but I believe in facts. Facts and reason. And there's no sense in dreaming up a conspiracy before we know the facts." The militia was lean in Eden-town—most able troops had gone to Baixa—but Lady Newton found two to send to the Old City. "There are plenty of senior Adepts there. They'll know what is happening and what to do."

"What about the baby?" Thomas asked. "What do we do without an Adept, with Cynthia almost ready to have a child?"

"In Baixa, we had plenty of babies without Adepts," Anya said. Everyone paused and looked at her; she didn't speak much. "When the Lady is ready to have the baby, we'll have the baby."

Cynthia smiled. "Anya's right. We'll be fine, Thomas," she said, patting his hand to calm him.

+   +   +

That autumn, a bit later than expected, Cynthia gave birth. Anya tended to her, and indeed knew the process. They had a daughter, born with a full head of her mother's brown hair. They named her Cydney, after a pet name Thomas had given to Cynthia, and immediately started calling her Cyd.

It was a difficult birth, and long. Cynthia stayed in bed for a week, but started working as soon as she was able, despite Anya's protests. "Without Adepts, we all need to help each other," she said.

The troops that were sent to the Old City never came back. Thomas finally convinced his mother to consider contingency plans, in case they were without an Adept for some time.

"I'm sure it's going to be fine," Lady Newton said.

"The only town we are in contact with is Over-town. They've sent troops to the Green Island, with no response. We need to consider the possibility that it's not going to be fine."

Between elders trained in old ways and students who had learned some medicine in school, they had a small group of nurses who could tend to the sick. They were comforted by the yield from the farms, which had been good that summer. Cynthia even opened the school once a week, acting as the teacher, though attendance was low.

"I wish I knew what was keeping them away," Thomas mused at the table one day, during breakfast. "It's still a community service that helps, even if there's not an Adept to teach."

"What is the point of it now?" Anya asked. She was nursing month-old Cyd at the time. "The learning was Adept, right? Learning to do Adept things? What you talk about, physics and meditating and words and money. There's no time for that now. It's time to learn to defend yourself, fight, grow food, make medicine."

"You're probably right. Maybe we could change things for now. Teach more useful things."

"They are all learning it from their families. The families

will stay to their land and survive. The town here, with the trees taken away, and the houses all next to each other, and the tiny gardens, they know it's not the way to live now. It only makes sense with Adepts to protect you." She paused. "It won't last long."

"I think you are having trouble translating from Baixan, Anya. I'm sure I don't understand what you're saying." Thomas poured himself some tea. "It doesn't make sense."

"I know what I am saying. I think you do, too." Anya looked at him. Cyd was nursing happily, eyes closed. "You aren't your mother. You know what is going on. You should be ready when we have to run away."

The next day, Cynthia woke with a high fever, and wasn't able to keep any liquid down. Thomas brought the elder Muriel to her; Muriel lit some pine incense and placed a poultice on Cynthia's bosom.

"The smell is invigorating," Thomas said. "I'm glad we brought Muriel in."

"It's not a good medicine," Anya said. "The sickness is too strong."

"What do you think we should do, then, Anya?" Thomas asked impatiently.

Anya stared at the wall as she rocked Cyd's crib. "I don't know."

Thomas spent every night by Cynthia's side. On her sixth day of sickness, at sunset, she woke for a short while. They held hands. "I'm very lucky," she said. "I have a beautiful daughter and a beautiful husband. You're always so good to me. You always look out for me."

"Of course," he said. "What else would I do?" Cynthia smiled and closed her eyes. Thomas watched her for some time in the dark, her chest rising and falling. When he woke the next morning, she was gone.

The sickness went all through the town. Thomas opened

the school for a few days, then stopped because no one would send their children to school. No one went outside unless it was absolutely necessary. Thomas woke every morning to the silent town and began the day's business. He would update the counts of sick and dead in his ledger, then have some breakfast. Mid-morning, he made posters of announcements, took them outside and posted them, then shouted them from the square, then went door to door and shouted through the doors to let the people know. Bury the dead quickly. Keep the houses clean. Keep the sick isolated.

This was his job now. He had become the acting mayor. Lady Newton took ill not long after Cynthia's passing. He stayed by her bed, and, every moment she was able, she filled Thomas with all the knowledge she could, pointing him to documents, insisting on protocols and practices and telling long stories. She reviewed the fine points of diplomatic engagement with other Administrators; the nuances of dispute adjudication in Eden-town, including the understanding of many unspoken, long-simmering feuds of which Thomas had been completely unaware; the locations of all ledgers, histories, and important records; the care and feeding of the bank.

Lady Newton had become chief financier of Eden-town with the departure of Sister Alice. Like the school, the bank had seen a drastic reduction in traffic, but there were still many accounts in place. Thomas, frankly, still found the bank to be the most confounding subject of all, especially now that the Adepts were absent. "What happens if the majority decides that the capital the bank holds is worthless?" he asked his mother.

"Can't you say the same thing about civilization, darling?" she asked him.

Thomas held her hand for a moment. "I know you don't like to talk about this," he said. "I want to know, though. Did we anger them, the old gods? Did we anger them when we stopped believing in them? Is this punishment?"

Lady Newton opened her mouth immediately to speak, but then stopped for a moment. "I don't know," she said. "I don't know. I love you, I know that for sure. The rest is just what we have to work with right now. Take it, or leave it. Do what you have to."

He smiled. "I love you, too." In the sadness and chaos of the past months, they had forgotten to maintain anger and bitterness toward one another. They had lost their rigidity, their dogma, both about the world and about one another. They had become friends again. She passed away, quietly, not two weeks later.

+ + +

When the sickness had run its course, everything had changed. Dozens and dozens had died. People didn't meet on the street to talk about the progress of the town or the war in Baixa or the world around them. They stayed at home, and they stayed alone.

It was late in autumn when the boats came. Old dugouts and canoes, a couple of pockmarked catamarans. They came into port slowly, almost with a sense of fatigue.

Thomas took a group of townspeople to the shore and found a group of soldiers from the boats, more than twenty. He recognized a couple of them from town: Daniel Bohm, the furniture builder's son, and the second-oldest Planck boy. The rest of them were new faces, soldiers from other parts of the Islands.

"Welcome!" Thomas said. "We're so glad to see you. We've had little news from anywhere outside of town. Daniel, have you come across misfortune? How goes the progress in Baixa?"

There was a bitter laugh from the back of the crowd. Thomas looked up and saw a large, unfamiliar, one-eyed soldier, who had just finished grounding the catamaran. The soldier was almost as tall as Albert and wore a chain shirt of the darkest iron Thomas had ever seen. "How goes the progress? The progress is over. Baixa's over."

Thomas approached him. "This sounds like dire news, I'm grieved to hear it. As I said, we've heard little." He extended his hand. "We'll help you however we can. I'm Thomas Newton, mayor and Lord Eden-town."

"Are you, now?" The soldier eyed his hand but did not take it. "Well, that makes everything fine then, doesn't it? Most of us dead and picked apart in Baixa, but the mayor and Lord Eden-town is here now to fix it all." He met Thomas's gaze. "You can keep your help to yourself, mayor and Lord Eden-town."

Thomas, unsure how to react, turned back to Daniel Bohm. "What happened to you?"

"All the Adepts," Daniel said. "It happened here, too, didn't it?"

Thomas wanted to say "no." He was still holding onto those words his mother said months ago. He wanted to stick to facts, the directly observable. It was comforting to do that. But in his heart he knew. "Yes. It happened here, too."

"When it happened, the Baixans turned on us. They over-ran the city."

"And they tore all the crippled Adepts, and all of *you*, all the mayors and lords, apart," the one-eyed soldier said. "They killed them, or made them slaves. And the rest of us, the soldiers, they just killed. We tried to retreat, hundreds of us. When we escaped the city and reached the forest, we thought we'd survived.

"But then we started the road to shore across the forest.

Where we came up against the bear-wolves, and the great cats, and the bugs that bring fever, and the poisoned plants. We didn't have an Adept to move trees or kill animals or heal us. The forest killed us better than the Baixans ever could. There were hundreds of us, and this is it. This is all that's left." The soldier looked again at Thomas. "So tell us how you're going to help us, now."

"Stay here, with us. You need food and shelter, which we have. And we could use a militia in these dire times. We can survive here."

"Survive here? Yeah, maybe." The one-eyed soldier spat on the ground. "I don't feel like being your militia, boy. Being militia for Adepts and mayors hasn't gotten me anything but grief. But maybe we'll stay here and take food and shelter." With that, he signaled to some of the other soldiers and began gathering their provisions. They hiked up toward the Castle.

Thomas grabbed Daniel to talk. "Who is he?"

"His name is Peter. He's from the Green Island. He worked for the Adepts for a very long time, even before the war. They were killing people even before the war. He told us."

"Help me make him understand. We have to work together if we're going to get through this."

"Thomas, listen," Daniel said gravely. He had been two years ahead in school. Thomas remembered him being quiet, pretty average at school, good at archery, and kind to younger students. "If Peter tells you to do something, you should do it. Don't get into conflict with him. He does horrible things. I've seen him do horrible things." He looked nervously up the hill, to where the other troops were headed. "I have to go."

Thomas watched him begin trudging up the hill. He watched the soldiers continue to travel to and fro, taking up gear. He hoped to catch Peter alone, to talk things through with him, get him to listen to reason. But the man never returned.

Thomas finally gave up and walked to the Castle himself. The soldiers had set up camp right in the middle of the square. They hadn't discussed any of it with him, which struck him as utterly improper. But he had no idea what to do. He went back into the house to check on Cyd.

+ + +

Peter came to the door the next day and knocked loudly.

"We need food. Food, water, drink, somewhere to shit."

Thomas had decided the night before that he was going to try to do this peacefully. They were all traumatized by the war, he thought. Best to give them slack for a while. "We can give you some food from our stores. There is a latrine space behind the hospital, which people aren't really using now."

"When do we get the food? We're fucking hungry."

"I'll have some men bring it right away. It may be an hour or two. It's mostly raw ingredients. Do you have what you need to cook?"

"We've been surviving in the wild for months. We can make do with the 'raw ingredients.'"

"Excellent," Thomas said. "We'll have to think through a long-term approach for feeding you all, but this will work for now."

"I don't care about the long-term approach. As long as my belly is full."

"Again, I think this would be a great opportunity to work together. We can supply provisions, and we need a militia. Don't feel like you need to decide that right away. Just a suggestion."

Peter glared at him. "We'll wait for the food." He walked away.

+ + +

The militia's tent city became a part of the square. At first, it was relatively quiet, as if military discipline still held sway. Over the weeks, though, the camp became louder and louder at night, with fights and drunken yelling. Thomas put the heavy shutters up on all the windows and fortified the doors. The people of Eden-town stopped going to the Castle at all.

Winter came. Leaves and dirt accumulated in the alleyways of the town. They had stopped being cleaned weeks ago, with the sickness. Thomas noticed boats starting to leave from the port, until the only ones left on the docks were the soldiers' fleet, a few vessels unworthy of sea, some hangers-on. No one asked or notified the mayor about their departure. One morning, as Thomas walked along the shore picking up trash, he saw Geoffrey and Harald Pauli sailing out to sea in a dinghy, Harald bundled in blankets, Geoffrey shivering against the wind as he manned the tiller. Geoffrey had a bow bound to his back, and Thomas saw what surely was a sword. *Geoffrey doesn't know how to fight*, Thomas thought. Harald saw Thomas and waved at him, and Thomas waved back.

Thomas held on to his duties; he visited the bank regularly, even though no one came to make deposits or withdrawals. For a while, he still sent communications out to Over-town. The messages back from Over-town got shorter and shorter, the last being, "Much sickness in the town. We will send a proper message soon." "All our love to Cynthia," it said, although Thomas had written of her death to the Kelvins some time ago. Then the first messenger never came back, and then the second messenger never came back.

One morning, on the way to the bank, he saw Peter

coming into his path. "Where are you going, over there?" Peter asked. "What's this?"

"I'm just going to the bank to tend to accounts."

Peter spat and looked livid. "You don't get it, do you? There is no more money. Stop wasting your time."

Thomas thought about walking on, but decided to discuss it. "The money belongs to other people, people in the town. I can't just let everyone down."

"Leave it alone!" Peter pushed Thomas back; Thomas lost his footing and landed on his back. "You already let everyone down!" Peter shouted. "All of you did. Stop pretending that it's still the same as it was. Get out of here and think about important matters. Like how you're going to feed us."

Thomas wanted to fight, but he knew he would lose. He stood and brushed himself off as best he could. He tried to look directly into Peter's face, but couldn't. He stared at the ground and said, "All this—the bank, the town working together—it feeds you, don't you realize that? If it falls apart, there goes your food, too." He tried to say the last part with as much authority and threat as he could, but his voice was shaking.

"That's what you want, isn't it? You want us dependent on you. You want us to behave and fight for you so that we stay fed. Maybe it works differently now. Maybe you feed us so we don't kill you." Peter's voice was terribly calm. "You heard me, get the fuck out of here."

Thomas went home. Anya asked him what happened, but he didn't answer. He went to his office. He brooded for hours, thinking about how he could beat Peter. Maybe he could organize farmers into a militia, or starve him out. Maybe he could figure out a strategy to have the soldiers depose him. Or maybe he would just punch Peter in his stupid damn face. He fantasized about beating Peter to a pulp, chopping his head off. Then he cried a little, and then the shame of that made him cry more. Finally he left the office and walked to the kitchen.

Mister Ewan and Anya were there, both sitting. They were eating some crusts of bread and a soup Ewan had made. "They raided the bank," Anya said, keeping her eyes on her soup.

He peeked out through a crack in the shutters. The doors and windows of the bank were broken through and through. Notes and pages of ledgers were strewn all around the square. They scurried about in the wind.

Thomas stared at it. "That belonged to the people, to Eden-town. They ruined it."

Ewan put a hand on Thomas's shoulder. "It's all right. Everyone knew the bank would go away sometime." Ewan meant it as a comfort, and that made it worse. Thomas took a bowl of soup and took a long time to eat it.

+ + +

Daniel Bohm knocked on the door the next morning. "Thomas, we need more food. Can you send us more food?"

"We've already given you months' worth. What are you doing with all of it? Our stores are running out."

"Thomas, you need to give us whatever you can. It's me and the other Eden-town guys that are keeping him from going berserk. He's going to tear everything apart if you don't send food."

Thomas stared at him. "I'll send what I can. But this isn't a free ride any more. If we starve, it's not any better than getting torn apart. Tell Peter that we need to negotiate some sort of long-term arrangement if you all expect to keep eating."

"You can't tell him that. There's no way you can tell him that."

"I'm not going to," Thomas said. "Because I've failed at

that. But you haven't. So you need to talk to him. Are you the Eden-town guys, or are you his mercenaries? Because this is about your town, too."

He took the glare Daniel returned and said, "I'm doing my part. I'll send more food. You need to do your part, too." He closed the door.

He went to the kitchen and talked to Mister Ewan. "Ask Roger to send more of the food stores to the camp. Save a survival ration for the town. I'll go down to market and start talking to the farmers. We'll need to figure out how to restock in the spring. I think if we all stand together we can negotiate some peace with them."

"I'll go to market," Mister Ewan said, and then paused for a while. "I think it will go better that way."

Mister Ewan left. Anya came in a little while later. "Where is Mister Ewan?"

"He went to market."

"You want some breakfast?"

Thomas grimaced. "I can make my own breakfast. I'm good for something, you know that? I just . . ." He trailed off. "I can make my own breakfast."

Anya shrugged. "I was just asking."

Thomas waited a long time. Hours passed. Eventually, he figured he had to go out. He didn't care who was concerned about that, and he didn't care if he was going to get killed.

There was a knock at the back door, Mister Ewan's door. Thomas answered it.

It was Daniel Bohm again. He was pale. "What's happened?" Thomas asked.

"The market. Peter took us there. To get food. He said to just take it. So we did, but some of the people said no. So they started killing people." His voice broke, and tears welled up in his eyes. "I'm sorry, I'm sorry. I didn't kill anyone. I didn't do anything."

Thomas began moving to grab his coat, his sword. "I need to go. I need to go and help."

"No, Thomas. No. They'll kill you. As soon as any of them see you, they are going to kill you. You have to leave."

"Leave? While people are getting killed? And go where?"

"I don't know, Thomas. It doesn't matter. You have to go away from here. They'll come here next."

Not knowing what else to say, Thomas said, "I can't just leave Mister Ewan. He was at market."

"They killed Mister Ewan." Daniel paused for a long time, looking at something in his mind. "I watched them kill him." He looked at Thomas again. "I have to go. You need to leave here. Please." And with that he turned away.

Thomas closed the door. He stood and stared. It was several moments before he realized he was staring at that place between the chopping block and the larder, where Mister Ewan would most often stand. He would stand there and talk to Thomas and Albert about school, or just watch them eat.

Anya came in. "There is noise outside in the square. It is no good. We need to leave now."

"I'm not leaving!" Thomas said. "I'm the mayor of this town, and I have a responsibility. Even if I'm outnumbered, even if I'm going to get killed. That's better than rolling over and letting this town die in chaos."

Anya gave a look of disgust. "And your daughter?" she said. "As soon as they kill you, they kill me and your daughter. But that is good, right? Because we will all die for the town. Even though there is no more town. It already dies in chaos, and you do not see. And you would let us die because you are blind and proud. Is that responsible?"

Thomas felt more rage at this moment than he had in any encounter with Peter, any moment of indignity with the soldiers. He thought, *how dare she?* And in that wave of indignation and self-absorption, he saw himself, too, and knew she was right. He deflated.

"We need to pack. Only the most important things," he said. "We'll have to sneak down the side just past the bank, in the back. It's hidden from the square and not too steep. And you're right, we have to be fast." He could hear the noise outside. It initially wasn't as loud as he had expected. There was an occasional shout, which seemed to come from one voice. It wasn't Peter's. Then there was another voice shouting in response to the first, sporadically. Then a third contributed as an accent. It was the sound of building rage.

They packed, mostly for Cyd. Thomas got some things from the larder, in case they were without food for a while. He went to his mother's library and got some books, one of important works and one with the town's records. Anya came across him and hissed, "If you tarry, we will die."

"I will accept that the town is dying in chaos if you will accept that it may come back to life someday." He shoved the books into his rucksack. He also packed his mother's stylus, to remember her by.

Just as they were leaving from the back door, the pounding started, loud, with shouting. There was a flicker of orange outside through the windows. Thomas looked at Cyd sleeping in Anya's arms. *She doesn't cry, she's amazing,* he thought. *It's all I can do to keep from crying myself.*

The back way was clear, and they made it to the path down the hill. They could hear voices around the back door not long after they were out of sight.

The path wasn't as treacherous as the rocky side, but it was isolated enough to be out of sight. They had to pay close attention as they descended. At the bottom, they saw that the Castle was already in flames, fire licking out the windows.

"Stop looking, it's gone," Anya said. "We go to the forest."

"No, I know a place," Thomas said. "It's a good place."

He led her west from the Castle. People stared from windows and doors toward the burning Castle, so it was hard to stay concealed. But Thomas knew how to sneak around. Once out of town, they went on for some time. "It's a farm," he said. "An empty farm where we can hide."

"The forest is better," Anya said. "But this is close to the forest."

They passed the Planck farm and got to the Todorov place. The militia stationed there had cleared out not long after word of the victory in Terra Baixa, and it had been sitting empty ever since, with Mal Planck on a small retainer to keep it from falling apart. Mal seemed to be doing less maintenance under the current circumstances, but it was still livable.

When they got there, Anya handed Cyd to Thomas and began tidying up a room for his daughter and locating fresh water. Cyd fussed a little on the transfer, then went to sleep again.

"This is a good place," Anya said. "They will find us eventually here, so we have to be ready to leave again. But it is good for now." She and Cyd slept in the Todorov mothers' room. Thomas stayed up for a while. He stood outside and stared at the sky, which glowed orange. The Castle must have been completely burning now, and the flames must have spread. He imagined the town burning. The sky glowed like all the world was burning around them.

It didn't seem real to him. The fear and despair and guilt burned through him. He was responsible for this. He was the mayor. He let the sensations wash over him for a while, and then suddenly he was able to let them go. It was less painful when he realized he didn't have to be a mayor any more. He could just be himself. He felt free, guilty to feel that way, but free.

Thomas took Albert's old room, where he'd slept over countless times before. The pillow still smelled like Albert.

The next day, they just hid. They sat in the house and kept everything closed up and quiet. Anya watched Thomas skeptically. "Just until things quiet down," he said. Cyd cried a number of times. *Cyd doesn't have to worry about what's responsible—it must be nice,* he thought.

There were noises outside throughout the day, the sound of many passersby. Thomas peeked out the window and murmured, incredulously, "They're leaving. It's their home, and they're being run out. They're leaving."

"They're going to the forest," Anya said. "That's the right idea."

They waited through the day. Anya quietly sang some songs. Then Thomas taught Anya some lessons about particle physics, which she received much more positively than he could have possibly imagined.

That night, Thomas sneaked over to the Plancks' house. "What the hell are you doing here?" Mal Planck said, shocked and furious. "Get out of here. You'll get my family killed."

"We're at Albert's, the Todorov place. We're keeping low. Just until we figure out what to do."

"Get out of here."

"Please, my daughter and her nurse. I don't care about myself, but I need to feed them. Please."

Mal looked at him, red-faced and lips pursed. "Wait here." He came back with two sacks of ready food, mostly eggs and potatoes. "Have your nurse start a winter garden. I can't feed you forever. They'll probably start taking food from us all. And have her come over from now on. No one can see you."

Over the next week, they fell into a routine, sleeping much of the day. Anya did well with the eggs and potatoes, and she gathered some plants from the forest to eat. Thomas ate some of the plants, but only at first. He ate none of Mal Planck's provisions. "Those are for you. You need them to feed Cyd," he said.

"You have to eat, too. We need you here with us, alive."

"No, you don't."

The stream of people from the town continued for a few days and then stopped. It became very quiet. Thomas kept expecting the soldiers to show up. Each day that passed without them, he imagined they were harassing the farms to the north first.

In the early morning and evening, he and Anya would try to tend the fields a little. There wasn't a lot they could do. Anya started a small garden, in the back of the house, out of sight. Thomas mended the fences; wild animals had gotten into the fields.

Thomas slept often. Anya couldn't convince him to eat, despite her increasing insistence and frustration. At one point, she cried, "If you die on me, I will kill you with my bare hands!"

Thomas smiled weakly. "I'll go hunt, all right? I'll go hunt an animal. And I will eat from that. I'll earn my food."

"You don't have the strength to hunt," she said. He was already getting started, though. He took one of Albert's bows and a quiver of arrows, put on his boots. He kissed Cyd on the forehead. "I love you. I'm so sorry." He went to Anya. "I'll be back. Good-bye."

"You idiot, don't do this. Just eat, damn you! Just eat." She was crying angrily. He smiled and waved at her and walked out.

He went out into the forest. He really did want to hunt, on some level. He walked into the forest for a while and came to a clearing. He sat down and decided to wait quietly. Then he felt very sleepy and rested his eyes for a bit.

When he woke up, the sky showed sunset. Several hours had passed. He thought about leaving, but he couldn't remember the way out. He didn't want to leave, anyway. He rested his eyes again.

That night, he heard the buzzing of insects and the chirping of frogs and the cries of wind. He heard Cynthia and his mother. They were spirits, and at first they were ashamed of him, but then they forgave him. He asked them if it was all right, if he could stop and rest. They were silent.

And then he saw Albert, emerging from the woods into the clearing. He actually saw Albert; he wasn't just a voice or a spirit. It was like he was really there. Thomas wasn't sure whether to believe what he saw. "Albert?" he called out.

Albert walked with a dreamlike look on his face. When he heard Thomas's call, he looked at Thomas in shock. "What are you doing here? You aren't supposed to be here."

"I was resting. What are you doing here?"

"This is my home," Albert said. Then he shook his head, like he was trying to get water out of his ears. "I'm, I'm going to my farm."

"We're there. My daughter and her nurse and me."

"You're there at my farm? Where's your mother?" Albert stared forward, trying to work something out in his head.

"My mother died, Al. Is it all right for us to stay there?"

Albert grinned then with what seemed like great relief. "Sure, of course! Sure it is. Welcome."

"Are you all right, Albert? Where have you been?"

Albert took a minute to answer. "Sort of. I was in Terra Baixa, and then I was on the Green Island." He looked at Thomas again as if he were seeing him for the first time. "I saw you, Thomas! I saw you at the Abyss." Then he hugged Thomas. "Are you all right, Thomas?"

"No, I guess not. I'm hungry. I'm glad you're here."

"Come on, we'll make some food." Albert took his hand

and started walking. Thomas realized where the farm was; they were walking toward it. He felt dizzy and leaned on Albert.

Albert was back. Thomas rejoiced inside. It was almost like everything was all right.

+   +   +

They reached the farm. "Everything's a mess," Albert said. "I guess that's because your mom died? They stopped taking care of it?"

"That's close enough. I'm sorry we didn't take better care of your farm, Albert."

Albert shrugged and smiled at Thomas. "That's all right. It gives us something to do." He burst into the front door with Thomas close behind. "Hello!" he cried.

Anya emerged from her room. She looked at Thomas with shock. "You're back? Who is this?"

Thomas smiled weakly. "This is Albert Todorov. I told you about him. He owns the farm."

"He's big," Anya said. "You're a soldier?"

Albert frowned. "I'm not a soldier," he said. "I used to be, but I'm not anymore."

"We need a soldier. If you aren't a soldier, you better shut up before you get us all killed."

"You shut up," Albert said, but teasingly. "You're Thomas's wife? I like you."

"Not the wife. The nurse."

Albert smiled at her, then moved to the kitchen. "What can we make for Thomas? He's hungry."

"Of course he's hungry," Anya said. "He's killing himself."

Thomas gave her an angry look, which she ignored.

"That's ridiculous," Albert laughed. "If I don't get to kill myself, then no one else does either." He found the eggs and the flour. "I'll make some flatcakes in the pan. That will fill us all up. Miss Nurse, can you fetch us some milk?"

"There's no milk," Anya said. "There's no cow."

Albert stared at her. "What happened to the cow? I guess there's no goat, either?"

"No nothing. I just started some vegetables, and in a few weeks we will have what the animals don't eat. That's it."

"Well, we can use water. Miss Nurse, would you fetch us some water?" Anya stared at Albert for a long moment, shrugged, and then went for water.

Albert made some cakes and insisted that everyone eat. Thomas did. At first, it was hard to keep the food down. But eventually he finished two whole cakes. The satisfaction of it made him feel giddy, his head spinning.

"I'll hunt us something good tomorrow. And I can go to Mal. I'll get some staples from him to tide us over until we are going strong again here. Or did you lose Mal, too?" he asked through a mouthful of flatcakes.

"The other farmer is there," Anya said. "He doesn't like us. He doesn't want his farm burned and his children killed."

"Who would do that?" Albert asked.

Anya sneered at him. "The soldiers, Albert. I guess you don't know, because you're not a soldier. But there are many of them, and you should start thinking about them. They burned the town. They killed a lot of people. They will kill you if you keep shouting like you do."

"I'm not shouting," Albert said, loudly. "So we have to do something about these soldiers?"

"I'm sure that will go well," Anya said. She stabbed at her plate without eating anything.

"I could try. They sound pretty bad," Albert said, taking in another big mouthful. "I say we just get the farm going first, and then we'll see what comes next."

"What comes next is that they will kill us, boy, and then they will burn the farm that you 'get going,'" Anya said. "You need to understand what's real here. You're setting us all up to die."

"Is that so, Nurse? Do you know that?" Albert boomed. "Do you know the future? I don't think you do. I think I'm the only one here who knows the future." He stared at them wildly. "So, since the one here who knows the future says we'll farm first, and then see what comes next, then maybe we should do that. Right?" Red-faced, he stood and went to the bowl of batter. "I'm eating more flatcakes. Who wants more flatcakes?"

Anya glared at Thomas with wide, shocked eyes. Thomas stared back, still barely strong enough to do more than shrug. Then he said, "I say we go with Albert's plan. And I'd love another flatcake."

"I'm having two more," Albert said. "And one for Thomas. And Nurse . . . What is your name, anyway? I can't keep calling you that."

"My name is Anya," she said. She said it so quietly. Her voice had something final to it that Thomas had never heard before.

Albert stopped his motion for a moment and looked right at her. "Anya, on this farm, no one will hurt any of you. Not soldiers, not me. Nobody. I swear this on the graves of my parents. Do you believe me?"

There was a silence when he finished, a cavernous silence. Anya opened her mouth as if to rebuke him, but then just met his eyes with an urgent, subtle gaze. After several moments, she nodded. "Yes, I do," she whispered. Then she composed herself and said, stiffly, "I'll have another flatcake."

"Great!" Albert said. "Flatcakes for everybody."

After they finished, Thomas took Albert to see Cyd. She had slept through Albert's arrival. "She'd sleep through the apocalypse," Thomas said.

Albert grinned, his eyes lighting up. "She's so cute!" he whispered. "Where's her mother? Is Cynthia her mother?"

"Yes, Cynthia's her mother. Cynthia died," he said. "I wish you would have met her. She was wonderful . . . kind, and bright—so bright! The conversations we'd have—and she understood. You and I, what we were, all of it. She was a good friend." He paused. "She took ill after Cyd was born. Sister Alice was gone by then. And then the sickness came." He paused. "And then she died."

Thomas drew closer to Cyd, put a hand gently on the crown of her head. "She's so beautiful," he said. "She's healthy." He looked over at Albert and saw tears streaming down Albert's face. "What's wrong?"

Albert looked at Thomas, then at Cyd, and then let out a howl, a bleat: a pure sound of grief Thomas had never heard from any human, much less Albert. He turned into the corner of the room, curled in on himself, and began shaking with great racking sobs. "No, no, no," he repeated over and over again, like a chant. Thomas led him out of the room.

He held Albert to his chest. "Shh, it's all right. She's fine. We're all fine. Baixa must have been so hard." When he said that, Albert began wailing again. Cyd woke up and started to cry, too. Anya, beyond surprise at this point, stood up from the table, lips pursed, and went to her. "Make yourself useful and clean up the dishes," she said to Thomas on the way in.

Thomas led Albert out of the room, then held him for a long time and didn't say anything, afraid that he'd cause upset again. He held him tighter and rubbed his shoulders. Sometimes, in school, he would dare to touch Albert between the shoulders like this, always amazed that it was an intimacy Albert would allow. Albert would always lean into Thomas's hand, and relax, and continue on with what he was doing as Thomas stroked his back. He could feel Albert rest against his hand.

Eventually, Albert calmed down, his sobs turning into sporadic shudders and hiccups. By the end, Thomas was rocking him a little. It was quiet from Cyd and Anya's room.

"How about we put you to bed?" Thomas said gently.

Albert shook his head. "I don't want to be by myself. Don't make me."

"All right, just sit here a minute." Albert did, and Thomas cleaned the dishes. He heated some water, and made a basin with soap. Then he filled the basin with the hot water and scrubbed the dishes, and dried them with some of Lini's linens they had found in a cupboard when they arrived. He then put them on a rack to finish drying.

He started humming a little and looked at Albert from time to time. "Do you want some tea?" Thomas asked. Albert, slack-jawed, flushed and spent and silent from the long cry, innocently shook his head. Thomas smiled at him. This was what he could be good at, he realized. He knew how to love and comfort Albert. He had been doing it for years. This was his new job.

When he finished the dishes, he took Albert's hand. "I'm in your room, the bed isn't very big. But your papa's bed isn't any bigger."

"I don't want to sleep in Papa's room," Albert said, shaking his head, on the edge of somewhere dark again.

Thomas rubbed the crown of his head. "It's fine, we'll be close in the bed, but it's fine. Like when we were kids."

They went to Albert's room. Albert stripped off his clothes in a pile on the floor. By the time Thomas picked them up, folded them, and put them on a chair, Albert was in bed and snoring already. Thomas climbed in and spooned him.

As he settled in, Thomas thought of all the concerns and troubles that were inevitable and dismissed them one by one. He was determined not to care, to just put his mind to this moment. He buried his face in Albert's shoulder and in the smell and warmth and feel of his skin.

They slept, with some occasional tossing and turning. In the middle of the night, Thomas woke, disoriented and unsure where he was. Albert had rolled onto the floor, but Thomas still had his hand on Albert's shoulder.

+ + +

The next morning was the best of early spring, sunny with some high and wispy clouds. Albert was back in high spirits. "This is going to be a great day. We're going to get this farm running again." He dug into the breakfast Thomas had made, eggs and flatcakes. Thomas had gotten up early and harvested some mushrooms and chives from the forest to put in the cakes. "Thomas, you're going to finish mending the fences. I'm going to thresh all the fields."

"All the fields?" Anya said. "All of them. Right."

"Yes, all of them!" Albert grinned. "What are you going to do, Anya?"

"I'm going to tend to the garden. And continue to feed and raise this boy's daughter," Anya said, pointing dryly at Thomas with her head.

Thomas took to the fences while Albert sharpened a scythe. The fences had gotten a little better with some of the early work he had done, but there was still plenty to do. He looked back at Albert from time to time and saw him swinging the scythe normally, almost lazily. Then, when the sun was high, he turned from his work to notice the fields were clean of the high grasses that had grown.

"That's impossible," he said to Albert when he found him. "You did all the fields?"

"I had a good morning," Albert smiled.

Lunch was eggs and flatcakes again, nearly the last of the store. "We won't have supper," Anya said.

"I'll go hunt us some supper this afternoon," Albert said.

"I'll go with you," Thomas said, excited.

Albert paused for a moment. "Actually, how about you get some more of those mushrooms and greens? Those were delicious. We could have a good supper with those. You could maybe find some roots, too."

Thomas nodded, a little dejected. "That's fine."

Albert patted his knee. "We'll go hunting together next time."

Thomas went out just to the edge of the forest and gathered. This was a good time of year for his favorite mushroom, small but meaty and concentrated with flavor. He found some young leafy greens as well, and a couple of roots. He had just put his full basket at the porch when he heard Albert calling him from the edge of the forest. Albert had killed a great boar. They dragged it toward the house, and worked together for some time to skin and clean the boar. Anya came out in late afternoon to check on them. "We have supper, Anya!" Albert cried, grinning, glowing, arms covered in blood and offal.

By the time they had the carcass taken apart, the sun was setting. Anya and Thomas took to roasting a shoulder in the clay oven. "I'm going to take some of this over to Mal. We should put the rest on salt."

"We don't have much salt," Anya said.

"I'll get some more from Mal."

Albert was gone for a while. When he came back, he was still smiling, but was a little more pensive.

"I talked to Mal. We worked it out. He and his boys haven't been able to hunt much, so they can use the meat. I'll take him more, and he'll give us some stuff we can use in exchange. See?" he said to Anya. "It's going well. It's been a good day."

"Did he talk to you about the soldiers?" Anya asked.

"Yes," Albert said. "I told him I'd take care of it."

The next morning, Thomas answered a knock at the door. It was Mal Planck. He was there with a goat, a couple of hens, and some bags. "This is flour, and seed, and salt," he said as he pointed. He looked at Thomas, eyes nervous. "We talked to Albert. If anyone can get that gang under control, it's him."

"Yes, he's back, it's a blessing," Thomas said.

"I'm not sure he's well," Mal said. "But he needs to be. He needs to save us. Do you understand? You make him well."

+ + +

They settled in to a pattern. Albert borrowed Mal's ox and tilled and sowed the fields. Thomas learned to milk the goat and tend to the chickens, and how to make cheese and yogurt. Anya's garden came up quickly, more quickly than Thomas would have said possible. All the crops started coming up quickly as well; they had ripened rows of barley and spelt within a month, which didn't seem possible. It looked like it would be an early harvest, and a big one. Cyd started to grow, rolling over, then pushing up. Albert would play peek-a-boo with her. Even Anya relaxed a little.

A week after his arrival, Thomas turned Albert around from their spooning position and began kissing him. Desperate for affection and out of practice, he awkwardly clawed at Albert's crotch. Albert pushed him back. "I'm afraid I'll hurt you," he said.

Thomas decided to try some of Albert's own damaged logic. "You can't hurt me while we're on the farm. You promised us that."

"You're right."

"So, there's nothing to worry about, right?"

Albert paused for a minute, mouthing silent and mysterious propositions and conclusions. Then he smiled sheepishly at Thomas and said, "I guess not."

There was a difference from before, an awkwardness. It felt like Albert was holding back something. Thomas didn't think too much about it; it all still felt so good to him.

They had all been there almost two months before Aengus came. He came up to the front fence while Thomas was cleaning some mushrooms and roots for supper. "Albert!" he shouted. "I know you're here. Albert!" He looked surprised when Thomas came up to him. "You're here, too?"

"I am. How are you, Aengus?" he said, giving Aengus a friendly pat on the good shoulder. "Are Will and Mila well?" He had heard that Aengus had settled down as a family with Will and Mila after coming back from Terra Baixa.

"Where is he? Where's Albert?"

"He's out hunting. Do you want to come in for a bit and wait for him? I'm sure he'd be glad to see you."

Aengus looked at Thomas for several beats. "He's all right?"

"I think he has some shock from the war. You all do, and that's to be expected." Talking to Aengus, Thomas remembered the old life, the Administrator life. He talked to Aengus like he would talk to a valued citizen. "I bet it will help him to see you. Please, come in. The barley's come up fast, and we actually have our first batches of ale ready. I'd love to have you try them."

"You and Albert are together now, aren't you?" Aengus asked. "And he . . . he never told you about us, did he?"

Thomas looked at him quizzically. "Albert hasn't talked a lot about the war, no."

He didn't know what to make of Aengus's reaction. Aengus seemed embarrassed and in grief. "I didn't think he would ever come back, Thomas. I would have waited for him. Do you hear me? I would have waited for him if I'd known."

"I don't understand what you mean. Did something happen in the battle? I'm sure he forgives you, Aengus."

Aengus shook his head. "It doesn't even occur to you, does it? Because it was always Albert and Thomas, since you were wee, all through school. Of course, he would just come back and settle down with Golden Thomas. Well, it was Albert and Aengus, too. As soon as your mama hauled you back to town after his parents were killed; all through Baixa, as well. He was mine, too. He was mine in war, when it mattered."

Thomas couldn't look at Aengus. He couldn't hear for the ringing in his ears. He felt dizzy. "Please stop," he said quietly. "Please go away. Please."

"I'm not trying to hurt you, Thomas." Aengus said, realizing himself. "I just . . ." He stopped and took a deep breath. "I just wanted him to know I would have waited."

Aengus walked back to his horse, mounted it, rode away.

Thomas went back to the porch, slowly, and took to cleaning the roots and mushrooms again. It was hard to focus on the mushrooms. After a while, Anya came to the door. "Cyd's down for her nap. What's wrong with you?"

"Nothing, I . . ." He paused, and in that moment he decided this didn't need to matter either. "Nothing."

+ + +

The next day, Albert stayed in for the afternoon. They had

plenty of meat curing, and he didn't need to hunt for a while. Thomas was making a boar stew while Albert and Anya were sitting on the porch drinking ale. Anya saw the horses first, coming from the Planck farm. "Here it is. Here they come," she said, agitated but also slightly self-satisfied. Thomas heard her and came to the door, drying his hands.

It was Daniel Bohm and Marcus, Mal Planck's son. They looked worried, ashen. "Albert," Daniel called.

"What?" Albert didn't move from his chair.

"We were talking to Mal about getting some food. He said that we were supposed to talk to you."

"Mal Planck? Marcus's father? He is your father, right, Marcus?"

Marcus nodded. "Of course he is."

"I told Mal to send any criminal soldiers to me, and that I would take care of it."

"All right," Daniel said, choosing not to take the bait. "Well, we're here because we were told to get food. So I guess you're going to cover the Plancks?"

"I didn't say I was giving out any food. I just said I was going to take care of it for Mal. That's your father, right, Marcus? The man you just tried to extort food from, that's your father."

Marcus said nothing. Daniel said, "We can't go back and say that. Peter will come back, and it will be trouble."

"Peter? Who's Peter?"

"Peter is the commander we came back from Baixa with, Albert," Daniel said, exasperated. "Look, we've been up on the north side of Eden-town for a while now . . ."

"Eden-town? There isn't any Eden-town," Albert said. "You burned it to the ground."

"Peter burned it," Daniel said. "But things have been better since then. We've been on the north side, and everyone has been cooperative, and no one's been hurt."

"Right, they've just been starving themselves for you," Albert said. "Starving so you wouldn't burn and kill them."

Daniel took a long pause. "He's terrible, Albert. You don't know what it's like."

"Seems like it's pretty easy to me, actually. You get free food while other people suffer, and you get to blame it on this Peter guy. Anyway, you send Peter to me."

"No, Albert, don't do this—"

"*You send Peter to me.*" The command issued from Albert, but something seemed to be playing tricks on Thomas's ears. It sounded like it came from everywhere. He looked around and everyone else seemed to be surprised, as well. "I will take care of it. Do you understand?"

"Please, no," Daniel shuddered.

"You send him to me." Then something changed back, and it was just Albert again. "It'll be easy. Send him to me, and you both can keep avoiding responsibility for these awful things you've been a part of. Marcus? Marcus! Look at me." Albert stood and walked toward them. "You send him to me, not your father, do you hear me? Can you manage that? Not to get him killed, his farm burned? Your father. Your farm." He had reached Marcus by the last words and spat the words into his face, which showed only fear and shame and hatred.

"I know everything you've done," Albert said to him, and then looked at Daniel. "I know everything you've both done. When this is over, you both leave. There's no place for you here anymore."

They climbed on their horses and rode off.

"When they come back, it will be all of them," Anya said, without much inflection.

"Yes. And when they do, I'll take care of it. You believe me, right?"

Anya nodded slowly. "Yes, I do."

"Then drink up," Albert said, taking a swig. "This ale is good. Nobody gets any of our ale without working for it." He grinned.

+   +   +

That night, all the soldiers came. They passed the Plancks' and came directly to the fence of the farm. Anya took Cyd in her arms and clutched at Albert's sleeve. "Where do I go? The baby . . ."

"You and Cyd stay in your room," Albert said. "I'm going to take care of it." Something in his speech sounded absolute and inevitable. She relaxed and nodded. "You can take care of Cyd, keep her calm," Albert said. "I need you to do that." Anya took Cyd to her room.

"I'm going with you," Thomas said.

"No. You don't need to see this."

"I can fight, Albert! Everyone forgets that. I can fight."

"I remember that, Thomas," Albert said. He seemed to struggle silently with himself for a moment. Then he gave in and said, "Don't fight until I say so. All right? Just stand back. Maybe there doesn't have to be any fighting." Albert didn't even seem to convince himself. They went outside.

There were dozens of them. Many carried torches, and the flames disturbed the cool night with smoke and hostile flickering. "We're here for Albert Todorov," said a voice from the crowd of men and horses.

"I'm Albert Todorov. Is that Peter? Peter, come on forward. Let's talk."

There was a pause and a shuffling as horsemen climbed down from their mounts and came forward. Peter, and five more, all with torches, all armed.

"I know you," Albert said. "Don't I know you?"

"I was in Baixa, boy. You knew your place better then.

I hear you're telling the farmers here not to give us food. Acting like you're in charge," Peter said. "That's a bad move."

"I'm not in charge of anything," Albert said. "I'm just a farmer."

"You're not just a farmer," Peter said. "You were one of us. You had a whole platoon. But then you cracked up."

"I used to be a soldier," Albert said, "but that was a while ago."

"Whatever you are, you're causing trouble. We don't want trouble in this place, but we're not going hungry either." Peter paused. "What am I going to do with you? I'll give you one chance. Give us what we need, and tell your neighbor to do the same, and everything will be fine."

Albert laughed. "That's very kind of you," he said. "I'm not giving you anything, Peter. And no one else is, not after tonight. It's time to stop harassing these people. It's time to stop crying about what you're owed and do some work. If you need food, cut down some trees and start growing some crops. Raise some animals. Hell, if you want, I'll help you do it. But that's how you get food from now on. The extortion stops."

"Bad move, Albert Todorov," Peter said. "Bad, bad move. We need to farm? Maybe we'll start by taking your god-damn farm." Then he noticed Thomas, apparently for the first time. "Look, our lord and mayor's here! This is making a lot of sense now."

"Thomas is my friend, and he's someone I protect," Albert said. "He has nothing to do with this."

"Of course not!" Peter said. "Of course the lord and mayor wouldn't find the biggest, hardest soldier he could find and use that blond ass to get that soldier on his side. Try to make a new land grab. Don't look offended, Todorov, I can understand it. He's pretty enough.

"But I'm not letting it happen. No more mayors, no more

Adepts, no more citizens running things. We burned down the town for a reason. We're starting over. And if this is the new mayor's house, then I guess we'll just have to burn it down, too. I don't care how big you are. There's only one of you."

"It's not too late to stop," Albert said, sadly. "Do you understand? Take a second, just a second. You can stop."

"I don't think so. I think it's just starting," Peter shouted. "I'll do you a favor. I'll kill you first, so you don't have to watch what I do to your lordship." Five more soldiers came down from their mounts, and the ten of them approached the gate.

"If you set foot on this farm in violence, it's the last thing you'll ever do," Albert said.

Peter laughed, kicked at the gate, and marched in.

Then Thomas heard a voice that said *get back*, and it was Albert, but it was Albert's voice like it was before, like it was coming from everywhere. And Thomas said aloud, "No, I'll fight with you." Suddenly, he was pulled back to the porch, and even though Albert stood in front of him, he knew the force was Albert, too.

And then a noise came from the forest, though Thomas couldn't tell exactly where. It was an animal, but Thomas couldn't tell exactly what kind of animal. He only knew that it was big and wild and terrible. And it grew closer, and with it came a shadow, and a wind. The wind blew past Thomas and toward Peter. And with it, Peter started screaming, the most horrible screaming, like the noise was eating him alive. Thomas squinted through the night and saw Peter being shaken and torn by something invisible. As he came apart, his screams became like the animal's howls.

The two soldiers next to him began screaming and coming apart as well. And then it was all tumult and movement, and Thomas couldn't tell what was going on. He made out something growing from the ground, plunging into the soldiers' trunks, coming out through their chests and shoulders and mouths. Every soldier that had crossed the threshold was being destroyed. The ones in back were still newly screaming, writhing, collapsing; the first ones, closer to Thomas, were swaying more slowly. Thomas realized that the first bodies were dead, that something else was doing the swaying.

The only body that stayed still throughout was Albert. He was still standing in the place where he started. Thomas could see only his back, silhouetted against the torches of the soldiers outside the gate. Those soldiers had darted back and forth, tentatively, when the screams started, but now stood stock still, looking at Albert's face. Thomas looked into the soldiers' eyes. It looked like they were gazing into something terrible.

And then Albert's voice spoke again, Albert's voice coming from everywhere. "The forest hurts you. So you tried to kill it and turn it into civilization, and then, when that didn't work, you looked for people to blame. Adepts, and mayors, and other soldiers, and civilization itself, anyone and anything you could think of. And you came here, because you thought I was another one to take the blame. But you missed the point. I'm the forest. I'm the one who hurt and killed you in the first place. And you can keep challenging me all you want, and I will just keep killing you. Because I am patient, and I am vast, and I do not care."

The soldiers that were left scrambled to their horses and rode away. In their haste, they left five horses without masters.

As they rode off, the noises and wind began to die down. Albert turned and walked toward Thomas. As he got closer, Thomas saw that he was covered in blood and soil. There were places on his face where the dirt was interrupted in streaks. It looked like the streaks had been cleaned by sweat, or tears.

"Would you take the horses back to stable, please?" Albert asked Thomas. It sounded like he could barely make out the words. "Don't touch the bodies." He walked around the side of the house. After a couple of minutes, Thomas could hear Albert cleaning himself in the basin near the rain barrel.

Thomas walked toward the horses. They had kept very calm, all things considered. He looked at the bodies as he crossed. Three men had trees growing through them. The rest were torn apart. He couldn't tell what used to be Peter.

He tied all the horses to the fence, then led them back one by one. They hadn't done a lot of cleaning of the stables, but they were still in good enough shape to get the horses in place and to bed them down. It occurred to him that the goat and chickens had some company, and he was glad of that.

When he was finished, he walked to the Planck farm. "We have horses now. We took them from the soldiers. You can take some, if you could use them. I was wondering if you had some spare feed."

"I do," Mal Planck said. "What happened to the soldiers?"

"Albert took care of it."

Mal was quiet for a while, then said, "I'll bring some feed over tomorrow." He closed the door.

Thomas walked back to the house. Anya was at the table, eating some cured boar meat and young pickles. "He wouldn't eat anything," she said. "He came in naked and wet."

"What did you say?" Thomas asked.

"I told him to dry off and to put some clothes on. Then I thanked him. Then I asked him if he wanted to eat, like I told you already."

Thomas went to their room. Albert was curled up in the bed, still naked, knees to his chest, facing the wall, clinging to a blanket too small to cover him.

Thomas sat on the bed and put a hand on Albert's back. "Something happened to you while you were gone," he said gently. "Something bad. It doesn't matter. I don't care. Thank you for saving us. I love you." He rubbed Albert's back for a while, until he felt Albert relax against the touch, just a little. Then he curled up against him and fell asleep.

+   +   +

The next morning, Thomas woke early, before anyone else. He went out to look at the gate in the morning light. He found that the bodies were gone. The places where trees had grown through soldiers were just the young trees themselves, bigger than saplings. Where bodies had been strewn about there were just gently rising mounds, covered in moss. It was more challenging to get to the gate, but not unmanageable. "It's beautiful, really," Thomas whispered to himself, then realized what he said and cowed himself into silence.

He went into the forest. He gathered some mushrooms and chives. He milked the goat and brought the fresh milk in, and he gathered some fresh eggs from the hens. He brought in some salt-cured boar.

He got a pan over the fire and fried the boar in the pan while he made up some batter for flatcakes. Richer ones this time, with the goat's milk and the mushrooms and chives. He took the strips of boar off and cooked cakes in the same pan. They bubbled up and turned golden brown on each side. He put the pot of tea he had been brewing on the table.

Albert woke up first and stumbled out of his room, eyes

still half closed. He had managed to pull on some breeches. Thomas kissed him, and held him until Albert almost fell back asleep in his arms. He directed Albert to the table and poured him a glass of milk.

Cyd had cried several minutes before, but when Anya emerged with her, she had the placid air of a baby who'd just fed. Anya held Cyd on her hip as she crossed the room, took a strip of boar, and began nibbling on it.

Thomas looked at all of them, at his family and his provisions for them, and his heart was full. And he thought to himself, *it's perfect, it's perfect.*

It was the end of the world, as it always had been, as it always would be. It was the end of the world, and it was perfect.

ACKNOWLEDGEMENTS

Sandra Spicher edited this book with the utmost skill, engagement, and professionalism.

Derek George provided stunning designs for the interior and cover.

Victoria Davis showed me how to begin, connected me to Sandra and Derek, and guided and supported me throughout.

Abby Webber gave the proof a meticulous proofreading.

Donna Flynn, Kira Lumiel, and Chris Pittman all read much poorer early drafts and provided thoughtful and valuable feedback.

Michael Craigue is my husband, my farm, my comfort spot.

www.ingramcontent.com/pod-product-compliance
Lightning Source LLC
Chambersburg PA
CBHW020640260626
47157CB00008B/2832